The Seventh
Miss Hatfield

The Seventh
Miss Hatfield

ANNA CALTABIANO

GOLLANCZ
LONDON

Copyright © Anna Caltabiano 2014
All rights reserved

The right of Anna Caltabiano to be identified as the author of this work has been
asserted by her in accordance with the
Copyright, Designs and Patents Act 1988.

First published in Great Britain in 2014 by Gollancz
An imprint of the Orion Publishing Group
Orion House, 5 Upper St Martin's Lane, London WC2H 9EA
An Hachette UK Company

A CIP catalogue record for this book is available
from the British Library

ISBN 978 1 473 20039 5 (Cased)
ISBN 978 1 473 20040 1 (Export Trade Paperback)

1 3 5 7 9 10 8 6 4 2

Typeset by GroupFMG using BookCloud

Printed in Great Britain by Clays Ltd, St Ives plc

The Orion Publishing Group's policy is to use papers
that are natural, renewable and recyclable products and
made from wood grown in sustainable forests. The logging
and manufacturing processes are expected to conform to
the environmental regulations of the country of origin.

www.annacaltabiano.com
www.orionbooks.co.uk
www.gollancz.co.uk

To the young man in the gray suit at Blackwell's,
without whom there would be no Henley.

Prologue: 1887

A young woman adjusted the veil of her hat to make sure it covered her face. She watched as the item she'd been waiting so long to possess was introduced. It was a portrait of a woman, the frame's gold leaf peeling with age. The woman in the painting was seated in an armchair, its royal blue a dramatic contrast to her crimson dress, the thick fabric of the dress even more vivid next to her olive complexion and dark hair. But it was the remarkable expression she wore that made the painting so special. Her almost-black eyes pierced the viewer with their gaze.

The veiled young woman at the back of the room narrowed her own eyes. She'd been caught up in the thrill of the auction house just from watching others bid in a flurry around her. She took a deep breath as the auctioneer brought in the final piece from the estate.

'You may not recognize this next oil-based picture, but that only adds to the aura of intrigue surrounding its story. Painted in the early 1500s, this portrait of an unknown Spanish lady was said to have been stolen sometime around 1515 from a ship docked in Spain. How the late Mr Hewett came to add this piece to his prestigious collection we don't know, but what we do know is that he had a discerning eye and we're starting the bidding at forty dollars.' The auctioneer winked from his spot on the stage at the chuckling audience below him.

The young woman raised her gloved hand, hoping to catch his eye.

'Yes, the young lady at the back,' he boomed. 'That'll be forty to you, miss.'

An older man up front lifted his walking stick in so slight a motion that it would never have caught anyone's attention had they not been looking for it, but the auctioneer's experienced eye took note. He barked out his next price, looking to the young lady at the back to see if she'd rise to the challenge. He saw her nod at him once and raised the price accordingly.

His eyes snapped back and forth, left and right, trying to keep track of the flying bids. The action was only between the man with the walking stick in the leftmost seat of the first row and the mysterious woman at the back. No one else appeared to be interested. As the auctioneer thundered another price, the man turned around, hoping to see who was bidding against him. Though a room full of people stared back at him, the woman at the back was not one of them. She'd hidden behind a pillar when she caught sight of his head turning. Having no choice, the man raised the price again. The auctioneer's eyes widened. At last the whirlwind stopped, the man's final bid hanging in the air.

'Going once,' the auctioneer announced as he looked to the woman at the back to see if she would bid again. 'Going twice ...' The woman shook her head once in a small gesture. 'Sold!' he declared as his gavel hit the block.

The man with the walking stick ambled up to a table at the side of the stage, along with the rest of the day's winners. All save one of the unsuccessful bidders slowly filed out of the room. The gentleman left his address with the clerk, adding strict instructions to come through the servants' entrance when delivering the painting. He strolled up the aisle between rows of now-empty chairs. Without knowing it, the man passed the young woman he'd just been bidding against and started his walk home.

The young woman was still seated in the same position she'd been in when the auctioneer was on the stage. She lifted her head in a cool manner, pulling the large brim of her hat down, and watched the man exit the auction house through the double doors before rising and following him out.

Always remaining no more than a few steps behind her quarry, the young woman took great care in concealing the sound of her footsteps. She followed him, turning familiar corners until they came to an opulent city house. It was one of those unmissable buildings with an elegant flight of steps leading up to a grand doorway, and she knew that the door itself only hinted at the impressive magnificence of the interior. Concealed in shadows, the young woman watched the elderly gentleman slowly climb the stairs. The front door was swung open by the butler, who came rushing out to help his master up the last couple of steps.

Light from the open door illuminated a single tear that slipped down the side of the woman's face, a tear that betrayed her momentary weakness. But as quickly as the door was opened, it soon swung closed again, and the woman was left in near darkness. A face in an upper window watched as her hand flew up to wipe the tear away, replacing it with a small smile on her thin lips. A low laugh escaped her then, lit only by the dim glow of the street lamps, whose flickering gas-flames cast a false sense of warmth upon the curious scene.

Chapter 1: 1954

Charlotte was always firm in her ways. I'd ask her questions again and again, but her answers were always the same. Her words never changed and neither did she.

I used to move her plastic arms into various poses and swap her dress to one of a different colour, but that never changed her. She was always Charlotte – for good and for bad.

Gran had Charlotte before me. She said she always remembered the Christmas she got her, how happy she was then. She also said that from that day on they were inseparable, but Gran isn't here any more, and Charlotte is.

Charlotte retained her eternal good looks while Gran's hair turned white and wrinkles cloaked her eyes, making them look permanently happy. Charlotte's hair was still a light golden colour, like the stitched-in thread on Mother's best dress. Her eyes remained a clear, piercing blue; nothing like what I remembered of Gran's watery eyes.

'Cynthia?' Mother peeked her head out from behind the front door. 'Do play somewhere safer than the front steps,' she chided. Upon seeing me sitting guiltily on the steps with Charlotte in one hand and one of Mother's pink tulips dangling from the other, she let out a long sigh. 'And stay out of the flowerpots,' she added.

4

I nodded. I hadn't meant to make Mother sad. Charlotte had told me that the tulip would go well with her dress, so I'd picked it for her. I hadn't really thought about what I was doing.

'So are you eating at Judy's tonight and then staying over?' Mother asked.

I nodded again, mumbling agreement.

'I'll pick you up in the morning, then. Or will Judy's mother drop you off? Or you could walk. After all, it's only a block away and you are eleven years old,' she said. As she disappeared back into the house, I heard her mumble, 'Where did you come from? When I was your age, I certainly wasn't playing with dolls.'

'I'm bringing Charlotte,' I said to no one, and my voice carried on the breeze.

The mailman's white truck drove up in front of our house. He only got out briefly to place a package at the foot of the steps before getting into his truck again and driving away. He didn't stop to notice me or Charlotte, but that was normal.

I hopped down the steps with Charlotte swinging from my arms, wondering what Mother had bought this time. Was it one of those pretty dresses she loved so much – the ones that made her look so beautiful?

When I picked up the package, I realized it was addressed to one of the houses on the other side of the street, not our house at all. It was the house across from ours, and I set the package down for Mother to deliver later.

Then I remembered how mad Mother had looked when she saw in my hand the tulip Charlotte had told me to pick. I grabbed the package again – it was only across the street and I was eleven already. All I had to do was ring the doorbell and put the package down. I could be a grown-up like Mother. Maybe then she would forget about the tulip.

I placed Charlotte down on the bottom step with care so she sat looking out towards the house on the other side of the street; I wanted her to be able to see me, and know that I'd be coming right back. I took a deep breath before bravely making my way across the street with the package. I placed it in front of the door and raised my hand to ring the doorbell, but before I could press the button, the door swung open.

A petite young woman stood framed at the threshold. She wasn't as young as my friend Judy's older sister, but she didn't look as old as my mother. She was wearing a cream-coloured sundress; her dark hair was pinned up, and it contrasted with her light dress in a way that made me gasp. I thought she looked like the angel from the postcard my mother kept taped on our refrigerator in the kitchen.

We both took our time examining every inch of each other while waiting for one of us to break the silence.

'Well.' The woman sighed as she finally picked up the package. 'What have we here?' Her voice was hushed for someone who looked so young and vibrant. Not frail, but as though she restrained it on purpose.

Her words put me on the spot and my breath caught in my throat. The lady looked down at me with kind eyes, trying to break my silence as she stated the obvious. 'So you brought me a package?'

I nodded, still not trusting my voice.

'You live across the street, don't you?' she asked, pointing to my house. I nodded again. 'Well, I just moved in a few weeks ago and still don't have many friends.' She sent a comforting smile in my direction.

I remembered the day she moved in. Mother was talking to her friends on the phone about our new neighbour. She baked a lemon pound cake that morning as a welcome gift, and took it with her when she went with her friends to greet our new neighbour. I watched from the window while they rang the doorbell and waited for a reply. They must have waited at least fifteen minutes, ringing several times but receiving no answer. Finally they gave up and left the pound cake by the door. When they came back in, they talked about how she must not have been home. But we'd all seen her enter the house that morning, and none of us had seen her leave.

'That Miss Hatfield … she doesn't appear to be the social type, does she?' I overheard my mother saying once over the phone. Yet here the young woman stood, looking anything but antisocial.

'Won't you come in?' Miss Hatfield asked. 'I just made some fresh lemonade,' she added when I hesitated.

Given her friendly tone, I couldn't bring myself to say no. Mother always told me not to talk to strangers, except when she introduced me to them. Then it was a different matter altogether and I needed to talk more, or else they might think I wasn't brought up properly. I knew I should be heading to Judy's house soon, but told myself this wouldn't take long.

I followed the lady through the doorway and into her home. I passed a grand old staircase that looked out of place in her untidy house. The banister wound up to the next floor and was draped with dust covers.

'I'm sorry my house is in such disarray – there's so much still to do!' she apologized. I looked at the mess around me and couldn't have agreed more, but kept my thoughts to myself.

7

She led me into a room she called the parlour and told me to have a seat while she fetched the lemonade and some cookies. I chose to settle into an old oversized couch while wondering if its atrocious colour was pea-green or cooked-celery-green. I decided that it most resembled the colour of the overcooked peas Mother served on Sundays, but all thoughts vanished when I actually sat down and realized that the couch looked far more comfortable than it actually was.

The other furniture in the room didn't appear to match the couch at all. Every piece was a different colour and texture, but the one thing they had in common was that all the pieces were what Mother would call 'outdated'. I supposed that was just a grown-up way of saying old, but I felt the word fit the room well. All the objects in the room, including the furniture, looked as if they'd been placed rather randomly in an antique store.

The walls were covered with maroon paisley wallpaper, which was peeling off in chunks. In some areas the colour was faded; in others it was stained with a harsh yellow that seemed to have bloomed with age. The coffee table in front of the couch where I was seated was actually an old steamer trunk made of dark aged leather – nothing like the couch or the wallpaper at all. It appeared to be from a much later time, and looked more modern than all the other objects and decorations in the room, despite the fact that it had obviously been well used. The trunk was a strange height; too short to eat from, yet too tall to have a conversation over once you were sitting down. Two chairs stood opposite the bright couch. One was covered with red velvet, but the other was stern-looking, made of a light-coloured wood with nothing to decorate it. The wall I was facing was dotted with ancient black-and-white photographs and dusty miniature paintings of people dressed in funny outfits. There was a photo of a stout man in a black bowler hat with his arm around a horse's neck; another portrait showed a woman with her hair piled up elaborately on top of her head. She was wearing a high-collared dress and appeared to be staring directly at me. All the other walls were empty.

The photos and paintings gave off an eerie feeling that made me uneasy. There was something wrong about all of those faces looking at me, but I just couldn't place my finger on why they made me feel so uncomfortable.

My thoughts were disrupted by a loud crash that sounded like glass shattering. The noise shocked me, and I involuntarily jerked up to a standing position. My head whipped towards the heart of the house, where the sound appeared to have come from.

I crept out of the mismatched parlour and walked deeper into the house. I felt like I was doing something I wasn't supposed to. When I exited the parlour, I found myself in a hallway cluttered with boxes, no doubt from Miss Hatfield's recent move. Two doors stood on each side of me and one large looming door ahead. No paintings or photographs decorated this hallway, unlike that one odd wall in the parlour. Of course, Miss Hatfield hadn't had time to unpack everything yet.

Hearing someone humming, I chose the door to my left, hoping to find Miss Hatfield. It opened into a room that only just resembled a kitchen. Like the hallway, it was buried beneath packing boxes with half-unwrapped plates and Christmas ornaments spilling out of them, as well as a good deal of additional mismatched furniture. But there was a stove and refrigerator in the corner.

Miss Hatfield was indeed there and, as I'd expected, she was the source of the humming.

'I–I heard something break,' I started. 'Uh, I hope everything's okay.' I had no idea what I was supposed to say. I didn't have a clue what I was doing here but had no choice except to stay, at least until after I'd shared some of her lemonade. It was only polite to do so, after having been invited into someone's house … at least, that's what Mother always told me.

'Oh, everything's fine. I was just warming up a batch of cookies I made this morning.' She smiled at me, looking up just briefly enough to wipe a stray lock of hair out of her eyes. Then she stepped over the remnants of a broken plate and reached into the outdated orange refrigerator for a pitcher of lemonade, which she set on the counter. 'Why wouldn't everything be all right?' I detected an underlying tone of hardness in her voice and shivered, but perhaps I only imagined it. 'I hope you like chocolate chip cookies, but in case you don't, I warmed some oatmeal ones, too.'

'Oh, I love chocolate chip.'

'They're my favourite too.' Miss Hatfield smiled. 'I can tell we'll be good friends. Why don't you help me bring the cookies and lemonade to the table?' She paused. 'There's no need to be formal. We can just eat in the kitchen if that's fine with you.'

I watched her place the cookies on a large plate decorated with big pink flowers. They were nothing like my mother's prize-winning peonies, which always took second place at the county fair, unmatched save for Mrs Blackwell's chrysanthemums. I didn't recognize these flowers. They had large centres that engulfed their petals, and their buds and blossoms were entwined, circling and looping around like vines. Each tried to outdo the other in beauty, and when they failed at that, they tried to do so in strength. It looked to me as if each bloom was trying to suffocate its neighbour before it became the one that was suffocated.

'Of course, Miss Hatfield.' The young woman froze and turned to look at me. She set the plate of cookies on the table, and took a few steps closer to me. I stood my ground, but every muscle in my body was telling me to flee.

'You know my name?' she asked, stretching her words out to form elongated syllables. It was all I could do to wordlessly nod, but then I got a grip on myself.

'M–my mother mentioned it when she came to visit you …' I said, my voice cracking and making my words sound like a question.

'Ah, yes,' Miss Hatfield whispered, putting me a bit more at ease. She sat in front of me. 'With her friends, am I right?'

I nodded again. I found it strange that she knew my mother had come with her friends. After all, she hadn't answered the door or even acknowledged their visit. How did she know?

'Such a silly group of girls,' she went on to say, though my mother and her society friends were far older than Miss Hatfield. 'They think they're so important just because they claim to be.'

'You know them?' I said, finding my voice again.

'Know them? I—' Miss Hatfield stopped, although I thought she was about to add something more.

'Miss Hatfield?'

'Miss Hatfield! Let's dispense with that right away. Please, call me Rebecca. I look over my shoulder for someone else when people call me Miss Hatfield.'

'Rebecca,' I corrected myself. I felt strange calling an adult – much less a stranger – by her first name. 'What do you know of my mother and her friends?' For some reason, I was curious to find out what she'd been about to say but didn't.

'I know enough of them,' she said cryptically.

I thought her evasive answer was odd, but didn't go overboard worrying about it. I reasoned it was probably just the kind of person she was. Most likely she didn't have anything to hide – why would she?

Miss Hatfield (as I continued to call her in my mind) suddenly stood up, knocking over the plate of cookies in front of her. In an effort to save them, I felt my body lunge forwards in sync with Miss Hatfield's. For a second we were the same person, reaching out for the same goal, but when the plate shattered on the floor and splintered into unrecognizable pieces, the moment fled.

I saw Miss Hatfield close her eyes for an extended second, and then she went about clearing up the broken shards without another word. Her actions looked a bit too jerky and tense to be natural, but again, it didn't feel like much to be concerned with at the time.

'There go our cookies, and another one of my plates,' she said, more to herself than to me. 'At least we still have our lemonade.'

Miss Hatfield was pouring a glass of lemonade when my eyes were drawn to a golden clock hanging on the kitchen wall. I was surprised I hadn't noticed it before. It was such a vibrant golden colour that it outshone every-thing else in the room. The clock looked like an over-sized pocket watch – the kind you need to wind up every morning like Gran used to have – except this one hung on a wall. It was circular like most clocks, but there was something different about this one. It had three hands, for the seconds, the minutes and the hours. But although the number of hours on the clock was the same as on every other, there appeared to be only half as many minutes marked as on a regular clock.

'The clock …' I frowned. I realized that the hand that should have been measuring seconds was moving abnormally slowly. I also wasn't sure what it was pointing to. There appeared to be a second series of dashes that were outside of the normal marks for minutes and hours that I was used to seeing on a clock.

'Ah, so you've noticed my pride and joy?' Miss Hatfield's voice drew my attention from the peculiar clock. 'It's my favourite thing out of pretty much everything here.' She moved over to where I was standing. 'It's mesmerizing, isn't it?' she asked, lifting it away from the wall and turning the dials on the back, causing the hands to move. Suddenly Miss Hatfield felt overwhelmingly close to me – too close for comfort. Luckily, however, she soon went back to the lemonade, while I stood frozen in my spot by the golden clock. I noticed a tiny inscription I was sure hadn't been there before, or at least I didn't think it had. The letters were too small for me to read. I assumed it was the name of the clockmaker.

'Um … Miss Hatfield?' I called.

'Rebecca,' she corrected.

'Rebecca, I think the time on the clock is wrong.'

'Oh, it's no matter. I'll fix it later.'

Miss Hatfield finished pouring the second lemonade from the heavy-looking glass pitcher. She stood on her toes to reach into a wooden cupboard above the counter and pulled out an empty vial, careful not to knock anything over this time. The vial was made of thick glass, worn smooth and flat in some areas. It was supposed to be clear glass, but the dust from the cupboard made it a smoky colour. She held the vial up to the light, turning it this way and that. I was tempted to tell her it was empty, but she appeared satisfied with whatever she saw inside. She unscrewed the top and held the vial completely upside down over one of the glasses. I didn't know what she was waiting for until one lone drop plopped in.

'Well, that's that,' Miss Hatfield mumbled to herself. 'It's all gone now.' She tossed the glass vial into the trash, seeming to not give it another thought. 'Here's your lemonade,' she said, handing me the glass into which she'd dispensed the drop.

My hand rose automatically to take the glass from her, but froze just in time. A range of thoughts went through my head, but none was as clear as this one: *What did she put into my glass?* Was it poison? Did she mean to kill me with it? Why me?

Miss Hatfield chuckled. 'Do you think I just put poison into your glass?' she asked, as if she knew *exactly* what I was thinking. 'You can rest assured that's not the case; far from it, in fact. Besides, why would I slip poison into your glass in plain sight, with you obviously watching? It's just a little addition to make the lemonade taste … better.'

I realized she had a point and took the glass from her.

'To a lasting friendship,' Miss Hatfield toasted. A thought crept into my mind. Should I ask exactly what Miss Hatfield had added to my drink? I shook my head free of that thought. I didn't want to look childish. Besides, Mother always told me that only children ask useless questions and we should leave everything up to the adults.

I clinked my glass with Miss Hatfield's as I'd seen adults do frequently, and downed the lemonade as she did the same with hers. The drink tasted like lemonade was supposed to, and why shouldn't it? I felt silly for having doubted her and worse for imagining her to be some kind of murderess. Of *course* she wasn't.

'I want us to be good friends,' Miss Hatfield said once we'd emptied our glasses. She sat at the table in front of me. 'You can tell me anything you wish, and in turn you can ask me anything.'

And so I did. I told her what I knew; my mother, my father, my teacher and my friends. I told her about Judy, at whose house I was supposed to be soon, to which she replied, 'Pish-posh.'

Miss Hatfield listened attentively to me, as if she wasn't an adult at all, but rather someone of my own age. She asked all the smart questions – the ones most adults call silly and pointless. When I told her about the presents I'd received for Christmas, she asked me how many and which was my favourite, not the total cost of them like Judy's mother had. But when it came time for me to ask questions about her, nothing came to mind.

'Surely there must be something pressing upon your mind that you want to ask me? Anything at all?' She smiled encouragingly.

I thought hard, but still I drew a blank.

'Maybe something about my house?' she persisted. 'Did you perhaps wonder about the antiques I have here?'

I responded that, in fact, I had. 'I especially like the portraits you have hanging in your parlour,' I found myself saying, though I really just found them creepy.

'Oh, thank you. I've been collecting them over the years.'

I nodded, waiting for her to direct the conversation. She continued, 'I have some other pictures of people I think you'd like even more. Do you want to see them?' Miss Hatfield asked as she stood up.

'Yes, I'd like that.'

I followed Miss Hatfield back to the parlour, where she crouched in front of the pea-green couch and unbuckled the steamer trunk. The heavy lid fell open in a flurry of dust, but once that cleared I could see stacks of photo albums inside – some older than the furniture around us and some brand new, as if they'd just been bought yesterday. Miss Hatfield shuffled through a stack of albums until she came to the one she sought, which was covered with pink lace and frills. It looked like a baby photo album – one of the ones that proudly declare *It's a girl!* on the cover to anyone who cared to notice.

As Miss Hatfield flipped through the album, her fingers lingering on its pages, I saw that it contained pictures of a mother and a father, and of a baby who grew as the pages of the album progressed.

'Where did you get this from?' My voice caught oddly in my throat, coming out sounding raspy. I couldn't breathe and wanted to run away, but somehow I couldn't make myself move from the couch.

'What do you mean? You don't think I stole this, do you? This is mine,' she insisted.

I felt myself shaking my head from side to side in disbelief. 'That can't be,' I muttered. 'That baby … is me.'

I was certain of it. The photos were of my mother and father and me. They showed me from all angles, but I was never once looking at the camera. Some had been taken through windows; others which were magnified had obviously been taken from across the street. I saw a picture of my parents walking me to my first day of school, but I didn't see their faces. Whoever took these photos did so without being noticed.

I flipped to the last page of the album. There was only one picture in the last slot; it was of me eating breakfast at home. I looked at what I was wearing and what I was eating. The picture had been taken yesterday.

My hands shook, the light pages of the photo album rustling with the tremors. I kept my eyes down as I tried to think of what I should do. I didn't dare trust my voice, but neither could I remain silent. I forced myself to look up into the distant eyes of the woman next to me.

'Who are you?'

Chapter 2

'Who am I?' She repeated the question right back at me. 'I'm Rebecca Hatfield.'

Her answer sounded small and far away. It sounded so well practised that it almost felt like the truth. But not quite.

'Who are you?' I repeated. As I stood up from my place on the couch, the album fell from my lap. Photos spilled out from its pages and floated down to the floor in the room's still air, but neither of us moved to pick them up.

'I'm Rebecca Hatfield.' Her answer was stronger now, firmer. But how could I believe a single word she said? 'I haven't lied to you. I've only told the truth. I *am* Rebecca Hatfield.' She gestured for me to sit back down on the couch, and maybe it was because she was an adult and I was a child that I complied.

'I was someone else, once—' Her voice was very faint now. 'But that was long ago. Now I'm Rebecca Hatfield.'

'I thought you just moved here,' I said, motioning to the photo album now lying in disarray on the floor.

'I did, but prior to that I visited quite often.'

'And what about the pictures of me and my family? You've been following me.'

I saw Miss Hatfield pause at my question. Rather than answer, she changed the subject and said, 'I need you for something.'

18

'Look, I'm sorry if I gave you any reason to think this was anything more than a polite conversation between two neighbours.' I stood up and began walking towards the door. I was suddenly aware of how much I sounded like my mother. I shook it off. 'But I really must—' The rest of the sentence died in my throat as my hostess suddenly slipped between me and the door.

'You don't understand,' she said breathlessly. There was something wild about her eyes now, something feral that didn't belong there. It made me catch my breath and take a step back.

'You're right,' I said. 'I don't understand and I don't want to. Nor do I need to. Please, I have to go.'

'There's no going back. You don't have a choice.'

'Of course I do. I always have a choice,' I said. 'Now please let me go. Someone's expecting me.'

'I've called Judy's mother to tell her you won't be going.'

'You called her? And she believed you?'

'I told her your throat started hurting and your mother thinks you might be sick.'

'My mother—'

'I also told her that your mother was out running a quick errand, which is why she asked me to come over to keep an eye on you. I said you just remembered you were to spend the night at their house and asked me to call for you, since your throat's too swollen to talk.'

'But I didn't hear you make that call,' I said, realizing that after I told Miss Hatfield about Judy and my plans for that night, she hadn't left my company at any point.

'You're right.' She paused and smiled at me. 'You are a clever girl, aren't you? A quick thinker. And your thinking has only improved with age. I made the right choice. I called before you came. I overheard you and Judy talking about your plans at the park yesterday.'

'So you knew I was coming?' I asked, uncertainly.

'I did,' she confirmed. 'It was easy to bait you to come to me. I know you play outside your house until dinner. I simply sent a package to myself, knowing what time the mailman comes around, and that he grows lazy in the late afternoon.'

I shook my head mutely, again in disbelief. This had to be a dream, or maybe some kind of nightmare. My voice finally came back.

'Why me?'

'I'm rescuing you from your life. I know you're miserable. I've watched you playing with your doll. You don't fit in with your friends or your family. You can't fit in because you're not meant to – you're meant for something greater than a normal existence.'

'So you spent time … years … planning all this?'

This time it was she who shook her head slowly. 'No. I was merely observant.' She laughed quietly.

I shuddered at the thought of a stranger watching my life through the lens of a camera while I was growing up.

'I–I've got to go home. My mother will be worried.' I tried to push past Miss Hatfield, but she stood her ground in front of the door. I didn't know whether I wanted to scream or cry in my panic. 'Please, Rebecca –' I thought if I used her first name as she preferred she might let me go '– you don't need me. You can find someone else for whatever this is about.'

'If only I could, but what's done is already done. I couldn't reverse it even if I wanted to. Immortality transcends time.'

'You're not making any sense. Please, I just want to go home. You're scaring me.' I began to feel frantic.

20

Thoughts raced wildly through my mind. This woman's mental state clearly wasn't stable, and quite frankly she terrified me. She hadn't tried to hurt me, but I didn't know what she would try to do next.

My head snapped around quickly as I looked at one wall, then another … I had to find a way out. I was getting desperate now. I caught a glimpse of something in a frame hanging next to an old faded watercolour painting of irises. It was such a curious sight that my head stopped moving as soon as my eyes passed over it. At first I thought it was another painting or a photograph, but there was something unsettling about it.

The scene was an interesting one, filled with the buzz of emotion and energy. It was of two young women having an intense conversation. One appeared to have grown tired of the banter and had moved her gaze towards the viewer. The other young woman looked flustered and was blocking a door as if denying the other young woman entry … or possibly exit.

The familiarity of the scene dawned on me, but I couldn't believe it at first. I forgot about everything around me and for that moment my whole world was centred on that framed image. My body was tautly strung as I walked towards the picture. It didn't take many steps to reach it, but each one felt like more than a mile to me. My hand unthinkingly went to my face, but what I felt wasn't me at all. My cheeks weren't as plump as they had been before. My face was longer than I had remembered it to be, and my chin seemed more angular. When I looked at my body, I was no longer a young girl. My body was proportioned more like Mother's.

I watched in horror as the woman in the frame copied my movements, motion for motion. When I touched the scene in the frame, the woman inside did the same. I found it cool to the touch and wondered if she did, too.

'What did you do to me?' My words were slow, as if they were someone else's. They were hopelessly caught, just as I was.

'Only what had to be done. I tried to tell you earlier.'

'You tried to tell me earlier? When? You couldn't try to tell me before you did … whatever you did?' My voice had a hysterical edge to it now, but for some reason it didn't sound like my own voice any more. It was much too old, and even my sobs were foreign to me.

I felt my knees buckle as my legs gave away beneath me. The hard ground met me halfway.

'I thought you'd have noticed,' Miss Hatfield said. 'Your improved vocabulary, your voice, even the way you walk – it's all changed. Now you must see why you can't go home.' Miss Hatfield crouched down beside me. I didn't want her anywhere near me. I wanted my mother and my father, but she was all I had. 'Your parents won't recognize you – you didn't even recognize yourself. This is for the good of everyone. Even you. You'll see.'

I felt Miss Hatfield grab hold of my shoulders and help me up before guiding me to something soft to lie on. I watched the world through a veil of tears as everything I knew became disfigured and mangled. The colours were all blurred together, running into each other. I felt as if I was slipping away into some strange dimension where I recognized nothing – not my surroundings, or my feelings, but most terrifyingly of all, not even myself.

Chapter 3

I woke with a faint thrumming inside my head. Everything felt like a bad, foggy dream, yet here I still was – in a stranger's house, looking at fingers too long and slender to be my own. I couldn't understand what had happened to me, couldn't get my head around the impossibility of it all.

I sat up to look around at the room and found myself on a plain mattress set atop a four-poster bed with an ornate golden headboard. There were no blankets on the bed or nearby. The logical conclusion was that I must have cried myself to sleep without even realizing where I was. Floral wallpaper peeled from the walls and ceiling, and tears or slashes in the paper revealed grey wooden boards beneath. Bunches of white primroses and blue flax swam in front of my eyes. Somehow I knew that these flowers had once made people feel comfortable and at home, but now they only made me feel lost and intimidated.

'Good, you're awake!' Miss Hatfield emerged unexpectedly from the floor through an old wooden trapdoor she'd pushed open with one hand while balancing a tea tray in the other. Her heels thumped against the wooden floorboards and made them creak in protest. 'Here you are, English breakfast,' she said, pouring tea into a cup decorated with flowers that resembled those on the peeling wallpaper.

I couldn't take the cup from her. Not after what had happened last night. The events of the evening had mostly become a blur, but the shock of finding myself in a different body with someone else's face still haunted me.

Miss Hatfield smiled what she probably thought was a sympathetic smile, but it didn't work on me. I remembered that she was the one accountable for all this.

'Take the tea,' she said. 'I didn't tamper with it. Besides, you'll need the caffeine. You slept rather fitfully.'

I was tempted to remind her that it wasn't every day that a stranger puts something into your drink that turns you into someone else.

'I can't trust you.'

'And with good reason,' she agreed. 'But remember, I've never lied to you.'

'You never told me the whole truth, either.'

She went mute at that, but after a moment of silence, she responded, 'Would you like me to start now?'

I wondered what kind of question that was. Of course I wanted to know the truth about what was going on and what all this had to do with me. I nodded, curious but still untrusting.

'Have you ever heard of Juan Ponce de León?' she asked me.

'The man who discovered Florida?'

'Yes. On 27 March 1513, Juan Ponce de León had his first glimpse of Florida …' I didn't understand why Miss Hatfield was giving me what sounded like a dull history lesson, but she shot me a look that silenced the words that were about to spill out of my mouth. 'On 2 April, he landed and took possession—'

'Why do I need to know this?' I blurted out, risking her anger in my frustration. 'It sounds like something from a

24

history book. It has nothing to do with me, or with what you've done to me.'

'And if it did, would you listen then?' It was a puzzling question. How could something that happened in 1513 have anything to do with me?

'Yes,' I said, reluctantly.

'Then listen,' she said. 'While he was there, Ponce de León explored the coast of Florida. He found many islands, one of which he named Islamorada, the purple island. In 1521, Ponce de León returned, this time with two ships, to colonize Florida for the Spanish. But while he and his party were building houses, they were attacked by members of the Calusa tribe. Ponce de León was injured during the battle by an arrow tipped with Manchineel sap, and the Manchineel tree is deadly. It can kill a man in four different ways – by breathing in smoke after a tree has been burned; by eating its fruit, which resembles a small apple; by inhaling the vapours the living tree releases; and by introducing the tree's sap into the bloodstream. The latter was what ultimately killed Juan Ponce de León. His men frantically tried to find arrowroot, the only known antidote for the poison, but to no avail. Finally his men brought him to Havana, Cuba, in a last-ditch attempt to find a poultice of arrowroot to save him, but Ponce de León died shortly after they arrived there.'

'This has nothing to do with me. You didn't poison me – you turned me into … this.' I motioned to my face. Never going home again and never seeing my parents or friends again felt almost like being dead. Dying from the Manchineel tree sounded easier and a lot less painful than what she was putting me through.

'This has everything to do with you – and me – if you'll just let me finish.'

25

I didn't know what to expect from this story. I had no idea what I should try to take from it, but having no other choice I could see, I agreed to let her continue.

'The story I just told you is the one most people are acquainted with, but it's only a fragment of the truth.' Miss Hatfield's voice became monotone, emotionless, as if she were reciting from an open book in front of her.

'In 1513, when Ponce de León discovered Islamorada, he also found a lake on the island filled with the clearest water he'd ever seen. Wondering if it were fresh, Ponce de León took a sip and was amazed to discover that it was. He invited his friend, Buono de Quexo, to try the water, but fearing the lake wasn't really fresh, he declined, preferring to stand guard in case the Calusa warriors decided to pay an unexpected visit. Instead, a woman by the name of Juana Ruíz, who had accompanied Ponce de León's expedition and was the first European woman to set foot in the New World, decided that she wanted to try the water herself. She agreed that it was the sweetest she'd ever tasted. Ponce de León marked the location of the lake on his personal map, in case his men ran out of fresh water. However, it appears he promptly forgot about it for the remainder of his first expedition.

'In 1521, when Ponce de León gathered men to return with him and colonize Florida, he realized that those who had accompanied him on his first voyage had aged gleatly over the course of the last eight years, whereas he received many compliments that he'd hardly changed and still appeared youthful. On his second expedition, one of the men, Francisco de Ortega, brought along his wife, Beatriz Jimenez, and she in turn brought her sister, Juana. While Beatriz had come to the New World to settle down with her husband and escape the tradition and social demands of Spain, her sister Juana had a very different reason for joining the expedition.

'Juana had heard from a friend about a woman with the same name as her who never aged and always had a youthful glow about her. She'd heard stories that this woman's perpetual youth was a gift of the magical waters of a lake she'd bathed in when she visited Florida. Juana knew it was a risk; there was definitely a strong chance the stories would turn out to be nothing more than that – stories. But it was a risk she was willing to take, for Spain held nothing for her any more. Not since her parents had passed away and her betrothed had married another because Juana couldn't pay a dowry. In a way, she had nothing to lose. All she had to do was stick close to Juan Ponce de León and find out if he knew anything about this lake.

'There came a day when Juana's patience and close following were rewarded. Ponce de León had gradually grown to trust her, and one morning he asked her if she would accompany him to a lake he'd found on his previous voyage. She agreed, of course, and as soon as they reached the lake, she dived right in. She swam around for a while, immersing herself in the water, and impatiently waited to feel different. Eventually Ponce de León asked her to help him search for kindling in the forest around the lake area to bring back to camp. He didn't want to leave her alone, but having come this far, Juana had no intention of getting out of the water just yet. She told him she'd be perfectly fine by herself and that she would wait for him. He tried again to convince her to come with him – the area around the lake was damp and he didn't know how far he'd have to go to find dry kindling. Ultimately, her stubbornness won out and he left alone, promising to return as soon as he could.

'As far as anyone knows, Juana spent hours floating on her back in the lake. She was still floating when the sun began to cast long shadows into the waters around her. The ripples she made in the water disfigured the shadows until she could no longer identify their shapes. As the water grew still, she peered at her own reflection. It remained unchanged. She was upset – even angry – that she didn't look any younger. She thought the waters hadn't worked the way they should have, but she still found herself bottling up some of the lake's waters.'

Miss Hatfield stopped speaking.

'And what happened to her?' I asked. I found myself caught up in the story despite myself, and was beginning to see where the connection to my strange situation came in.

'The story goes that when Ponce de León returned, he didn't find anyone floating in the lake. He searched the banks and looked all over for her. Just as he was about to head back to the camp, believing that she'd left without him, he realized that the small leaf-covered tree trunk he'd just stumbled over was too soft to be merely wood. He crouched in the mud and rolled the object over. It was a body – Juana's body. Not even the smears of mud on her cheeks could hide her sickly pallor. She had claw marks on her face, as though she'd either scratched herself with her own fingernails or been involved in some sort of struggle. Her cheeks were bloodied and her expression was one of utter horror – the only evidence of the nature of the last thing she saw. No one really knew how she died. Some speculated that she went mad and took her own life, while others swore that the Devil himself was in the forest.

'The physician Ponce de León ran to fetch said that in her grasp was a glass bottle of some sort. He thought the bottle might be a key piece of evidence in the mystery of her death, so he tried to take it from her hand. Though she'd been dead for many hours, her grip was still equal to that of the strongest man. It took three men to prise the vial from her fingers, and when they did, her fingers creaked as they opened, and a sigh escaped from her lips as if she were still alive. After her burial, which was a quick and small affair, the glass bottle went to her closest living relative – her sister Beatriz – who put it on her mantelshelf, where it remained, untouched, until the day she died.'

'And where do I fit into this?' I asked. 'You're still not telling me why you did what you did.'

Miss Hatfield barely glanced at me before lapsing back into her story. 'The glass vial was passed down through family members and friends who didn't know what they held, until in 1608 it reached a certain Rebecca Hatfield.'

'1608?' My mind froze for a second as all the implications of Miss Hatfield's sentence unfolded themselves. 'You were alive in 1608?'

Miss Hatfield laughed, the corner of her eyes crinkling daintily.

'Don't be silly,' she said. 'I wouldn't be born for another 224 years.'

'But that's still—'

'It was just someone with the same name.' Miss Hatfield paused to collect her thoughts. 'She was making herself a pot of tea one day when she knocked over the glass bottle. The neck of the bottle hit the opening of the kettle just so, the cork stopping the bottle flew off, and a drop of the water fell into the tea. Poor Rebecca didn't notice, and promptly re-corked the bottle and set it back onto the shelf above her. She drank the tea without thinking, and it wasn't until a few months had passed that she realized something was amiss.'

'How did she know?' I asked.

'I'm glad you're finally taking an interest in my story.' A small smile flickered across her face, and she continued, 'She'd cut her hair sometime after drinking the tea, and though months had passed since then, her hair didn't appear to be growing any longer. Rebecca had cut her son John's hair at the same time, and was shocked to realize that her hair had stopped growing, though his had not. When half a year had passed, she knew something was wrong, but she kept her secret to herself. When five years had passed, she saw her husband's face gain wrinkles and her son's grow into maturity while her own didn't change, and she knew she had to do something. She could no longer remain in denial. She thought of talking to the town priest or to her husband, or maybe even to her child, but she knew they wouldn't believe her. She couldn't escape what was happening to her and there was no way out. So, one fateful day, she left home and never looked back.

'For years she lived alone in the wild. She learned to fend for herself and keep others at a distance. She lost track of time; the only way she knew one year from another was by the passing seasons and the growth of the trees around her. They protected and sheltered her from the elements as well as from mankind, and for that she was thankful.

'Many days, she dreamed about how it might be to go back home. She knew it wouldn't be as if she'd never left. She wondered if her son had finally moved out of the house and married a pretty young girl. She wondered if her husband was still blacksmithing, though his once-strong hands might now be stiff and feeble with age. That wondering was like a seed in her mind; once it was planted, it soon occupied her every thought and invaded her dreams.

30

'Rebecca woke up one night thinking enough was enough. She would only visit the town as a passing stranger and check up on her family. It wouldn't do any harm. Curiosity gnawed at her bones, and she felt compelled to make the visit.

'The next day she rose early and began the walk to town. By the time she got there, the path's dust and dirt cloaked her form so entirely that she believed she wouldn't have to hide her face. She was treated respectfully as a weary traveller, and when she asked for directions was told the way to her own house.

'Though she thought she knew the town as well as she knew her own son, she found the place completely changed; it had morphed into something more. The old buildings had been extended, making them look bigger and grander. The dirt paths were beaten out and smoothed, so as not to trip the children who ran along them. When she arrived at the home the stranger had told her was where the Hatfields lived, it looked nothing like the house she remembered. She thought the stranger was probably mistaken, or possibly had directed her to her son's house, since his family would also be Hatfields. Just to make sure, she decided to knock on the door for good measure.'

Miss Hatfield smoothed out the wrinkles in her dress, and I found myself growing impatient, wanting her to continue this strange tale. She finally began again. 'When the door opened, a woman with a baby at her hip peeked her head out and frowned. Rebecca told her she was looking for John, since she believed the woman was prob-ably his wife and might be startled at the sight of such a dusty female traveller knocking on her door for no apparent reason. The woman looked at her in confusion, saying no John lived there. Thinking she had the wrong house, Rebecca then asked her where she might find the Hatfield residence. The woman looked even more confused, and replied that she was Sarah Hatfield and the residence was indeed that house. Rebecca, refusing to believe her, asked to see her husband, who soon came to the door. He introduced himself as Richard Hatfield, and when asked where John was, he too was confused at first. He scratched his head for a moment, until a certain light of recognition dawned in his eyes. "Are you doing some type of family history research, ma'am? My great-grandfather's name was John." He clearly thought all of this strange, to say the least, and stared at her, waiting for an answer …

'Rebecca finally realized what must have happened but, needing further proof, she asked Richard, "What year is it, please?"

'"Why, it's the year of our Lord 1713, of course," was his reply. At this, Rebecca was visibly shaken. It's said she asked him where the nearest river was, and then walked there, all the way muttering, "1713," to herself.'

'And what happened to her after that?' I asked.

'She found a rope somewhere on her way to the river. Once she got there, she tied one end of the rope around her waist and the other end around a heavy rock, and then waded into the river with it cradled in her arms. A child from the town saw her do it and ran to get help.'

'And then?' I couldn't help myself. I had to know what happened to Rebecca, and why Miss Hatfield was named after her.

'She was never seen again,' she said. 'Her body was never found. It probably sank with the rock and never surfaced.'

'And why were you named after her?'

'Named after?' She smiled. 'I've never thought of it

that way.' She was almost mumbling now. 'I wasn't always Rebecca Hatfield. I had a different name, once. I … just don't remember it.'

'You don't remember your given name?' I was astonished that someone could so easily forget something as important as that.

'I used to remember it,' she said, more to herself than me. 'I used to whisper it to myself at night, so I wouldn't forget it. But it appears I finally have.' Her voice was remorseful and tinged with sadness. I had the strangest urge to comfort her, but I instinctively knew this was one thing I couldn't help her with.

'I was born almost one and a half centuries ago, in 1832.' She'd obviously started her own story now. It was a ridiculous statement, but I had no choice other than to go along with her fantasy for the moment, and besides, it was no stranger than the fact that my appearance had changed completely overnight. 'My childhood wasn't perfect, but it was happy enough. My parents were of the upper class, so I didn't have to worry about my future. It was all laid out for me; I just had to continue living according to their plans.' She glanced at me and saw that I was now thoroughly drawn into her tale. 'This isn't a story. Those were days strung together with a beginning, but no middle or end.'

'How are you still alive now?' I couldn't help but ask her.

'It all happened in a few hours,' she said. 'A lady was pushing a pram around the same park where I took my morning stroll. I wasn't alone, of course – it was improper back in those days for a young woman to be in public unaccompanied. My older brother was chaperoning me, but he was talking to an old friend from his university days, and his back was turned.

'I don't quite know what possessed me, but I said to the woman with the pram, "Excuse me, madam. Your baby looks so adorable. May I hold him?" I'd only glimpsed the dear baby's face and a lock of his golden hair, but his dimples made me smile and think of my little sister's dimples when she was that age.

'"Why, of course." The woman smiled warmly and reached into the pram. She placed him gently into my arms which suddenly registered the unexpected shock of weightlessness. When I looked down, glassy eyes stared back, and I almost dropped the baby.

'Upon a closer look, I found that it wasn't a baby at all, merely a doll that resembled one. Its hair was stiff and coarse, and I wondered how I could have mistaken it for my sister's soft, golden tresses. I remembered her lying perfectly still in her last earthly bed. Her eyes were closed, but I recall how the wind had tousled her locks. I was the last one to touch her; I smoothed her hair as gently as I could with trembling fingers. I watched as two men shovelled dirt upon her coffin, scoop after scoop, until she was buried deep below our feet. And yet I couldn't erase her face from my memory. How could I, when even though she was with us for such a short while, I loved her so dearly?

'"How could you?" My words came out harsher and deadlier than I expected. It was a cruel joke this woman had played, especially when she must know of the loss my family and I had suffered this November past. How could she be so insensitive, when she and everyone else in the town knew of our pain? It had been plastered all over the newspaper for everyone to see. But although we received flowers by the bundle and condolence letters by the stack, how could anyone have truly understood how we felt?

'Perhaps I was being unfair. I didn't recognize her – maybe she didn't know what had happened to us. "I–I'm sorry," I said to her quietly. She couldn't possibly understand what my family had gone through; there was no reason for her to. I had no right to talk to her in that way. I handed the doll back and turned away from her, tears streaming down my cheeks as I walked back to my brother.

'"You think I don't understand, but I know." I felt a gentle hand on my shoulder, which caused me to look back. "I miss my darling boy," the woman said, not meeting my eyes. "I miss him so much that sometimes I feel as though I'm breaking from the inside out. The only thing holding me together is the thought that he wouldn't want that, and neither would your sister."

'"Your boy," I asked. "What happened to him?" In a way, I didn't want to hear the answer, but for some reason I knew I had to ask the question.

'"Walter didn't wake up, just like your sister," she said, and I saw how wrong I was to have judged her as I did everyone else.

'She introduced herself to me as Miss Rebecca Hatfield, and asked if I would like to see a photo of her son she kept at home. Knowing it might help her cope with her loss, I agreed without thinking twice about letting my brother know, for he was still engaged in conversation with his friend. Besides, I thought I wouldn't be gone long.

'Miss Hatfield led me along block after block. It felt strange without a family member accompanying me. I was used to being watched over, and this felt like freedom to me.

'The house we came to wasn't stately in the least, although I've done it up over the years and now I'm quite fond of it, especially this room. But back then its gable was crooked and its colours drab. The shingles were falling off the roof and there was no porch to speak of. I was surprised she could have afforded a photograph of her son. Once she led me inside, however, I found the tidiness and warmth that permeated the house made it much more welcoming than my own. There was none of the polished-yet-cold atmosphere I found in the way my mother kept her house; similarly, Miss Hatfield turned out to be much less distant than my mother.

'Miss Hatfield brought out a cake she'd baked, along with – of course – some tea, which I later learned had a drop of the lake's waters in it. I remember we talked for at least an hour. What of, I don't rightly recall, but I suppose I told her of my life, just as she disclosed parts of hers. I say parts, because though I failed to notice it then, she was keeping portions of the truth from me and twisting her story to suit herself and her objectives. She introduced me to the idea of immortality through the same stories I told you, and some more we haven't got to yet. She explained to me the simultaneous gift and curse it was to live for ever. At the time I thought she was merely delusional, and that she was making those stories up. I still wish she had been.

'She told me that now I was just like her, and there was no turning back. She said I was destined to become her and that we would live out our endless lives together. At one point I became so scared that I asked her to stop. I accused her of things I dare not repeat even now. I begged and pleaded with her, but to no avail. Miss Hatfield said I needed to know the truth, now that I couldn't go back. And so I grabbed the nearest thing to me, which was the knife she'd cut the cake with, and held it up at her with a shaking hand.

'"Stop!" I remember crying out. "Please stop. I can't bear it." My words tumbled out through my sobs. But Miss Hatfield only laughed.

'"This is for your own good. Do you think I'd be doing this if it weren't?" There was a dark glint in her eyes. "Go ahead, kill me," she dared. "I'd rather die than keep living this way." She put her hands around mine, which were shakily grasping the knife's handle, and brought the tip of the blade closer to her chest. "Go ahead."

'"Just stop it," I remember begging. "Please."

'Her hands still around mine, she jerked the blade away from her. All in an instant I felt relief, and then that, too, was shattered when she plunged the knife into her chest. I can still hear her little gasp in my ear when I close my eyes. I remember crying out, but hearing no sound save for her final utterance: "Walter."

'Death appeared glad to be able to finally reclaim her after all those years. He'd been waiting for her; watching until he found his moment. The fifth Miss Hatfield turned to dust before my eyes. There was nothing left of her existence save for the thin sheen of blood on the cake knife.'

'And that's when you knew the stories she told you were true,' I said.

Miss Hatfield nodded and I found myself understanding how she felt.

'But why did you take her name?'

'It was one of the things she explained to me, before … it happened. She told me that we become each other, since we were the only people we could trust. We need a life to turn to when we lose our own, and by taking on the name, we take on a history and another life.'

'So now … Who am I?'

'You are me and I am you. We're exceptions in time.'

'And I'm now Rebecca Hatfield.' I meant to ask it as a question, but my remark came out sounding more like a statement, much more certain than I was.

'You're the seventh Miss Hatfield.'

Chapter 4

'This still doesn't explain who I am ... *what* I am.' I gestured to my face. 'If I'm immortal now, why am I in someone else's body?'

'You're not in someone else's body,' Miss Hatfield said in a matter-of-fact manner. 'You're still in your own.'

'But this person is ... older.'

'It's your older self, and that has nothing to do with immortality or the lake's waters. That has to do with the clock and is a different matter entirely.'

'The clock? What does the clock have to do with anything?'

'I used the clock to move time forward. You weren't immortal yet, since I had not yet given you the water. This aged you, while I, being immortal, did not age. After I gave you the water and turned you immortal, I again moved the clock, but you and your body had already entered an immortal state and therefore did not age.'

She paused as if collecting her thoughts and continued. 'The clock ... It gives us a place in time,' she responded cryptically. 'Immortality displaces us from time as you used to know it. We're visitors in every time and don't have one of our own, so when others become so suspicious of our true nature that we must relocate, we use the clock to do so.'

'You mean time travel?'

'You might call it that. But travel indicates a journey with a beginning and an end, and we have neither.'

'We?' I asked. 'The Miss Hatfields collectively?'

She shook her head. 'No, just you and me.'

'But what of the others? Don't they live by the same rules and in the same way?'

'They used to,' was her answer, until I pressed for more.

'How do they live now?'

'They don't,' she said coarsely, in a way that quite differed from the kind of person I thought she was. 'The fifth Miss Hatfield left me all alone with no instructions other than to destroy any trail that might lead to us. The others are also deceased.'

'But they were immortal—'

'Immortality from the waters of the lake can only protect you from illness and death by natural causes. You can still die in an accident.'

'And that was how they all died? In accidents?' I pronounced the word carefully, in spite of the fact it tasted bitter in my mouth.

'Yes, accidents,' she said. 'I told you the story of the first Miss Hatfield, who drowned herself, but that wasn't the end of the misfortunes faced by women of our name. The second Miss Hatfield died in a fire aboard a ship heading to Wales. The third was tried in a town court and found guilty of witchcraft because people noticed she wasn't ageing. Missing children and failing crops were blamed on her, and her death marked the beginning of the Salem Witch Trials. The fourth Miss Hatfield died in an asylum because she asked her fiancé to accept her for what she'd become, and still find it within himself to love her for who she was now. Needless to say, he thought she carried bad blood and helped them lock her away. It's not clear exactly how she died, but it was probably the torture they put her through which ultimately did her in. And the fifth Miss Hatfield, of course … Well, I've told you about her end.'

'If time has no meaning for us, can't you go back and save the other Miss Hatfields from their deaths?' I asked.

'If only it worked like that.' I heard Miss Hatfield draw a soft sigh. 'But unfortunately, it doesn't. Or at least no one's figured out how to do it yet. It's probably physically impossible. Once you become immortal, you don't have a place in time. You or I can save a mortal from an untimely death, but death always has his way; he soon finds another means to claim what's his,' she said. 'I can't even go back to stop the fifth Miss Hatfield from slipping the lake's water into my tea.'

'But if a mortal goes back in time—'

She cut me off coldly, simply saying, 'They can't.'

I felt myself frown, trying to understand. 'They can't? What do you mean?'

'Mortals can't physically go backwards or forwards in time past the limits of their own lifespan. They can't move from their places in time since they belong there, and nowhere else. They're tied down.' Miss Hatfield noticed my brow furrow deeper and tried to explain the idea to me more clearly. 'Time isn't a river, as most people think. It's more like a lake or a pond, in which multiple times exist simultaneously. One time doesn't just begin and end suddenly. They all coexist as parts of a whole. One person belongs to a series of times in their lifetime. They leave a part of them behind in each, but each part is slightly different from all the others, even though they belong to the same person.'

I was still a bit confused, but thought I was beginning to grasp what she was saying. 'Which is why people change gradually over time?' I asked.

'Precisely. To a mortal, it looks as though people change slowly over the course of their lives, but the reality is that people leave a different version of themselves behind in each moment of time. Mortals can't see the whole human or perceive these different versions of each person.' Gradually her words began to make more sense in my mind as they painted a very different world from the one I'd thought I existed in. I was beginning to get a glimpse behind the façade of time that we all had created for ourselves.

'We immortals disappear from other times, even from the times during which we were alive. We only have one version of ourselves. If you went back to your time, to your house, you wouldn't find yourself there. Your mother and father think you've gone missing. They wouldn't even recognize you as the little girl they're looking for.'

I shuddered and tried to wrap my head around what she was saying.

'And the clock? You still haven't explained how it works,' I pressed her. 'When and how did you receive such a thing?'

Miss Hatfield tried to hide her grin with the back of her hand. 'Please excuse me for being amused, but you must realize that the word "when" has little meaning to me now.' She actually laughed slightly, and I saw what she meant.

In the life – if you could even call it that – she lived in, of which I was now a part, I had to remind myself, there was no past or future, not even a present except her current location in time.

'Finish your cup of tea and come downstairs. I'll show you how it works.'

I'd completely forgotten where I was, much less that I was holding a cup in my hands. I downed the tea, now cold as water, in a few gulps. I trained my eyes on Miss Hatfield, desperate for more knowledge about who I currently was. Her story made a strange kind of sense – it *felt* right – but I couldn't quite bring myself to believe it all.

I helped Miss Hatfield gather our cups onto her tray and followed her back down through the house the way she'd come, into the kitchen. Setting the tray on the table, I paused in front of the clock, which I realized held much more meaning to me now than it had when it last caught my gaze.

'It's a simple contraption, really.' I turned to see Miss Hatfield behind me, staring as intently at the golden clock as I must have been until she spoke. 'The twelve hours on the face of the clock signify the months in a year; there are thirty-one minutes, indicating the days in a month. But of course, the clock deals with months that don't have thirty-one days and it deals with leap years as well—'

'But what are those increments marked on the very edge of the clock's face, beyond the minutes?' I asked.

'The seconds.'

'And they stand for the years?' I guessed.

'Yes. They start right above the twelfth hour at 1527, the year the clock itself was made. The time beyond that is untouchable even for us,' she said. 'There are ten years between every hour, forwards or backwards.'

'Then surely there's a limit to how far forward you can go – what's that mark to the left of 1527?'

'When the second hand passes over that mark, a new cycle begins, overlapping the one just completed. Just as there's no end to time, there's no end to the clock. Therefore, 1527 is also 1647, 1767, 1887, 2007, and so on.'

'Where did the clock come from?' I was dumbfounded at the idea that this simple-looking object could somehow control time.

'I'm afraid I don't know the history of the clock itself,' she said. 'I think one of the earlier Miss Hatfields found it and just passed it along with the rest of this stuff.'

'So everything in this house belonged to the former Miss Hatfields?'

She nodded. 'Even the house itself is a living relic, modified and arranged to each Rebecca's tastes. It's changed in so many little ways over the years, but its foundations remain the same, and stay strong because of that. There's something about the house that comforts me. Perhaps it's the fact that it's seen all of this before – the frightening moment when you finally realize what you've become, and that you won't be going home ever again; the silent hours when you feel lost in time and in life, but also the odd instant when you look back on your life and immortality and realize you've come to terms with it all.' Miss Hatfield had a faint, faraway smile on her lips. I'd have described it as sad and lonely, but nonetheless it was a smile – the only glimmer of hope I'd seen so far on her otherwise dull and emotionless face. 'I do hope you decide to keep the house and add to it the things you valued most in your former life. As an immortal, you'll find yourself looking back on it and wishing you had more of it to live. Collecting things from our long-gone lives is one way we keep our sanity in a world that changes before our eyes. People die, technology improves, objects are replaced … It can be difficult to keep up, but in this house, everything's the way you want it. You don't have to maintain appearances here, and you can surround yourself with familiar things.' Miss Hatfield picked up a painted miniature of a girl walking her dog from the tabletop. Her eyes were focused on the miniature, but I could tell she wasn't really seeing it. Her eyes looked right through it, to something else entirely. She set it down. 'For a few minutes, you can almost pretend that none of this ever happened.'

'Of course I'll keep the house. I don't think I have anywhere else to go except here,' I reminded her. I was still angry with her, but I was becoming resigned to my fate. There was no alternative that I could see. 'Besides, you're now the only person from whom I don't have to hide a portion of myself. I'll need you – and you'll be here waiting for me, won't you?'

'I can't be sure about that,' she said, catching me off guard. I knew I couldn't leave her, since I was bound to her now, but it hadn't crossed my mind that she might leave *me*.

'Wh–what do you mean?'

'Don't you think it strange that each Miss Hatfield dies in an "accident" soon after she finds the next one? Are they really just accidents, or is it time trying to protect its secrets?'

'You're not saying that you'll leave me, are you?'

'Not willingly, but I can't control destiny.' Her gaze was downcast. She refused to look me in the eye for a few moments, but then suddenly her head snapped up. 'I'll do whatever I can to prepare you for what's ahead.'

'Thank you,' I said, for I didn't know what else to say.

'It's your right. I owe you at least that much. But first there's a little job I need you to do for me. For us.'

Chapter 5

'I look like a sixteenth-century pageboy in this.' I was astounded by the clothes Miss Hatfield had dressed me in.

'My aim is to make you look like a lady.'

'Not even my mother wears anything remotely as old-fashioned as this,' I complained. The clothes Miss Hatfield had chosen were beyond absurdity. They puffed up in odd places and were skintight in others.

'Hopefully this corset will change your current sixteenth-century-pageboy appearance into that of an early twentieth-century lady,' Miss Hatfield muttered, pulling the garment around my middle and over my hips. 'Hold on to the bedposts. I'll have to lace this up quite tight in your case – you're quite behind in developing your figure.' She yanked on the laces and the corset's stays contracted around my midsection. 'My mother started putting my sisters and me in figure-developing corsets from the time we were six, and our neighbour chided her for starting so late.' She jerked the laces again and I gasped as my breath was forced out of my lungs. 'This will just have to do,' she said. 'You're petite, but luckily this will probably still fit you.' She pulled an elegant-looking dress down over my head as I peered into a dirty full-length mirror, trying to see what I'd been transformed into.

My body swam in the endless sea of fabric draped over me, but even the crack running from the top of the mirror to the bottom couldn't mar the sheer beauty of the garment. It was of a colour similar to burgundy but a bit brighter, which somehow made it more emotionally uplifting.

'This was your dress?' I asked Miss Hatfield.

'Yes,' she said. 'But I do think it looks much better on you than it ever did on me.'

I looked from my face in the mirror to Miss Hatfield's behind me, and in addition to the similar smile we both wore, we looked so much alike now that we could have been mistaken for sisters.

'The colour contrasts quite nicely with your pale skin and auburn hair. It's beautiful,' Miss Hatfield said. I smiled gratefully and reached a hand up to touch my hair, which she'd piled up on top of my head like another mop of dark fabric.

My mother called my hair colour that same shade Miss Hatfield had – auburn. I always called it brown, but she would shush me, insisting it was auburn. Easy for her to say, I'd thought, since her hair was a light blonde – the kind everyone wanted and admired. She'd called my hair beautiful, too, but I noticed with a pang that her words had already begun to fade into a distant memory.

'You look like a true Gibson Girl,' Miss Hatfield proclaimed. I wasn't entirely sure what she meant, but took it as a compliment.

'Are you sure the corset isn't too tight?' I asked her, to the sound of her laughter.

'Of course not. You should be wondering if it's not too loose.' She laughed softly again, then grew serious once more. 'Do you remember everything I told you?'

I wanted to tell her I wasn't ready, but she'd promised this would be only a short job. I asked her many times why she couldn't buy it from its owner, or even steal it herself, but she would only mumble that the owner would never sell it and she could be recognized.

I tried to convince myself that all I had to do was go in, grab the portrait, and come right back out. I was doing the right thing, especially as the man had stolen the portrait from Miss Hatfield in the first place.

I didn't know much about this portrait I had to take from the man's house. All I knew was that it was a painting of a young woman, and that it was somehow important to Miss Hatfield and this whole mess I was in.

'You remember how to get to the house?' Miss Hatfield asked me for what must have been the third time at least as I followed her into the kitchen.

'Go down Second Avenue and turn right onto East Sixty-Sixth Street, then cross Third, Lexington, and Park Avenue. It should be the first house on the left,' I recited, exactly as I'd learned. As Miss Hatfield wound the golden clock to the correct date, I watched in wonder as its hands spun around in circles, stopping where she wanted it to. There was no question in my mind that it really did work – my older, stranger face was proof of that – but somehow I still couldn't believe that such a simple-looking instrument could transport someone like me through time.

'Very good,' Miss Hatfield said, but she was still wringing her hands with worry as she led me to the door. 'I'm sure you'll be fine, but just in case – don't talk unless you absolutely have to.'

I nodded. 'I think I'm ready.' I took a deep breath in front of the closed door, scared what it would reveal once opened.

'I think you're ready, too,' Miss Hatfield said, and she opened the door with a flourish. 'Miss Rebecca Hatfield, might I introduce you to the year 1904.'

I was only vaguely aware that my mouth was gaping open at the sight before me. A huge Victorian-looking house stood tall and grand where my own once stood … or would stand … Well, let's put it this way – where it stands somewhere else in time.

The intricacies of the whole new concept of time that Miss Hatfield had explained to me were only now beginning to unfold in my mind. I was currently in 1904, but I hadn't actually travelled back in time. I'd simply travelled to another part of time. I had to keep reminding myself that time was a lake, not a river as I'd once believed. A period of time doesn't start when another ends. They coexist.

I stared in awe as a horse-drawn coach drove past. It was truly remarkable to see a world changed so drastically, when I'd thought it would probably be quite similar to the one I'd left behind.

'Now go,' Miss Hatfield said, pushing me through the front door. 'It'll be done before you know it, and you can tell me all about it when you get back.'

So I started to make my way down Second Avenue. Miss Hatfield had explained why she couldn't come with me to the man's house – she could be recognized by someone – but I didn't understand why she wouldn't walk at least part of the way there with me. Then it dawned on me that this was *her* time or, at least, there might still be people alive who remembered her. I'd completely forgotten that even Miss Hatfield had a time of her own long ago. But I realized that if she'd not gone to the park that day and instead had continued living her previous life, she would have still been alive today in 1904. That was why she knew so much about the period – it had been close to her own. And though her parents were probably dead, many of her siblings and friends could still be alive. I couldn't blame her for not coming along. I wasn't sure I'd be returning to my home either, now that I'd moved on.

Lit street lamps glowed in rows of pure light. People were scurrying from place to place, eager to get home quickly to their families. The steady dark and evening cold followed swiftly on their heels, overtaking me and everyone else in its still blanket.

'Evening, miss.' My head whipped right at the sound of a voice, and I caught an elderly man tipping his hat at me.

'Sir,' I responded as politely as I could, remembering all I'd learned from Miss Hatfield over the last few hours of intensive cramming about this day and age.

I knew I must have looked at least a bit out of place, as I felt very conscious of myself and my movements; very much like an alien in this strange land. I picked up my pace, hoping to get this over with as quickly as possible.

'Go down Second Avenue and turn right onto East Sixty-Sixth Street, then cross Third, Lexington, and Park Avenue,' I muttered to myself as I saw Park Avenue disappear behind me, much too slowly for my liking. 'It should be the first house on the left.'

It was a large house, much grander than most of the others I'd seen on my walk. It had three rows of windows, fine curtains barely visible behind them. Stately steps led up to the front door with its large brass knocker. It looked quite intimidating.

I tried to circle the block, to attempt to find another entrance, but there were intimidating iron-wrought gates probably set up for the very purpose of discouraging thieves and people like me. Luckily, it wasn't long before I found the servants' entrance.

The servants' door was plain and made of unpainted wood, and made me feel somewhat more at home than the grand front entrance had. I looked behind me instinctively, but for what, I couldn't say. I knew I wasn't doing anything wrong by taking back the painting since it was Miss Hatfield's to begin with. I supposed I couldn't rely on anyone else agreeing with me, though.

Not finding anything or anyone behind me, I walked up to the door silently and tried the handle. It swung open, and I was surprised it wasn't locked or barred in some way. It was dark, but listening to the silence, I could tell that the hall was empty of servants. I closed the door behind me, not wanting to attract any undue attention, and felt for a wall with my hands. Finding one, I proceeded to try to feel for the opposite wall, but my hand crashed into something hard instead.

Gritting my teeth and nursing my hurt hand in the dark, I tried to feel out what my hand had hit. Thankfully, it was the opposite wall, so I was in a narrow passage of some sort. Miss Hatfield had told me that the servants' entrance in most houses almost always led into a hallway that connected to a maid's closet and the back stairs, and then to many other places in the house. I just had to get to the back staircase.

With one hand trailing along a wall and the other out in front of me so as to not bump into anything else, I walked cautiously forward. The boots Miss Hatfield had made me wear tapped ominously on the uneven wooden floor, and more than once my long dress caught on splinters or rough edges.

My left hand felt a sudden dip in the wall and I was sure I'd found something, hopefully a door. With my other hand, I searched for a doorknob and, finally finding one,

I swung the door open to reveal even more darkness. My outstretched hand found a cold, slightly slippery surface, and recoiled in disgust. I didn't know how I was going to find the back staircase in this gloom, and I knew I had to find it quickly before the servants returned to the hallway I was in.

Tap. Tap. I sucked in my breath and pressed myself against the wall, hopelessly trying to hide from whoever was walking down the hallway towards me. A steady glow of candlelight drew near as the person approached, but suddenly it stopped in its tracks. I couldn't see whoever was carrying the candle, but it was obvious that they could see me.

I knew I had to do something, and fast, before whoever was carrying the candle figured out I wasn't supposed to be there. Remembering that Miss Hatfield had dressed me to play the part of a wealthy man's daughter, I decided to put on an act.

'Well, what is it?' I asked the figure in the shadows. 'Has someone finally brought me a candle to help me navigate through the dark?'

'Y–Yes, miss.' A woman, by her voice.

'It's about time. I think I might have ripped the hem of my dress.'

'I'm sorry, miss,' the timid voice said, but I still couldn't make out her face in the gloom.

'Show me back to the parlour,' I said, guessing that would be an acceptable destination for a stranger, and also might be where the painting was located. It was worth a shot.

'Yes, miss. Please follow me.'

The woman took my hand gingerly and led me along the narrow hallway. All I could see in front of me was the now dim glow of the candle. I was strangely comforted hiding behind a persona that wasn't my own. If someone had asked me to act like myself, I think that would have been harder. It was as if I'd lost myself and forgotten who I used to be. I wasn't Cynthia any more, and I couldn't be her even if I wanted to. Perhaps that realization was going to be useful here.

We came into the light together. It was blinding compared to the darkness I'd been in for the past few minutes. As my eyes grew accustomed to the brightness, I began to take in a few of the details that surrounded me once the maid had escorted me to the parlour.

Wall fixtures greeted me with arms holding candles to light up the room. The working fireplace in the middle of one wall and the cream-coloured wallpaper gave the room a less stuffy appearance than I'd expected. Large windows faced out onto the street, but in the dim glow of the lamps outside and the flickering candles inside, all I could see was my face reflected in the dark glass.

I turned from the window and continued my survey of the room. There was a painting hanging above the fireplace and, upon closer inspection, I realized it was in fact the one Miss Hatfield had sent me to find – the portrait of the Spanish lady stolen from her by the man who owned this house. It was right in front of me. All I had to do now was take it and run.

My arm was outstretched, almost touching the portrait's gilded frame, when I heard someone clear their throat behind me. I quickly turned around.

An older man in a grey waistcoat was standing in front of me. One hand rested on top of an ornate walking stick, and he was staring at me with austere eyes. I knew without a doubt that he was the man Miss Hatfield had told me about – the owner of the house. A few steps behind him was a younger man, dressed all in black, looking similarly grim.

'What do you think you're doing?' the older one asked me sternly. The tone of his voice chilled me instantly. I tried to think of something to say, but before I could answer, he went on, his voice taking on a surprised tone. 'Why, Margaret, you didn't tell me you'd arrived early.' The man suddenly laughed and drew me close in an embrace. 'And you didn't even greet your old uncle. When did you arrive? An hour ago? You must tell me about your journey. Are you warm enough? Have you been offered a drink?'

I was thankful he talked so much that he didn't let me answer his questions. I hadn't expected to be caught, and I most certainly hadn't expected this sort of greeting. I was in utter shock and didn't know what to say or do.

'Riding on the train alone must have been horrible for a young woman of your age. I do hope you'll forgive your old uncle for that. I would've driven down with my new automobile if I hadn't fallen ill. Eh, physician's orders. What can I say?' The man paused – barely – for breath, then went on babbling. 'Why, it's been so long since I saw you last, Margaret. Just look at you! You're a young lady now, not the little girl I once knew. You were only knee-high the last time I saw you and you've only grown more beautiful,' he gushed, making me feel more uncomfortable by the second.

I was thankful when he finally paused and looked back at his grim-looking companion, as if suddenly remembering he was there.

'Margaret, this is Father Gabriel, the new local chaplain from the town near our country home. He's doing us the honour of staying with us while we're in the city. I almost forgot that you two haven't had the pleasure of meeting.'

I looked at the man standing a step behind him. The black clothing he wore now made sense, though he looked young to be taken seriously as a chaplain. As I gazed into his hard eyes, I gauged that he couldn't be more than thirty-five, yet the serious way he held himself suggested he was older.

'Though Father Gabriel has only been with us a short time since Father Dominic's passing, he's made himself indispensable, and it feels like we've known him for ever. He appears to have that effect on people.'

'A pleasure to meet you.' I found the chaplain's voice to be warmer than I'd expected. 'But as I was telling Mr Beauford right before we found you, I'd best retire for the evening to be up for the early mass tomorrow. If you wish, you may join us.'

I thanked him, before he quickly turned on his heel and left. I was now alone with the old man.

Mr Beauford hesitated, as if just recalling something. 'You haven't seen Henley yet, have you?'

I shook my head, wondering who I'd be introduced to next. I only hoped whoever it was didn't talk nearly as much as the man currently standing before me. 'Henley! Boy!' the man yelled to no one in particular. Muttering to himself, he rang a bell in the corner of the room. A scant minute later, the same servant who had escorted me to the parlour appeared.

'Sir?' She nodded towards the man and cast a confused – but polite – glance at me.

'Bring Henley down to greet his cousin. This is my niece, Margaret, whom we've been expecting,' he said. When he named me as his niece, the woman eyed me up and down, and I felt her cold judgement. Whether she reached a conclusion she liked or not, she quickly uttered, 'Yes, sir,' and promptly set out to find this Henley the man wanted me to greet.

The man, Margaret's uncle – whoever she was – made small talk, trying to engage me in conversation at any cost, but my mind was elsewhere. I needed some way to escape, but I couldn't leave without the painting. I knew I was being rude by not conversing with him, but he didn't appear to mind.

'There he is,' the man said. The tone of his voice changed all of a sudden and made me look up from my thoughts.

The same servant was standing near the door, now ajar, but Mr Beauford's gaze was on the younger man coming through it.

The young man looked nothing like the older, stooped-over man in front of me. His steps were filled with a lively spring, and there was something within him that made him glow like the embodiment of a happy and vigorous life. His face, however, conveyed a different message. His clear eyes had a strange sort of light in them, and his lips twitched as his hard eyes examined me. I suppressed a shiver, not wanting him to get the better of me.

'Henley, say hello to your cousin,' Mr Beauford said, still cheerful. He was oblivious of the tension that had passed between his son and me.

'Hello, cousin.' His voice sounded detached from the rest of him, but his father didn't appear to notice. His lips flickered momentarily but, apparently deciding on a smile, he grinned. I drew a shaking breath, then replied with what I hoped was a polite but tart nod. Something about him made me uncertain – I just didn't know what to make of this intense young man.

Mr Beaufort motioned with his cane to the servant, who was standing silently to one side, and said, 'Please escort Miss Margaret to her room.'

'Yes, sir.' It appeared to be all she ever said. She mutely motioned for me to follow her. Having no notion how to extricate myself from this ever more complicated situation, I allowed her to lead me up the main staircase and along multiple hallways before she cracked open a random door.

'I hope this room is to your liking, miss.' She lit the candles in the wall fixtures one by one, and I watched the room come alive.

'Yes, thank you,' I said distractedly, hoping to dismiss her and finally have some time to myself. This was becoming complicated, and none of Miss Hatfield's lessons had covered being mistaken for a member of the family.

'Would you like me to help with undressing?'

I told her I would see to it myself and excused her, shutting the heavy wooden door behind her. I sighed, realizing it was the first time I'd been alone for a while. I was stuck. I had no one I could talk to, no direction to go in and no one I could trust. Just myself.

I was still confused, only barely starting to comprehend the recent events that had occurred. But I knew I could never return to the way things had been – the only way to endure it was to continue and move forward, trying to survive.

I closed my eyes, letting my emotions run untempered through me. For the first time, I simply let go. Sadness. Uncertainty. Despair. Shock. They rushed at me as soon as my defences fell and I found myself surrendering to them. For the first time I let myself feel it all, including one emotion I felt above all else – terror.

My back fell heavily against the door, making no sound except a rustle of fabric as my dress slid down the wood and I collapsed into a crumpled heap on the floor.

Chapter 6

I woke to a knock at the door and stumbled out of bed to answer it. I wondered vaguely how I'd managed to drag myself to bed the previous night, but I felt more rested than I had in days.

'Yes?' I said as I opened the door.

'Sorry to wake you, miss.' It was the servant I'd met yesterday. 'But Mr Beauford asked for your presence at breakfast in an hour and sent me to assist in dressing you.'

I fumbled for words, and once I'd found some, managed to croak out a single phrase: 'How kind of him.'

The servant slipped into the room before I could stop her and audibly gasped at what I was wearing. I must have taken off Miss Hatfield's dress and corset before I fell asleep, being careful not to crease it, and now I was wearing only the undergarments Miss Hatfield had lent me.

They'd been quite comfortable to sleep in. But it was obvious that the woman in front of me didn't think they were fit to be used as sleepwear.

Nellie, as I learned was her name, took every care to dress me properly and in a manner 'befitting of my station'. She found the dress I'd worn yesterday and smoothed it out before dressing me in it once again. She took pains to put my hair up exactly as it had been the night before, and once again I became the very picture of a well-bred gentlewoman.

I thanked Nellie and was making my way downstairs when a small laugh erupted from my lips. If only my mother could see me. What would she think of her little daughter dismissing servants and dressing like a Gibson Girl, as Miss Hatfield had described me? I wondered if she'd even recognize me.

As I rounded the curve of the staircase, I almost crashed head first into someone coming up.

'Pardon me,' I started to say as I was regaining my balance, but the words dried up in my mouth as soon as I saw who it was. Henley. Without so much as an apology or anything more polite than a low chuckle, he turned and left, continuing up the stairs.

I stood dumbfounded, trying to work out what had just occurred, before deciding to follow him. What was the matter with him, anyway? I hadn't given him any reason to act as rudely to me as he just had, and as he had the night before.

I kept to the shadows in case he looked back and held up my skirts to make as little sound as possible. My footsteps were light summer rain compared to his, which echoed down the hallway. I had no idea what I was going to say when I confronted him, but I knew it was necessary.

I paused in the hallway as a door swung shut behind him. I heard his footsteps pacing the floor on the other side and swallowed a lump of fear as I wondered what he must be thinking about. Perhaps he suspected the truth – that I wasn't Margaret but rather some impostor.

I cracked open the door without thinking about it any longer. I was worried I'd become petrified by my thoughts, and it was obvious to me that I had to confront him now. It was the right thing to do, and if I didn't do it now, I wouldn't be safe any longer.

I waited in the doorway until he noticed me. He stopped pacing and his body froze as if I'd cast a spell on him. 'Shut the door behind you,' he commanded, and I complied without thinking. He took a first step towards me, but appeared to think better of his plans and instead walked to a window at the far side of the room. I was standing in a bedroom with a large bed in the centre, as mine had. Its sheets and bedspread were pristine and immaculately made up. I immediately knew this room wasn't his.

'You knew I was coming?' I asked him, when I realized he'd been waiting for me.

Henley remained mute, his back turned towards me. The morning light refracted through the window and bathed his figure in an unearthly glow. Early sunlight ran its fingers through his dark hair and made the distance between us miles and years, not just feet. I stood transfixed, staring at Henley. I wanted to reach out and touch him to make sure he was actually there. He was so still – inhumanly so. I was struck by a surge of emotions I didn't understand.

I turned around to leave quietly. It had been a mistake to follow him. I had nothing to say to him. I couldn't tell him the truth, so what difference did it make if I hid behind a lie? He didn't know who I was. He would never know.

'Wait,' he said, catching me off guard. 'Please.' It was the hint of desperation in his voice that ultimately made me decide to stay. I could tell he was as confused and unsure as I was, despite his confident demeanour.

'I have nothing to say to you,' I found myself telling him.

'You don't have to say anything.'

His answer surprised me. I'd guessed he would question me until he found out what he was looking for, such as where I came from, why I was here, who I was.

'But I have something to say to you.'

I was hesitant at first, but he gestured to an empty seat next to where he was standing at the window, and so I sat down.

'I don't know who you are,' he began, 'but I know you're not Margaret. You're not my cousin.' I immediately opened my mouth to object, but I couldn't figure out what I was supposed to say. I had no proof that I *was* her, because we both knew I wasn't.

'A letter came in the post the day you arrived. It was from her, apologizing that she wouldn't be able to spend the summer with us as she'd just fallen ill and was in bed with a fever. She wrote that she hopes to come later in the summer, but not until at least a month has passed, as her physician warned her against travelling in her condition. You're not her,' he stated again. 'So who are you?'

I looked down, suddenly knowing what I had to say. 'I can't tell you, but it's important that I be here. I don't mean any harm to you or your father, or to anyone else in this house, but I have to be here.' It was painful not to tell him the truth, I admit, but lying was the right thing to do. I couldn't drag him into this, and I didn't know him well enough to judge whether I could trust him with something that was beyond unbelievable. The story of the Miss Hatfield who had been put in an asylum was still bright in my mind.

'I believe you, I think. But what should I call you now?'

I thought in silence for a minute and suddenly looked up into the clearest blue eyes I had ever seen. 'Margaret,' I said. 'For now, call me Margaret.'

He nodded. 'Then, Miss Margaret, I don't know why you're doing this, and I don't know why I'm agreeing to play along, but I won't tell anyone. I'll keep your secret. You can trust me.'

I wondered if I really could. Henley only knew a small portion of the truth, but it was far beyond what anyone else knew, with the obvious exception of Miss Hatfield. I was trusting him with a part of me.

Chapter 7

'Margaret, please pass the marmalade,' the old man said.

I'd learned from Henley that his father's full name was Mr Charles F. Beauford. I had rushed down to breakfast after my confrontation with Henley, only to be the earliest to arrive at the table. At first, seeing the deserted seats, I thought I'd missed the meal entirely, but then Nellie walked in with pastries and other breakfast treats and apologized, saying that Mr Beauford was almost always late to meals, especially breakfast due to attending morning mass. She added that Mr Beauford expected me to start early and not wait for him or Henley. When I asked about Father Gabriel, I was told that he always preferred to take his meals alone in his room, and consequently would not be coming to breakfast. However, Miss Hatfield had instructed me that it was rude for guests and hosts alike to start eating when not all the seats were filled, so I decided to wait until Mr Beauford arrived regardless. Henley had some matters to attend to before he joined us for breakfast, and had asked me to tell his father that he'd be late as well.

'Would you like some jam, too?' I asked, smiling at the heap of food already on Mr Beauford's plate.

'Yes, please. It's as if you just read my mind.' He let out a deep, throaty laugh. 'So, have you packed yet?' he asked. Seeing my puzzled face, he added, 'For the country, I mean. Or have you already prepared from home?'

'The country?'

'Haven't you heard?' I turned around at the sound of Henley's voice. For a split second I wondered if he'd dare reveal my secret. 'They lost her luggage at the station.'

'Ah, yes. Someone must have mentioned something to me,' Mr Beauford said.

I felt slightly sorry for him as everyone around him was lying and he was oblivious to it, but then I remembered he was the only person in the room who wasn't aware of this … abnormality in his life, and perhaps it was a blessing. That's what I'd taken to calling myself – an abnormality in life. After all, that was what I was. I wasn't supposed to be here. It wasn't supposed to be like this. It would have been better if Henley still thought I was his cousin, but I had no control over what he'd worked out for himself. Besides, he only knew a very small part of the whole truth.

'Then you must take Margaret shopping, Henley,' Mr Beauford said. Henley agreed, while I tried to decline. 'No, I insist,' Mr Beauford declared. 'I'll be occupied this afternoon, unfortunately, but Henley can take you out. Surely there must be some place in this city that will make fine dresses to your liking.'

Henley nodded, his eyes never leaving mine, and I found myself agreeing before too long. Our plans were set, and Henley and I would leave immediately after breakfast.

On my way out of the house, I found myself drawn towards the parlour. My feet stopped in front of the painting and I had no choice but to look into the woman's eyes. How could I have forgotten about it so quickly? The portrait was the reason I was here. All I had to do was take it and leave. I couldn't get tangled up in this world. All I had to do was grab the painting and leave.

'She's a beauty, isn't she?' I spun around as I heard a soft laugh from behind me. 'It's just me,' Henley said, holding his hands up. 'No need to be scared.'

I didn't bother telling him that it wasn't him that scared me. It was the thought that someone had guessed my intention to steal the painting.

'But enough admiring that dusty old thing. We've got a life to live, places to go, and the servants have to take that thing down anyway.'

'They have to take it down? Why?'

'My father wants to have it moved to our house in the country. God only knows where he'll put it. It's already stuffed with cobwebbed paintings and various antiques he can't bear to part with once he buys them.'

'So it's coming with us?'

'Well, not at the same time, naturally. It should arrive before us with our other things.'

I exhaled, thankful I didn't have to come up with an excuse to stay behind, but concerned that I was being railroaded into travelling with these people.

'We've got to get going,' he said. 'The carriage is already out front waiting.'

I huffed, trying to show him I wasn't happy with this, but he just laughed and led me outside. 'I don't know why you're agreeing to this,' I said, scrunching up my dress while climbing into the back of the carriage. I didn't know how ladies of this time put up with their skirts. I wondered why they didn't have more cars either – Henley's father said he owned one – but of course I kept my questions to myself.

'What if I said that I'd like to see you in something pretty?' His eyes twinkled as he settled into a seat directly in front of mine.

'Then I'd ask you why you don't think my current dress is pretty enough.'

He laughed. 'But you can't go on wearing the same dress for months, or however long it is you intend to stay with us.'

'What makes you think I'm planning to stay a while?'

'A stranger comes into your home one night and impersonates your cousin. Why would you think she'll leave anytime soon?' He had a point, based on what he knew of me, but I didn't want to think about spending months with these people.

'Well, I wish as much as you do that I could go home.'

'I don't wish you to go away,' he said slowly. 'I just want to know more about you.' He tapped the outside of the carriage twice and it started moving.

'And that's the one thing I can't tell you anything about. I can only tell you who I'm not.'

'Then why this house? Why us?'

'Would you be disappointed to know that it has nothing to do with you or your father? It has nothing to do with your family or your house.' That wasn't true, of course, but I didn't want him to work out the real reason for my arrival.

'Then what made you come here?' he asked, sounding as if he really wanted to know; as if he cared.

'I can't tell you,' I said. 'It's too close to the truth.'

'The truth?' he asked, as if he already knew the answer.

'Yes, my truth.'

'Then I'm free to analyse who you're not,' he decided.

I nodded, fearing what he might say and, simultaneously, what he might not.

'You aren't from around here.'

'Why do you suppose that?' I asked him.

'You looked afraid when the carriage started moving and then quickly concealed your fright, as if you were trying to hide it from me.' He was more observant than I'd thought. I'd have to be more careful around him. 'You look as if you've never seen New York before.' If only he knew how close he was to the truth. 'Consequently, you must not be from the city.'

'I guess I'm not.' I smiled at him. Try as he might, he'd never figure me out. He would never guess my real story.

'Here we are,' Henley said as the carriage pulled to a stop. 'I think you'll like Mrs Wetherby's designs. Even my mother, who I'm told was at times the most impossible woman to satisfy, loved Mrs Wetherby, and claimed she's the best seamstress in the entire state.'

Henley exited the carriage on his side, then came around and helped me out. He led me into a quaint shop where we were greeted at once by two ladies. Their dresses were plain compared to the multitude of elaborate fabrics in the shop. A full-length mirror in one corner of the room made the store appear bigger than it was. It mirrored the neat baskets and bundles of fabric, making them look never-ending.

'Hello, Mr Beauford,' the shorter woman said, already eyeing the dress I was wearing. She was stouter than the younger girl who stood meekly behind her, an arm's distance from the woman. She had a pleasant, ruddy glow to her face. The older woman continued, 'I hope we may be of service, whatever you're looking for. Is it a new morning dress for your lady friend here? We just received a shipment of French fabric, and I dare say the lilac silk would be quite becoming on her, especially layered over a light blue … Don't you agree, Kitty?' The girl behind her quickly nodded in agreement.

'Well, not exactly, Mrs Wetherby,' Henley said. 'We were hoping for something a bit more ... extensive than that.'

Mrs Wetherby frowned at his words, trying to understand what he meant.

'This is my cousin, Miss Margaret.' He motioned to me.

'How do you do,' she said with a nod.

'She'll be staying with us in the country, but unfortunately her luggage was lost at the station, including all her dresses,' Henley explained.

'Why, that's horrible, absolutely ghastly of them!' Mrs Wetherby interjected. 'That's why I never trust those conductors with my luggage. You never know—'

'Ah, yes,' Henley interrupted her, trying to get her back on track. 'As you can imagine, she'll need an entirely new wardrobe of at least twelve dresses by the time we travel.'

'And when would that be?'

'We hope to be off early tomorrow morning.'

'Tomorrow morning? It would be impossible to have everything ready by then. Garments take time to make, you know. They don't appear magically, ready to be worn—'

'Yes, I do realize that, of course, which is why I hope you can ready at least one dress, one nightdress and ... whatever else she would need.'

I saw a light blush colour his cheeks and didn't understand why until I realized what they were discussing. For an accomplished young man who appeared to have everything he ever wanted or needed, I found it funny that Henley couldn't say the word 'underwear' – or even 'undergarments' – without feeling embarrassed.

'The rest can be sent to us in the country,' he concluded, his cheeks still pink.

'Then yes, we could have a few of the necessary garments ready by the morning, but you do understand that there will be an increased cost. We'll be sewing all night.'

He nodded in an understanding manner. 'Price will be no problem. Just enter it on our account. My father and I will only have the best for Miss Margaret while she's in our care.'

Mrs Wetherby nodded and clicked her tongue as she started directing Kitty to gather fabric of all different colours and textures. As soon as her back was to us, I turned my attention towards Henley once more.

'I really don't need all that,' I told him.

'Of course you do. What will you do without a wardrobe? Live in that dress?'

'Well, I don't need twelve dresses!' I hissed.

'You're trying to pass as my cousin, aren't you? Margaret would never travel with only a handful of dresses, not even for a short trip.'

I studied him closely, but Henley's face betrayed no emotion. His expression was calm and his eyes gazed past me, as if we were discussing the weather. 'Think of it as a gift from me.'

Henley's eyes were still looking anywhere but towards me when Mrs Wetherby called me over to take a look at the fabrics she and Kitty had laid out on the table. The different materials painted the table in an array of colours, each more beautiful and richly designed than the last.

'They're all so gorgeous,' I breathed.

'You look like you need help with choosing,' Mrs Wetherby said.

I accepted her offer gratefully, and one by one she held up each swatch of fabric, only for me to tell her that it wasn't quite right. 'They're all beautiful. They're just too much,' I said finally, utterly overwhelmed.

'So you want something simpler.' She pulled a few fabric swatches from the back of the store. 'Here's the lilac silk I mentioned earlier. It would look gorgeous with your hair colour.'

Indeed, the fabric was something to behold. It was the lightest purple I'd ever seen, almost translucent. Where the light laid its fingers, it shimmered like the surface of water before it let the light pass through.

'We can stitch it over a light blue like this,' she said, holding up a swatch of blue fabric underneath the translucent lilac. The pairing created a mirage that glistened in and out of focus like water in the desert, and I found myself saying yes to this choice, transfixed by the sight before me.

'I knew you'd like it. Now, how about these?' Happy with her success, Mrs Wetherby pulled down bundles with more vigour. My eyes swarmed with colour after colour, like a maddening kaleidoscope, ever changing. In the end, I picked the softest colours, a light cream, a light blue and a dusty rose among them.

'We just need to measure you, and then you two can be on your way.' Mrs Wetherby beckoned me in front of the full-length mirror. She bustled around me with a measuring tape while calling out numbers to Kitty, who stood close by, recording everything in a book.

'Mrs Wetherby,' a voice hesitantly called from the front of the store. I'd forgotten that Henley was there waiting for me. 'Mrs Wetherby?'

'Yes. What is it?' She looked up from her work.

'What do you think of this?' Henley was holding something up, but with the glare coming through the glass behind him, whatever he was showing us was obscured by the light.

'Bring it over here. My eyes are failing me.'

Henley walked towards her carrying a bundle of fabric in his arms. 'What do you think of this?' he repeated.

'I'd forgotten about that one. No one asks for that colour any more, but it would make a beautiful evening dress,' Mrs Wetherby said. 'What do you think?' she asked me.

The fabric had a faint sheen to it, like satin, and was a dark green, a shade of emerald. It was gorgeous, actually, and reminded me of the dress Miss Hatfield had lent me. It had the same texture, but instead of dark red, it was a deep, vivid green.

'I think it'll look stunning with your eyes,' Henley said.

My eyes trained themselves downwards and it was my turn to feel a warmness spreading through my cheeks.

'Not to mention with that blush of yours.' He laughed and Mrs Wetherby joined in.

'I'll make an evening dress out of this.' She looked to me as I nodded, a little too eagerly, perhaps. I felt myself getting swept up in all this, but couldn't stop myself. 'Will four nightgowns do?' This time she looked to Henley instead of me.

'Yes, that'll be fine,' he said. 'Will that be all, do you think?'

'It most certainly is. Kitty and I will begin work on your order at once, and will send the first part of it directly to your house by sunrise tomorrow. The rest we'll send to your country residence just as soon as they're completed.'

'Very good. Thank you.' Henley nodded as we walked out.

'Do come again!' Mrs Wetherby called through the store's open door. 'And Miss Margaret, it was a pleasure to make your acquaintance!' Her voice was so loud that heads on the street turned our way to see who exactly this

Miss Margaret was. Apparently finding me peculiar, they stared until we got back into the carriage.

Once seated with a barrier between me and the crowd, I let out a sigh. Henley chuckled as I shot him a look. 'What?' I asked him.

'You think it's all over.'

'Well, isn't it?' I was confused. 'Aren't we going back?'

'Not yet. At least, not for a little while.'

I groaned inwardly as he continued to laugh louder.

'No need to make that face. All you have to do is say yes to everything they show you. That's the simplest way out of it.'

'But it's too much. I don't want you to buy all these things for me.'

'Remember, everything's a gift.'

'That's too large a gift for me to accept,' I insisted as Henley shook his head at me.

'I've never met a woman who dislikes shopping as much as you do. Other women your age would be overjoyed to receive all the new dresses they could wish for. But you … I can't understand you,' he said slowly. 'You look like most women most of the time, but occasionally it's as if you came from another world entirely.'

It scared me how close to the truth he was coming. 'Maybe I'll learn to enjoy shopping sometime, but for now, I'd rather do as little as possible of it.' I tried to smile, to shake off the uneasiness his words had stirred within me. 'Why are you helping me?'

Henley stared out through the carriage window, so I couldn't read his face. I'd resigned myself to not getting an answer when he turned back to me.

'I used to love stories of adventure and books about regular people like me waking up one day and deciding to seek treasure, find their fortune.' Henley's eyes crinkled in a smile. 'I suppose I was like every boy in that way. I wanted adventure.'

'What happened?' I asked.

Henley looked confused.

'You said you *used* to love stories of adventure. What happened?'

'I grew up.' Henley's words were hard, but he still had a smile on his face. 'I put away the copy of *Treasure Island* I'd kept on my dresser for years. I knew I had to put my childhood away and become an adult.'

I felt my brows furrow and Henley laughed at my confusion.

'When you turned up, I guess I took advantage of the situation. There you were, a mysterious stranger impersonating my cousin, with some secret reason to visit our house … How much more adventurous could you get?'

I liked the way Henley laughed. It was carefree and bubbled up from within him like a child's. I shook my head, shaking off any hint of heaviness with it.

'So, where are we off to next, then?'

'The hat store,' he said.

I couldn't help but frown. 'I think I can do without one.'

'Nonsense. It's the fashion for women right now. We'll buy you a few, at least.'

'A few? How about just one?'

'And make my father look bad by not treating our guest like gold? Especially when it's his niece.'

'Fine, but I'm not happy about it,' I said, which only made him laugh more. I sat mutely for the rest of the short carriage ride.

'We're here,' Henley announced when the carriage stopped again.

'I know, but I'm not getting out,' I decided.

'You're not getting out?'

'Yes, that's right – I'm not. You can't make me take your gifts.'

Henley tried to reason with me. I knew I was acting childishly, but I was stubborn. My pride couldn't let me back down.

'Fine,' he said suddenly, surprising me. He got out of the carriage by himself and walked into the hat store. From outside, I saw him briefly talk to the store clerk before coming straight back to the carriage.

'What was all that about?' I asked him.

'It's what happens when you're stubborn and won't accept gifts gracefully.' I was puzzled, unsure exactly what he meant by that. 'I bought out the entire store.'

'You *what?*'

'Now, that's no way for a young lady of your breeding to speak,' he teased. 'I simply bought out the store.'

'You mean you bought every single hat in that shop?' I tried to wrap my mind around the idea that I was in the presence of a young man, roughly my age, who could afford to do that.

'And a few pairs of gloves,' he said. 'You know, it would have been much easier if you'd come in with me and picked out the ones you actually liked.'

I closed my eyes, trying to dissolve the annoying fellow in front of me, but when I opened my eyes again he was still sitting there with an infuriating smirk on his face.

'Please say we're done with shopping now.'

'If you say so.' His smile dripped into his voice. It was so contagious, I couldn't help but feel an identical one spreading across my own face. 'But we're not done with our outing just yet.'

'Oh! What more is there to do?' By this point I was practically begging him to take us back home. To *his* home, in *his* time, my thoughts silently reminded me. I was still on a mission, but it was so easy to get sidetracked, especially with this fascinating young man doing his best to impress me. Or embarrass me. I wasn't sure which.

'We're two young people in a great city – there's always more to do. I gave the coachman instructions to drive to my favourite place in all of New York. I think you might like it.'

The smile on my face only grew bigger. It was as if I'd known Henley for ages. I didn't know anything about his childhood or his favourite things, but those were trifles when I felt I understood who he really was at the core of his being. It was clear to me that he was actually quite uncomplicated, and voiced his opinion plainly. Henley was a man of this time, but his voice and personality would have fitted in anywhere, and probably at any time.

Chapter 8

'Here we are,' Henley said. 'That wasn't so bad a ride now, was it?'

The coachman helped Henley step down from the coach, and then Henley ran around to the other side to help me down. 'Thank you,' I murmured, recovering my hand from his.

'Anything for my dear cousin.' He winked and I hoped the coachman didn't catch it.

'So where are we going?' I asked as I looked around. There were yet more shops dotting the street, but Henley had promised I was going to be spared from more shopping for now. There was a fountain at the other end of the street, but it didn't make sense that he'd ask the coachman to stop here if that was our destination.

'You haven't figured it out yet?' He grinned. 'It's right in front of you.'

I looked up to see the sign for Hallman's Ice Cream and Confectionary and gave him a questioning glance. 'This is your favourite place in the entire city?'

'It would be yours, too, if you'd grown up eating their strawberry ice cream.'

I smiled, imagining Henley as a little boy eating ice cream. He did strike me as a strawberry kind of boy. He wouldn't want something as decadent and rich as chocolate, but neither would he settle for something simple like vanilla.

'Come on inside – that's where the magic really is.' He held the door open for me and I stepped into his childhood. We took seats at a table near the back of the room. I saw at least three little boys, any of whom could have been Henley when he was younger. I sat on a chair with legs and back made of wrought-iron struts that wove around each other in a dizzying dance. The table was of the same design, and Henley placed his hat on it.

'So I suppose you want me to order the strawberry?' I asked him.

'Whatever you'd like,' he replied, sounding most like a gentleman's son. 'But if you'd share one with me, dear cousin, I would be most grateful.' He snickered at his false formality.

'You may have some if you wish,' I teased back. 'But if I like it, I'm expecting you to act like a gentleman and let me finish it.'

'You have only to ask.'

When Henley left to place our order, I finally had a chance to survey the room more closely. There was a counter at one end, where Henley was currently waiting to be noticed. The man behind the counter was wearing a tie with a white and red striped shirt rolled up to his elbows, a long apron tied around his waist. Behind him were candies and sweets – every child's fantasy – in pot-bellied bowls filled to the brim. Cakes were displayed underneath the counter, shielded from greedy fingers behind thin glass. The sweet scent of sugar and molten chocolate transcended any point in time, and it drew me back to my mother's baking. I could almost hear the sound of sugar sifting.

A cold hand pulled me out of my reverie. My mind sprang back to my body as my head jerked up in response to the foreign touch.

'What are you doing here?'

I looked up past the veneer of a woman's hat veil into the cool eyes of Miss Hatfield. 'I–I'm with a friend,' I said. I didn't know how to explain myself and I was so acutely conscious of all the bodies in the room around me, I could almost feel their movements as my own. I thought I sensed the tug of a man crossing his leg on the other side of the room and the shifting of a woman's hand to her glass. I knew we had to be careful what we said, so no one would hear the real meaning behind our words.

Miss Hatfield's eyes followed mine as they darted to Henley's back at the counter.

'So I see.' There was a slight pause before she continued. 'Come to me as soon as you can get away. We have much to discuss.'

With those quick words, Miss Hatfield turned and left me nodding to her back.

'Here it is.' The glass of ice cream clinked against wrought iron as Henley placed it on the table. My head turned from Miss Hatfield's receding back to Henley's face.

'No wonder you asked me to share with you,' I said, taking care to smile and not betray my surprise at what had just happened. The glass cup had at least four scoops of ice cream in it.

'You thought I was fooling you!' He put on an offended expression, which made me laugh. I reached for a spoon, but he snatched it away from my grasp. 'And now you think you can fool me. I saw you talking to that woman.'

I felt the colour draining from my face as my mouth slowly opened, my mind racing frantically as I tried to come up with something to say.

'Relax,' he said. 'I know who she is.'

I felt my hands tremble and instinctively grasp each other for support. How did he know her? And what did he know about her?

'She's an old friend you don't really want to see any more, right? We all have some of those,' Henley said, and a sigh of relief escaped my lips. 'Is she from the same place as you?'

'Sort of, but not really.' I tried to dodge around the truth.

'A mystery, indeed.' Henley wiggled his eyebrows. I wanted to laugh, but felt exhausted after my moment of panic. I reached for the spoon again. This time Henley passed it to me and I started eating the ice cream while I tried to piece together who he really was.

All along he'd been trying to figure me out, but I suddenly realized I didn't know him, either. When I first met him, he was just a wealthy man's son who had everything he could possibly want, and therefore was nothing like me. Now I saw that Henley was also a little boy, somewhat stuck in the past, always ordering strawberry ice cream as he'd done when he was younger. I felt confused. Who was the real Henley Beauford? Was he the little boy I was seeing today, or the gentleman's son I'd met yesterday? What if he was neither, but something else entirely? I didn't even know why I cared. I wouldn't be here long – I couldn't be. I had to get the painting and leave before anyone else figured out I didn't belong here. But still, I couldn't resist the temptation to learn more about this man. Perhaps I needed someone to ground me in this strange world I'd found myself in.

79

'Is it my turn to ask you questions now?' I asked him.

'I'm not sure you've answered mine at all.'

'I've answered them to the best of my ability, kind sir.' The corners of my mouth twitched, as I fought to hide a smile.

'You haven't even told me your name.'

'Of course you know my name – I'm your dear cousin Margaret,' I said. I saw him roll his eyes at me as I continued, 'You know me perfectly well.' Henley opened his mouth to speak, but I interrupted him. 'And as your cousin, it feels odd that I know nothing about you.'

'So what do you want to know?'

'Something about your childhood.' I knew I was asking about his childhood to better play the role of his cousin, but I found myself actually caring. I didn't know why, but at that moment in the ice cream parlour, it felt important to me.

'Well, I was raised by my father, mostly, and whatever governess he'd employed at the time. They never lasted long, and as soon as I reached an acceptable age I was sent to boarding school.'

'So you grew up being passed from hand to hand?' I tried to imagine what that would have been like, but found I couldn't. I'd grown up with a mother and father always there for me. My world was miles apart from the one Henley had grown up in.

'It wasn't that bad,' he said. 'It's expected, being the oldest – well, only son. I had a lot to learn before I could take over my father's affairs. Still do.'

'But what about your mother?' I asked him. 'Didn't you say that she loves Mrs Wetherby's dresses?'

'Used to,' he was quick to say. I knew he saw my brow furrow when he started explaining. 'My mother ... my mother passed away.'

I was mortified. 'I'm so sorry. I didn't know. I never should have brought her up … I should have realized when you didn't mention her—'

'It's fine,' Henley said. 'She passed away when I was still a baby. I don't even remember her. All I know of her, my father told me.'

'It must have been difficult growing up without a mother.'

'In some sense it was, but I never knew what I was missing.' He tried to gloss over it lightly, but his voice was strained. 'When I was younger, still a little boy, I rarely saw other boys' mothers – their governesses usually accompanied them. But when I did see their mothers, all they ever did was pat their boys' heads and tell them to be good. I never thought I was missing out on much as my father did the same thing to me. I never knew how it felt to have a mother.'

I nodded. 'What was your father like?'

'The same as he is now,' said Henley with a laugh. 'My father was older than my friends' fathers, so we never did anything the other boys did with theirs. Not once would he play ball with me; he just told me to go and work on my Latin exercises with my tutor, and that's precisely what I did.'

'So you were never close to your father?'

'Not in the sense you mean, no. We never did anything together. I learned to prefer solitude.'

A chuckle escaped my lips and he raised his brows at me. 'You prefer to keep to yourself, yet here you are helping a stranger,' I explained, not wanting him to think I was laughing at his childhood.

'You're not a stranger,' he said, and it was my turn to raise my brows at him. 'Of course not – you're my cousin.'

He smiled his devilish grin and I had to laugh along with him again. But then his face turned serious. 'I–I have a question I must ask you.'

'What is it?' I feared the worst.

'Are you going to eat that?' He pointed to the remaining ice cream which was slowly melting, as was his serious demeanour. I pushed the bowl towards him as his countenance cracked and a smile escaped again. The smile made its way to his eyes, and it was contagious. A smile spread across my face, too. I couldn't help it.

Chapter 9

I listened to Henley's laugh echo off the pavement, and mine soon rang with it. 'And after that, Miss Wetherby swore never to gossip again ... Though she never did hold true to that promise!'

We were taking an aimless walk around some of the more obscure parts of the city. The streets were narrow and deserted save for the occasional person hurrying to their destination. No one paid us any mind.

'Oh, look at that.' I pointed to a rainbow of colours cast on the pavement in front of us from a store window.

'It's beautiful,' I heard him murmur.

We followed the streaks of coloured light back through the store window to a single ring. It was breathtaking. As the setting sun struck its facets, it basked in an unearthly glow. Shards of light played off one another and flung themselves onto any surface they could find. The band was silvery. White gold, maybe? Sterling silver? Platinum? But the gem in the middle, flanked by two small diamonds, was what caught my eye. It was an astounding blue, as bright as the ocean's surface; it sparkled with the vivid light of a million stars trapped inside.

'It's the colour of your eyes,' I said automatically. Henley's eyes crinkled, as he burst out laughing.

As I realized what I'd just said, I felt a warmth rise up my cheeks and I looked down, embarrassed.

'Do you want it?' he asked, after a moment of thoughtful silence.

'Oh, no. You're not going to buy me that. You've already spent far too much money on a perfect stranger.'

'That's not what I asked,' he said. 'Do you want it?'

'No.'

'You know, you're not a convincing liar.'

'I'm a stranger to you. You wouldn't know if I was telling the truth or not.'

'You're not a stranger any more, and I already know you well enough to tell that you're lying. You *do* want the ring.' Henley marched into the shop with me chasing after him, right on his heels.

'May I see the ring in the window?' he asked the store clerk, who promptly brought it out.

'Is this for your fiancée?' the clerk asked, looking towards me, but Henley didn't bother to correct him.

'Do you like it?' Henley asked me, slipping it onto the ring finger of my right hand. It fitted perfectly, which both frightened and delighted me. 'I'll take it,' he said, after looking at my face for a considerable amount of time.

'You can't,' I said. 'You've already bought me a whole wardrobe and an entire hat store. This ring must cost a fortune, and I'm not going to let you spend that kind of money on me.'

'It's a gift,' he said again, just as he had about the dresses and the hats.

'Well, I'm tired of your gifts. I've accepted my fair share of them today. You are *not* getting me that ring.'

'All those gifts were from my family to you, my dear cousin. This gift will be from me.'

'I can think of a better gift you could give me.'

'Is that so?'

'The gift of not buying me that ring.' I wondered if he'd agree to that, or laugh at it, thinking it nonsensical.

'Would you like that more than any of the other gifts you've received?'

'Yes.' My answer was an honest one.

'Then I guess I won't be taking it,' Henley said to the clerk, who had been painstakingly wrapping the small ring into a slightly larger box.

'Yes, sir,' the clerk said, as if he was used to this sort of indecision.

'Thank you for your time,' Henley said as we left the store.

'I think that was the best gift anyone's ever given me,' I told him, earning myself a grin.

'I'm glad you liked it so much. It's a unique gift, isn't it?'

I agreed. 'Does that mean we can go back now?'

'I don't see why not.'

We returned to the carriage. As we climbed aboard, I realized I was finding it easier to navigate my skirts and layers, now that I'd had a little more practice. With a knock on the side of the carriage from Henley, we were once again rocked into heavy motion. Oddly, I now found the horse's steps comforting, beating out a familiar pattern.

Conversation in the coach was small talk compared to the meaningful conversations we'd been engaged in earlier. Our previous exchanges had been filled with almost-truths that were closer to reality than some truths were themselves. Anything would sound trivial in comparison to that. We arrived at the house after a journey only a few minutes longer than the one which had taken us into the heart of the city.

A man in traditional black and white livery answered the door immediately. 'Welcome home, sir,' he said. He glanced at me and gave a curt nod. 'Madam.' His voice didn't have the slightest hint of emotion, his tone dead and still. 'Packages have arrived for Miss Beauford,' he said to Henley as if I wasn't even in the room. 'I've taken the liberty of telling the porter to place them all in her room.'

'Very well. Thank you, Jim.'

'Sir.' Jim bowed his head and disappeared.

'Well, he's not exactly a homey sort of fellow, is he?' I commented as I watched his retreating back.

'Homey?' Henley laughed. 'Jim thinks of duty first.'

'Duty? It's almost like slave labour.' I was joking, but the words flew out twisted, and before I could shut my mouth I'd already said them.

I looked tentatively at Henley, wondering what his reaction would be. His face was smooth, betraying no emotion at all.

'I don't think the servants would think of it as that,' he said quietly. His tone changed abruptly. 'Now, run along to your room and see what the porter brought.' He shooed me away to my room as he, too, made his way up the stairs.

I heard rustling even before I opened the door. Nellie was scurrying back and forth between heaps of hats and whatever else was tucked away beneath those heavy box tops. She stopped when she saw me and sank into a deep curtsy before speaking. 'Miss, your hats and garments have arrived.'

'So I see,' I mumbled under my breath, forgetting to keep my thoughts to myself. Towers of hats swayed dangerously. Scarves in Nellie's hands fluttered in the breeze coming through the open window. It looked as though she'd sprouted wings as she skirted from tower to tower, but for some reason the image didn't amuse me as much as it should have.

I crossed the floor to the window and caught a glimpse of the brash blue tail of a bird. It was a fleeting sight – not even a second long – but the colour stayed with me. I knew I would never see the same colouring on the same bird in the same way. I would never see beauty in that exact same manner. It only existed in that one fleeting moment, and then that, too, was gone. In a normal life, I felt that blue would have been the thing that would let me continue living. It would have been the first colour I'd see behind my eyelids in the morning, and the last colour I'd see in my mind's eye at night. That vivid hue would have been the one thing that spurred me forward into life, when nothing else could have moved me. That flash of blue was a symbol for my life: quick yet enduring.

I reminded myself that my entire so-called life would now be filled with moments like this. It would be comprised of fleeting moments – one life after the other, but I'd never stop being Rebecca Hatfield. I would never die.

Suddenly I felt robbed of that blueness. Its fleeting beauty was meaningless to me now that my days had no end. I was robbed of death, and in some ways of life as well. That blueness would never be my last thought; the last thought at the end of it all. Instead it would just stay with me, flitting in and out of my dreams and reality until it, too, would be forgotten, as everything else eventually would – my name, my identity and that bold, striking blue that reminded me of how to live.

I closed the window in a move I wished to be swift, but still a breeze stole into the room. It was so sweet it made me feel alive; something I realized I hadn't felt in a long time. I closed my eyes to take it in. Its hand reached out to touch mine ... but then it vanished, for breezes are as fleeting as birds, life and blueness.

'Miss, you must let me close the window for you next time.'

'Very well,' I told Nellie, but I asked her to draw the curtains shut. I didn't want to see another bluebird, another reminder of what had been taken from me.

I sank onto a portion of the bed that wasn't covered by boxes and hid my face. I wanted to block out the world around me but found that I couldn't, however much I tried.

'Miss, do you have any specific instructions regarding what to pack?'

'I don't really care—' I saw the appalled look on Nellie's face. 'I trust your judgement is all I mean, Nellie. Please, just pack what you think is best.'

'Very well, miss.'

The only sound in the room was faint rustling as Nellie packed in the corner. I couldn't help but pay attention to the movement of her hands. They were so precise and sharp. No small movement was wasted. But every so often her hands paused and clasped each other, as if they somehow knew they couldn't find the support they needed on their own. Those were the times when she glanced up at me. Our eyes would meet briefly, until she dropped her gaze. She looked like she wanted to say something, but, not finding the right words, she remained mute, and each time continued her work with a sense of renewed diligence.

'What is it?' I asked.

'Nothing, miss,' was her reply, and she didn't even glance up while saying it.

'If it's really nothing, what's that look you keep giving me?'

'I'm sorry, miss, if I gave you a look. I wasn't intending to.' Her response was automatic, as if it had been drilled into her from when she was little. It held no emotion and was devoid of anything resembling life, but then she looked at me once more.

'There it is again.' My words sounded harsher than I'd intended and I apologized to her.

'Please don't apologize, miss.'

Seeing I'd put her in an uncomfortable position, I wanted to apologize again, but I held my tongue as that was the thing that had caused the problem in the first place.

'You want to say something to me,' I said. 'Please just say it.'

'Miss, I can assure you that you wouldn't want to hear my thoughts—'

'And that's where you're wrong. I do, but how can I if you won't even voice them?'

'It's not my place to. My master—'

'I won't tell if you won't.' I was taken aback by what I'd just said. My voice was my mother's; I sounded exactly like her. Those were the same words she always said to me when she gave me a cookie before dinner. 'I won't tell if you won't.' But I had to focus on where I was at that precise moment. 'Please, just be honest with me.'

I could see Nellie giving in as she sighed. 'Sorry, miss, I just don't see any reason for you to be unhappy,' she said.

'What do you mean?'

'I saw how you looked out through the window. It was as if you'd seen a secret the world keeps from us. Something we're not meant to know – something so sad …'

I wondered how Nellie would react if she knew how close to the truth she was, how close she was to the secret the world keeps from its people, one that had changed my life for ever. But I knew I wouldn't wish that knowledge on anyone.

'Now please, miss, you be frank with me,' she said. 'What do you have to be unhappy about?'

I opened my mouth, but I couldn't find it in myself to lie to her when she'd told me her thoughts so openly. This time, it was me who didn't know what to say.

'You have everything one could possibly want – and you've always had it,' she continued. 'You don't need to worry about tomorrow like the rest of us do. You can sleep peacefully at night, knowing you'll have many more tomorrows ahead of you – all happy, and you without a care in the world. But what about us? The ones who don't have your easy life and money? All we do is wonder what tomorrow will bring. We worry even though we know that none of us can change it. You're blessed not to have that life.'

Her words sank into me, hurting like the fragments of truth they were. They cut and stung, leaving untraceable marks on my skin.

'I–I'm sorry, miss.' Nellie's voice was small. 'I don't know what came over me. I shouldn't have spoken out of turn. Please don't tell my master—'

'No. I needed to hear that. But will you listen to what I have to say in return?'

She nodded, if a little tentatively.

'I know it may not feel this way to you, but if you have everything one could possibly want and you never know the feeling of lacking, do you ever even notice that you have everything? And if you sleep peacefully every night, do you really know the meaning of the word "peaceful"?' My eyes burned with unshed tears, but I didn't want to cry in front of someone I barely knew. I strained my voice even more, because I knew I had to finish. 'Isn't the wonder of tomorrow ultimately what prods us along?

90

Without it, won't we drag our feet, knowing that there will never be an end?' I looked at Nellie's face to see tears appearing in her eyes.

I felt raw and naked, unprotected without something to cover me. My mind – my emotions – were all laid out in front of her. I was painfully exposed under her eyes, but although I was waiting for her to judge me, the words never came.

A knock at the door startled both of us. My eyes stared straight into Nellie's panicked ones. Wordlessly, she wiped her eyes dry and turned to answer the door.

'Sir.'

'May I see Miss Beauford?' The voice was Henley's.

Nellie looked to me for an answer and I nodded my approval. Henley came in, leaving Nellie to slip out of the room and quietly shut the door behind her.

A minute passed, and neither of us moved. I sat motionless on my corner of the bed and he froze by the door. He placed his ear to it and after a few seconds of listening proceeded to my side.

'You can never be too careful with servants,' he muttered. 'They never cease to gossip.'

'I trust her,' I said, thinking about the moment I'd just shared with her. 'Will she be coming to the country with us?'

'You want her there?' he asked. 'You do know there will be a handmaid already waiting for you, don't you?'

'But can I bring Nellie?'

Henley paused. 'Why not? You can inform her of the new arrangement tonight.'

'Thank you.' I smiled.

Henley just shook his head, a small grin growing on his lips. 'Most peculiar,' I heard him murmur as he made to leave the room.

'Didn't you have a reason for coming to see me?'

'Pardon?'

'Did you have something to tell me?'

'Oh, no, I was just checking that everything had arrived safely,' he said as he backed out through the door, closing it as softly as Nellie had.

It suddenly felt odd to be alone in this room. Around Nellie I was Miss Beauford. Around Henley I was a familiar stranger. I wondered who I was to myself. Was I still in some way Cynthia, or was I Miss Rebecca Hatfield?

I took a deep breath and closed my eyes. I decided that I had to be in the present – wherever that was; and I had to be me – whoever that was. I couldn't go back home or live someone else's life. I was stuck here until I could get my hands on the painting, so I might as well make the best of it. I was acutely aware that the only other person in the world who knew exactly what I was going through and how I felt was Miss Hatfield, so I decided to visit her that night and tell her about the changes that must be made to our plan.

After I told Nellie that she would be joining me in the country and sent her off to pack, there was another knock on my door. Remembering after a moment that Nellie had gone, I opened the door myself to see Henley leaning against the wall on the other side of the hallway. He stood up immediately upon seeing me and straightened his back. He cleared his throat and ran his fingers through his hair.

'Um …'

It was the first time I'd seen Henley unsure of himself. He didn't look like his normal composed self as I watched him search for words.

'I–uh … I remembered what I came to ask you earlier.' Henley looked like an overgrown child as he stared down at his feet. 'My father asked if you would accompany us for a walk?' His intonation lifted at the end of the sentence, like a question. When Henley's eyes met mine, his cheeks were flushed. 'I just forgot to tell you … Would you like to come? I'd … I'd like it if you could.'

I told him I would love to and hurried to get myself ready. Henley chuckled at my disarray as I grabbed his arm and we darted out of the door to meet Mr Beauford.

Chapter 10

As we walked, it wasn't uncommon for the people we passed to acknowledge Mr Beauford in some way or other. The women nodded politely while the men tipped their hats, calling out greetings. Mr Beauford responded the same way to everyone he met. He simply waved them on about their lives, and that was that.

'Now tell me, Margaret,' Mr Beauford said, patting my hand as we strolled through the busy streets and into the park. 'How's your mother doing?'

I opened my mouth to say something – I've no idea what – but was thankfully interrupted by Henley, who was walking in front of us and spun around on his heel.

'Oh yes. Margaret was telling me yesterday how well Aunt Emmeline is faring.' Henley gave me a meaningful look to which Mr Beauford appeared oblivious. 'Weren't you?'

'Do tell,' Mr Beauford said, 'How is my dear sister doing?'

'Well—'

Henley cut me off, trying to relieve me of the burden of having to lie to his father.

'She's doing just fine.'

Mr Beauford looked at his son with stern eyes. 'Let Margaret speak for herself. I want to hear about my sister from her own daughter, not you.'

Henley looked at me with worried eyes.

'Now, Margaret – how is your mother spending her days? Is she still at it with her hobbies?'

'I'm afraid she isn't, Uncle. She's caught the flu.'

'Oh my. I should write to her, then,' Mr Beauford said. Henley looked alarmed, but was hesitant to interrupt again.

'I don't think that'll be necessary,' I said. 'I believe Mother almost prefers it – this way she gets some time to rest.'

'She was never much of the social type,' he agreed.

'But when she's well, she enjoys her needlepoint from time to time and has picked up painting.' I felt triumphant that I was able to pull this off. To impersonate someone's niece was one thing, but to lie to a person about their own sister was a completely different matter!

'I think what Margaret means is that her mother has picked up painting *again*,' Henley chimed in once more. He threw me a look as if to say that I shouldn't be speaking when it wasn't absolutely necessary, but started laughing when he saw the bewildered look on my face.

'Yes, yes.' I glanced at Mr Beauford to see if he'd realized something was amiss, but all he did was pat my hand once more.

'Henley Beauford?' a voice said from behind, the words clipped and punctuated with a precise British accent. 'Is that you?'

All of us turned at once to see a man dressed formally in a frock coat and silk hat. He wore an ascot tie and kid-leather gloves that were the lightest grey I'd ever seen. Their colour was so light that they looked like morning shadows.

'Willie, whatever are you doing here?' Henley appeared to know the man well, but nevertheless still offered him a formal, distant handshake.

With a closer look, I saw that the man was no older than Henley. Although his clothes made him look far older than he actually was and his hat cast a wide shadow over his eyes, anyone could see he was a very handsome man.

'A pleasure to meet you again, Mr Beauford.' Willie shook Mr Beauford's hand in turn.

Mr Beauford murmured a quick, 'How do you do?'

'What brings you to America?' Henley asked.

Willie was silent, as if ignoring Henley's words. His eyes darted from Henley to me and back again in quick shifts. It took me a while to understand why he wasn't responding, but I realized he was waiting for Henley to introduce me.

'Oh, I'm sorry,' Henley said, as if finally catching on. 'Excuse me. This is my cousin, Margaret. Cousin, this is Willie. We went to school together.'

'A pleasure to meet you.' He tipped his hat in my direction as I smiled.

I wondered why he didn't offer me his hand to shake, as Miss Hatfield had told me this was common courtesy for men as well as women. I decided to ask Henley later, casually, when we were alone.

'Business, mainly,' Willie replied to Henley's question. 'We just bought a few more factories in the south. I'm to stay in New York one more day before sailing home.' He paused. 'How's the steel business? And how's your family?'

'Steel is boring, as usual,' Henley said. 'Buying more factories in Georgia, you say?' I noticed that Henley didn't really answer Willie's question. I wondered exactly how involved Henley was in the family business.

'Well, yes. There was a fire a couple of months ago in which two of our main factories were destroyed. We have to make up for that loss, and the textile business in England is booming ...' Willie paused when he glanced at Mr Beauford

96

and saw his expression. 'I won't bore you with the details when you're obviously out for pleasure.'

'Nonsense. We have some catching up to do—' Henley started, but Mr Beauford interrupted him by clearing his throat.

'I'm sure you do, but I don't want to bore Margaret with all this talk about business,' Mr Beauford said.

I had to fight off a smirk as I realized that Mr Beauford was trying to use me to get out of talking with Willie.

'Why don't we leave you two to talk and Margaret and I will continue our walk.' Without waiting for an answer, Mr Beauford took hold of my arm and set off walking at a faster pace than before.

Henley and Willie appeared content to catch up on all the things they'd missed, so neither objected – not that Mr Beauford would've listened if they had. Henley threw back his head and laughed, catching my eye as I left with his father. He looked pleased to see me going on ahead rather than talking to his handsome friend. We could no longer hear their excited tones when Mr Beauford finally began to slow down to our original pace.

'You know, you're a good influence on Henley.' Mr Beauford turned to me and was the first to break the silence. 'You're helping him see his life in a new way. I don't think I've heard Henley laugh this much since his mother was still alive.'

He stopped and looked straight ahead. I heard him suck in a breath.

'He was just a baby. He wasn't ready to lose her. And I wasn't ready to, either.'

The arm clinging to mine shook with tremors and his whole body began to convulse.

'Oh God,' he whispered. 'Oh God, Ruth.'

Nothing could have prepared me for the sheer strength he exerted to wrench free of my arm, the force of which sent me stumbling backwards. When I regained my balance, Mr Beauford was already out of reach and running down the street as fast as his legs would carry him. He dropped his walking cane and his hat flew off his head, but he didn't appear to notice.

'Ruth! Ruth!' He was screaming at the top of his lungs now and passers-by stopped to look at him.

Mr Beauford shoved aside ladies walking with their lace parasols and knocked over a grocer selling strawberries on the street. I tried to run after him, but after only a few steps I realized that the dress and shoes I was wearing would only hinder my movement. Instead I turned and headed back the way we'd come as fast as I could manage, hoping to get Henley's attention.

'Henley!' The people on the street probably thought I was as mad as Mr Beauford, for they scampered out of my way as I approached Henley and Willie.

Seeing me with half my skirts bunched up in one hand and mud colouring the other half, Henley immediately knew something was wrong.

'Are you hurt?' He took me by the shoulders and forced me to look at him. 'What is it? What's wrong?'

When I told him about his father running off yelling, 'Ruth,' Henley's face blanched. He told me to stay where I was, but as soon as he ran off after Mr Beauford, I tried to follow him.

Nothing had ever scared me as much as the look on Henley's face the moment I told him about his father. He acted in a way I'd never seen before. He didn't even pause to think before he ran.

My shoes hit the ground in a beat as erratic as my heart. I was only semi-conscious of the hem of my dress ripping as I tripped over it, but at least now I could move faster. Faces blurred past and I couldn't tell whether it was how fast I was running that made them fuzzy, or the tears that were spilling onto my face.

I didn't know why I was crying. I felt frightened and nervous – I didn't know what to do with myself, and I wasn't sure what was happening.

I didn't know where I was going, but Henley's bobbing head in the distance assured me I was still heading in the right direction.

It wasn't until he slowed down at a gate that I noticed how much my feet ached. My shoes really weren't meant for this. Nonetheless, I willed myself to go on. If Henley could do it, so could I.

My heart stopped when I saw Mr Beauford kneeling in front of a grave with his head in his hands. Henley was there with him, talking softly and stroking his back.

'You didn't mean to do it—'

'But how does she know that?' Mr Beauford snapped back at Henley. 'All she saw was a man chasing her.'

'But surely she thought you must have mistaken her for someone else.'

'I could have sworn she was Ruth,' Mr Beauford muttered to himself, ignoring Henley. 'She looked like her. She even walked like her. It was only when she turned around ...' Mr Beauford paused, apparently overcome by all that had happened. 'She wasn't Ruth.'

'Ruth ... my mother is dead.' I knew how much it pained Henley to say those words, but I admired what he was prepared to put himself through for his father. 'She can't be here. She's dead.'

'I–I'm sorry.' Mr Beauford finally looked up at Henley. 'I'm so sorry.'

'We should get your uncle home.' I turned to see Willie standing beside me. He had followed us to the graveyard.

Before I could mutter an assent, Henley nodded. Willie and Henley helped Mr Beauford to his feet. Mr Beauford looked frailer than ever. My gaze was drawn to the shadows and lines that constructed his face, but I could barely make out his eyes, sunken in like caves.

When we arrived home, Henley put his father to bed with Willie's help. I wanted to go with them, but my feet stopped working in the parlour. I heard Henley tell one of the servants to call the family physician and also the chaplain, since his father refused to see the physician until the chaplain visited his bedside. Father Gabriel came swiftly, as if he'd been awaiting Mr Beauford's call, and the physician also arrived before long. Shortly after the chaplain left Mr Beauford's room and the family physician took his place by his bed, both Willie and Henley appeared in the parlour.

It was the first opportunity we'd had since the incident to collect ourselves. Willie's silk hat was crumpled, while Henley had lost his altogether when he ran. I noticed that Willie's silver cravat pin was missing and his silk-faced lapels were all creased now. I decided that in the rumpled clothing Willie and Henley now wore, they finally looked their true ages.

Willie took off his coat and plopped down into an armchair.

'Nothing like chasing people to get your daily dose of fresh air,' he said.

I knew he was trying to lighten the mood, but Henley only stiffened even more. He stood frozen at the door until the butler showed the physician in.

When Henley followed the physician upstairs, Willie turned to me. 'Good God, I can't imagine what he's going through.'

I nodded. 'Especially as he's his father's closest living relative.'

'Close only in terms of blood …' Willie trailed off and looked at me intently. 'But he has you.'

I'd forgotten again that I was supposed to be Henley's cousin, but Willie's words grounded me back in my reality.

'Yes …'

I wondered what Henley would do once I left, for my leaving was inevitable. I'd be gone as though I'd never existed here, and Henley would live on in his time and eventually die. The world would keep existing without him. There would just be an empty space where he once was. It would be the same for him, of course – I would simply vanish.

'He's lucky to have you,' Willie said. 'I never really understood how much you meant to him.'

I was puzzled by that. I wasn't sure if Willie had met Henley's actual cousin, but if he had, surely Willie would have mentioned it when we met.

Willie laughed. 'We talked about you when we were in school. We talked about our entire families. I knew how distant Henley was – and still is, it would appear – with his father, but I never knew how close you two were. Come to think of it, he didn't say much about you at all. Just that he had a cousin out of the city, an only child he hadn't seen since he was younger.' He smiled at me. 'He failed to mention how close you are. It's apparent to anyone who sees you two together. With you he looks …' Willie tried to find the right word. 'Alive. His eyes – his whole person – are brighter around you.'

I couldn't find the words to respond to that, so Willie and I sat in uncomfortable silence. We watched as a servant showed the physician out. The family chaplain went in again, but Henley didn't return.

101

'I'm worried about him.' It was Willie, again, who started the conversation.

'I am, too.'

'Have you seen his father act this way before?'

'He's been distant, but I suppose he always is.' I tried to be tight-lipped with my answer, as I didn't want to say anything that was untrue. I couldn't guess how much Willie knew.

'I don't know him as well as you do,' Willie said. 'You're related by blood? He's your uncle, am I correct?'

I remembered what Mr Beauford had said about his sister and my supposed mother and replied that he was, indeed, correct.

'He was never there during Henley's childhood,' he said. 'We both went to a finishing school in the Moors, days away from London. Parents would visit, and those who came from abroad, whose parents couldn't readily visit, they received care packages.'

I nodded, interested in hearing about this part of Henley's life, a part that had been hidden from me so far.

'Even I received packages from home and my parents lived in London. But for whatever reason, Mr Beauford just wasn't interested in that kind of contact. The only thing Henley would receive from home was the occasional telegraph notifying him of money being wired into his account for his birthday.'

'Just that?'

'Well, what do you expect from someone like Mr Beauford?' Willie's outburst surprised me. 'Everything he does is done because it suits him – even this sudden piousness. The only reason that man's taken an interest in religion these past few years is because he knows he's going to die. A relationship with his own son doesn't suit or benefit him enough.' Up until now, Willie had at least been tactful when discussing things he didn't agree with, but there was no hiding the malice in his voice when he talked about Henley's father – my uncle, I kept reminding myself.

'I'm sorry.' Willie had seen the look of surprise on my face. 'I know he's your uncle. I shouldn't have said that.' He made a move to leave.

'No—' I touched his elbow, making him pause. 'Please stay. I know that Mr Beauford – my uncle – hasn't always been there for Henley when he's needed him. I agree with you.'

I saw Willie relax.

'I was just worried that—'

'I know,' I said. 'But right now we have to be here for Henley. Regardless of what my uncle's done, he's still Henley's father, and we must stand by Henley, whatever happens.'

I briefly saw a shadow flitting beneath the parlour door and wondered who could be listening. Thinking it might be a servant, I prayed they hadn't heard much of our conversation. But as quickly as I noticed it, the shadow was gone. Perhaps Father Gabriel had left Mr Beauford's bedside and was pacing through the house, waiting to be called back in.

When I looked up again, Willie was smiling. 'You're right. You're absolutely right, Margaret.'

It made me cringe to hear Willie call me Margaret. In the short time I'd known him, I'd grown to really like and respect him. I didn't want to lie to him, but knew I had no choice.

'Let's go and see how Henley's faring. Whatever the physician said, it couldn't have been good.' Willie took my arm as we went up the stairs. 'No matter what, we have to keep our friend's best interests at heart.'

Henley was seated outside Mr Beauford's bedroom. With his head bowed in his hands, he didn't see us approach. Willie impulsively moved to comfort Henley, but Henley didn't even acknowledge him.

'Henley, what did the physician say? It couldn't have been that bad.' I heard Willie say the exact opposite of what he'd said to me just a few moments ago. 'You'll see. He'll get better. He's having a bad day – all he needs is some rest.'

'And how is *your* family?' Sarcasm dripped from Henley's voice.

'Faring well, indeed,' Willie replied. I knew he wanted to say more, but out of consideration for what Henley was going through, Willie kept his response short.

'Your father must be proud,' Henley said. 'You're finally working in the family business. It must be a dream come true for him.'

I couldn't help but notice the dry tone of Henley's voice and I wondered if Willie could hear it as well.

'Not as happy as Mother is with Mary's debut into society. She's almost as excited about Mary's first season as Mary is!' Willie betrayed no sign of having heard the dark notes in Henley's voice, and he ploughed on, apparently trying to distract Henley. 'I think Mary's more enraptured by the idea of having a season than with the actual season itself.'

There was an awkward pause as Willie and I both waited for Henley to say something. When it was clear that he was just going to sit there staring at us with blank eyes, I tried to jump in, but Willie spoke again before I could.

'Mary always had that fantasy of marrying a wealthy titled lord after only her first season. Remember when you two used to make up stories about that? I blame you for encouraging her.' Willie laughed, but Henley's expression remained unchanged. 'We would all end up buying neighbouring houses, though we'd spend so much time with each other that we might as well be living together …' Willie trailed off in the face of Henley's persistent silence.

A servant I didn't recognize left Mr Beauford's room, carrying an empty glass on a tray. She nodded at Willie and me as she passed.

I caught Willie's gaze, and he understood without me having to tell him that I wanted some time alone with Henley. He obliged, smoothing his crumpled hat in his hands before entering Mr Beauford's room. Although he closed the door behind him, I could still hear the mixed mumble of voices. I couldn't distinguish individual words, but Willie's reassuring tones were soothing.

I knelt down in front of Henley, who had his face in his hands again. We sat there in silence, listening to each other breathing, and to the muffled voices next door. Then he gathered himself together.

'I–I don't know how I feel,' Henley said. 'I'm terrified for my father, yet … there's a part of me which can't feel anything for this man I hardly know. I know it's horrible – I know I'm not supposed to be numb like this. He's my own father—'

'Henley. It's all right,' I said. 'You don't have to feel a certain way. I know you have conflicting emotions, and that's normal. You don't have to justify anything to yourself or to me and Willie. We're here for you and that's not going to change. Your father will be all right. What did the physician say?'

Henley drew a shaky breath. 'It's just that I can see him slowly going insane. I know it and there's nothing I can do about it. When I was younger, I remember asking him about his love of collecting antiques. He said he collected them because they're immortal; they were here long before us and will remain long after we're gone. But his collecting has become an obsession, not a love.' Henley jerked his head up to look at me. 'He's been driven insane by his fear of dying. It's all he ever thinks about now. He practically has that chaplain by his side day and night, as if that alone will ward off death. Father Gabriel even appears to be indulging my father, pretending he actually takes an interest in the things he collects. He's using him, thinking that if he yields to my father's every whim, my father will give his chapel more money. That's what everyone's ultimately after, isn't it? His money. That's why they give in to all his desires … even this sickening fixation of his. I–I actually thought it would pass … that he'd somehow get better, but today … Today I really saw what his insanity can do to him. I saw the way the people in the park looked at him. I've never seen eyes like that. They judged him. They labelled him and I know he wouldn't want that. I know he's a greater man than that, and he deserves more. But I know he's not well, either.'

'Margaret, Mr Beauford has asked for you.' Willie was at the door.

I nodded and stood, but paused at the doorway and looked back.

'Come on, I'm afraid you look paler than your father,' Willie said as he grabbed hold of Henley's arm. 'To bed with you, and that's not a suggestion.'

Henley didn't resist and I watched him stagger down the hall next to Willie, just as Mr Beauford had staggered along beside us.

I closed my eyes for a long second and entered Mr Beauford's room.

106

'Close the door behind you.' His voice was stronger than I'd expected it to be.

After I'd closed the door as he instructed, I sat in the vacant seat next to the bed. Unsure of what to do, I folded my hands in my lap before spying a glass of water on the bedside table and asking him if he'd like some.

'No, thank you,' he said. 'If I were thirsty, I'd be drinking water right now. I'm not sick, you know, I'm perfectly capable of picking up a glass. It was just a misunderstanding. All I did was mistake someone for Ruth.'

'But Ruth … She's not here any more.'

Mr Beauford looked away from me. 'Pass me that pillow beside you,' he said.

I did as he asked and he put it behind his back to help him sit up taller.

'I miss her,' he said. 'I just don't know why she won't come home.'

'She's—'

'Yes, she's dead. Was that what you were about to tell me? But she's not, you see. I saw her a few years ago.' Mr Beauford nodded to himself as he spoke. 'She was standing right there.' He pointed towards his window. 'I remember it as if it were yesterday.

'I was wearing my smoking jacket, for it was hours after dinner. I was thinking of retiring to bed when I glanced out of the window and saw her. I saw Ruth. She looked exactly the same as when I'd last seen her. She was standing on the sidewalk, right there. At first, I wondered if I'd drunk one too many glasses of brandy after dinner, but when she looked up at me, I was sure it was her.

'I remember the moment our eyes met. She looked scared. I wanted to tell her there was nothing to be scared of, but when I opened the balcony doors, she was gone.

107

'I ran out of the house to look for her. I looked for her for hours before Jim found me and brought me home. He tried to convince me that I'd mistaken someone else for her.' Mr Beauford laughed, scaring me. 'But there's no mistaking that face. Ruth was – and still is – the prettiest girl I've ever laid eyes on. She has a special air about her.' Mr Beauford smiled up at me and reached over to pat my hand. 'You look a bit like her, you know. You two would have got along. She has some sense of humour … You'd love it. Everyone does.'

I stood and began to back away towards the door when Mr Beauford started using the present tense for Ruth, as if she were still alive.

'You need your rest, Uncle. We'll visit you in the morning,' I said, but Mr Beauford didn't seem to hear me over his own laughter.

That evening, I dismissed Nellie early, then waited in silence in my room until dark. Shadows flitted about, cast by the single candle I'd lit at dusk. They snatched at my feet and grabbed at the empty air around me. I knew one of the shadows was mine, but somehow I couldn't find it. Footsteps crept about, making the old house groan as if it were tossing and turning in its sleep. Then all at once the house was still, and all its inhabitants were fast asleep.

I took the candle and felt my way along the wall to the door. My steps were strangely sure, even though I'd only been in this house a short time. It was as if my body had memorized the house itself, and when the house breathed, my body breathed with it.

I managed to find the back stairs and, from there, the servants' hallway from which I'd first entered the house. It was as cramped and cold as I remembered it being. When I opened the servants' entrance, relief washed over me with the cool night breeze. I blew my candle out, thankful to have the gas street lamps to guide me to Miss Hatfield's house.

'Go down Second Avenue and turn right onto East Sixty-Sixth Street, past Park Avenue.' I still remembered Miss Hatfield's directions to the Beauford house, and I muttered them to myself for company as I followed them in reverse and made the lonely walk back to Miss Hatfield's.

Having knocked at least four times, I told myself I'd wait a few seconds more before turning back. Where else could she be, after all?

'Miss Hatfield?' My voice had a rasp to it I didn't recognize.

She didn't look at all surprised to see me, even though it was around one in the morning. She invited me in as if I was calling in the early afternoon. 'I'll just go and brew some tea,' she said, and I nodded, amused. As if tea would bring a tone of civility to our discussions of stealing a painting.

I sat down on the overstuffed pea-green couch in the parlour, just as I'd done the first time I met Miss Hatfield. I wondered whether I'd have guessed anything at all of her past if she hadn't told me. Would I have thought even for a moment that there was anything amiss? I realized that her smooth demeanour betrayed nothing – not even time itself.

'I hope you like Earl Grey,' she said as she poured. I held the hot cup in my hands, waiting for Miss Hatfield to speak, but the silence dragged on.

'This tea … It's delicious.'

'I was surprised to see you at the ice cream parlour today.' Miss Hatfield's abruptness startled me and made me swallow hard. After all that had happened, I could hardly believe our shopping trip had only been this morning.

109

'I–I was surprised to see you, too.' My mind scrambled to find a way to tell Miss Hatfield that I hadn't been distracted from my mission.

'Why were you there?'

'I could ask you the same question.' Even I was surprised by my defensive words. Perhaps she had something to hide herself.

'What I do to reminisce about my past is none of your concern.' Her tone was chilling, her face a white mask. 'But you completing your task is, unfortunately, mine.'

'I was there to get more information about the painting.'

'In an ice cream parlour?' Miss Hatfield was quick to squint her eyes at me, but I tried to brush it off.

'The painting that was stolen from you,' I began, 'it's being moved to Mr Beauford's country home.' I went on to explain that I'd posed as Mr Beauford's niece Margaret so that I'd be taken to the country as well, in the hope of securing the portrait.

'I see,' she said. 'Taking the painting appears to be a more difficult task than I anticipated.' Miss Hatfield eyed me more closely, as if trying to decide whether the mission was really all that difficult or if I was just incompetent. 'If you can't bring it back to me, destroy it.'

'The painting? Destroy the painting?'

'Yes.'

I was startled by this new instruction, but tried not to show it. Instead, I talked further about posing as Mr Beauford's niece.

I waited for Miss Hatfield to praise me for blending into the family and devising split-second adaptations of our plan, or even to question some aspects of my tale, but her face remained grave.

'He has a son, doesn't he?' Miss Hatfield asked.

'Who? Mr Beauford?' Her question startled me.

'Yes. I don't know his son's name – but he seems convinced you're his cousin?'

'I–I don't know him that well, but I don't think he's suspicious at all.'

Miss Hatfield squinted at me again. 'Wait for my instructions once you're at the country house,' she said, then paused. 'And ... who was that young man you were with?'

I knew she was talking about Henley in the ice cream parlour, but I was surprised to learn that she didn't know he was Mr Beauford's son. I wondered where I should start. Yes, I'd already told her the necessary details concerning the painting, but there was so much more I needed to say. I wanted to tell her about Henley, but I knew Miss Hatfield would disapprove. I decided to make nothing of it.

'He's just some gentleman's son.' I took another sip of tea so I wouldn't have to add anything more.

'You two appeared to be having a riveting conversation. Where on earth did you find time to meet him?'

I forced myself to inhale a deep breath, hoping that would calm me. How long had she been there watching us? How much did she know?

I opened my mouth, unsure what to say, but Miss Hatfield spoke first.

'Don't let him become a distraction. You have a lot to focus on as it is. We don't need another complication.'

I nodded, not trusting my voice.

'I thought you knew better.' She closed her eyes and rubbed her temples as if she was a hundred years old. 'I should have spent more time teaching you about the consequences of various actions for us.' She paused again, then looked right into my eyes. 'Do you remember what I told you about the fourth Miss Hatfield?'

111

'That she died in an asylum?'

'Her fiancé locked her up.' Miss Hatfield's voice was hard and emotionless.

'And she died in there because they tortured her?'

'Precisely. She thought she could trust someone. That was her downfall. Foolish, really. Idiotic.'

Miss Hatfield's strong words made me swallow a bitter lump in my throat. She spoke as if she believed love was a choice that could be made willingly, and I couldn't find it in myself to disagree with her. What did I know of love, anyway?

'Love will weaken you,' she said. 'We're not like other people. We're not made like them. You won't even be able to physically tolerate staying in one period of time for long. Your body knows it's not supposed to be here in this time. It's uncomfortable. Unnatural, even. And you're not only putting yourself in danger, but also me. Loving him will cost you my life as well as yours. It's a selfish thing and you can't afford to give in to it.'

When I couldn't respond, my hands tried to keep busy. They found a loose thread at the seam of my dress and began to work at it, dragging it out so it appeared to grow in my hands.

'Don't fall in love with him,' Miss Hatfield said. 'If you do, it'll lead to your downfall.'

She stood up, signalling the end of our conversation.

Dawn chased at my heels as I crept back into the Beauford house. Once in my room, I changed into my nightgown so Nellie would think I'd slept, but in reality I spent the rest of those placid hours awake and worrying about what was to come. And, despite Miss Hatfield's warning, with thoughts of Henley.

Chapter 11

When Nellie crept into my room in the morning, I was already sitting upright in bed.

'Oh, miss, I'm sorry not to have been here when you woke.' She was quick to apologize and continued apologizing when I told her I'd been awake for hours before she arrived.

Nellie opened the curtains and pulled out a morning dress for me to wear to breakfast.

'Will this do?' she asked, holding up a dress with blue flowers on it.

'Yes, that'll be perfect.'

I'd learned that it was easier to say yes than to explain to Nellie that I simply didn't care what colour my dress was, or what kind of peonies I would prefer on my bedside table, or anything like that. She didn't know that I had more on my mind.

'Did Mr—' I realized I didn't know Willie's last name. 'Did Willie spend the night here?'

Nellie's hands froze when I called Willie by his first name.

'I didn't realize you and Mr Garner were so familiar with each other.' Nellie's mouth was agape, but she quickly began apologizing again. 'E–excuse me. That's none of my business. The younger Mr Beauford did ask Mr Garner to stay the night.'

'No need to apologize,' I said. 'I'm afraid it skipped Henley's mind to properly introduce us, so I never discovered his full name.' I remembered how Henley had in fact forgotten to introduce us altogether. 'And Henley? How's he faring after the scare he had yesterday?' I knew what had occurred in the park would already be common knowledge. The servants knew most, if not all, of what occurred among the folks 'upstairs'.

'I'm not sure how he is faring, but he did go out riding early this morning before breakfast. He should be back by now.'

I rushed to get dressed and ran downstairs to see Henley. I knew that if he was back, he'd probably be at breakfast.

'Someone flew down the stairs ... and not too gracefully, I might add. I could hear you all the way.' Henley was seated at the head of the table in Mr Beauford's absence, looking at me. It reminded me of all Henley would someday inherit.

I playfully swatted at Henley before taking my seat next to him. Across from me, Willie was already devouring a piece of toast overladen with marmalade.

'We could hear you thundering along from a mile away,' Willie chimed in. 'How unladylike.' He wrinkled his nose in a comical way.

'And did you know she hates to shop? Or to have things bought for her?' Henley said.

'Nonsense, all women like to be showered with gifts!'

I couldn't help but notice how familiar Willie was getting with me. I knew yesterday's events had a lot to do with that. The frightful experience had brought us close, but still, we'd only met the day before. I paused, remembering that he also believed I was Henley's cousin.

'You're lucky you're too far away to swat,' I said, and

Willie wiggled his eyebrows in a way that reminded me of Henley.

A lot of the things Willie did reminded me of Henley. I accredited that largely to their similar upbringing. But there were many things Willie did that startled me. I realized that I expected him to act like Henley in a time when it was unusual for people to act like Henley.

When a servant took their plates, I saw that difference again. Henley thanked her, while Willie didn't even acknowledge her.

I tried to let that go. Willie had somehow brought Henley back to his former self and I was thankful for that.

'How's your father?' Willie asked suddenly. I held my breath, expecting Henley to relapse, to return to how he'd acted yesterday, but to my surprise he answered the question directly.

'He's well enough to travel. Dr Hanville said the fresh country air will be best for him.'

'Is he coming to breakfast?' I enquired.

'I asked them to take up a tray for him when he woke. They said he wanted to come down, but I thought it would be best for him to conserve his strength.'

I was struck by his wording and couldn't help repeating after him. '*They* said?'

'Yes,' Henley said. 'They … a couple of the servants.'

'He didn't ask for you?'

'I saw him for a few minutes when he first woke.' He sighed. 'Then he asked for his chaplain.'

'Father Gabriel?' I asked.

'Of course, Father Gabriel.'

I hesitated as I wondered what I should say next. 'So what are we doing today?' I asked Willie, when I realized there wasn't much more we could say about Mr Beauford.

I knew Henley and I were supposed to be leaving for the country this morning, but I was sure that everything would be postponed due to Mr Beauford's bad turn.

'We?' Willie asked.

'Yes, we,' said Henley. 'I know you're leaving tomorrow, but you must at least stay the day.'

I smiled when Henley backed me up.

'So, what are we doing today?' I asked again.

'Why don't we go boating?' Willie suggested.

'That sounds like fun.'

I'd never been boating, but tried not to let on to that fact. Henley didn't appear to mind what we did, so we decided to go to the lake at Central Park.

'Jim.' Henley waved the butler over to his side. 'We'll be going to Central Park today. Have the coach ready in a few minutes.'

'Yes, sir.'

I'd never get over how quickly the servants appeared and vanished at Henley's beck and call. I knew they had to be ready, for they could be called at any moment, but I couldn't quite figure out how they managed to be everywhere at once. I added this to the lengthening list of things in this time to which I knew I would never grow accustomed.

'I think I'm ready,' I announced when Henley and Willie appeared dressed up in their outing attire.

Willie wrinkled his nose at me and looked down at my bare hands.

'I don't believe so,' he said. 'Where are your gloves?'

'In my room, I think … or maybe Nellie's ironing them.'

'Nellie?' Willie looked from me to Henley and back again. 'Who's Nellie?'

'My maid.' Those words felt heavy in my mouth, but I couldn't find another way to answer the question.

'First Jim, then Nellie,' Willie grumbled. 'What is it with everyone remembering the help's names?' He continued, a bit louder, 'They're paid to do their jobs. We don't need to remember their names.'

I was surprised at the fuss he was making over me remembering Nellie's name. Of course I'd know her name. Why wouldn't I?

Willie was still mumbling when he left the room. I made a move to follow him, but Henley grabbed my arm.

'You should go and get your gloves,' he said.

'I never wore them when we went out before—'

'You should go and get them.'

'But—'

'Please,' he said, then walked out to join Willie, as if he'd signalled the end of our discussion.

I bit my lip, conflicted about the change in Henley when he was around Willie. I didn't like being told what to do, but in a strange way I understood Henley was only trying to keep up pretences and play the role he had always played before I showed up.

I ran back up to my room to fetch my gloves. They were folded one on top of the other on my dresser like nesting doves. When I grabbed for them, they both flew to the ground. I picked them up and ran back downstairs and out of the door. I jumped the last few steps into the carriage.

The footman snapped the coach door shut behind me and the carriage lurched into motion.

There was silence as we rode. I couldn't help but feel slightly responsible for it, after the business of me remembering Nellie's name. Henley and Willie had been friends for far longer than I'd known either of them, and I wanted them to remain that way.

'Oh, look – there's the ice cream shop.' I pointed out of the window as we passed it.

'And look at all those people crowded inside. Some of them are our age – they just can't let go of their childhoods!' Willie scoffed and I glanced at Henley. I knew that comment must have hurt him, but he betrayed no sign of his feelings.

A few more minutes of uncomfortable silence went by. The carriage rocked from side to side steadily, repeating the only pattern it knew.

'Miss Dorothy Jones's Séance Parlour,' I read from a sign attached to what looked like a regular house.

'Pardon me?' Willie looked up.

'Miss Dorothy Jones's Séance Parlour.' I pointed outside. 'I didn't know séances were popular enough for someone to have set up shop here.'

To my surprise, Willie responded, 'Séances are always popular,' he said. 'In fact, Mary once begged Mother and Father to invite those people to our house. First she wanted a psychic. Then it was a medium.' Willie laughed and Henley joined in.

'And did she succeed?' Henley asked him.

'Of course not – Mother had a fit. But I don't think Mary's quite given up on the idea. God only knows why she romanticizes contacting the dead.'

I was glad to hear Henley laughing again – things were slowly getting back to normal.

'We should visit.' The words just tumbled out of my mouth. I wasn't sure why I wanted to go, but my recent experiences had shown me how different the world was compared to my beliefs. Who knew what might happen?

'The séance parlour?' Henley suddenly looked troubled and I cursed myself for bringing up such an idea. I'd momentarily forgotten his father's incident yesterday and the fact that Henley had lost his mother.

'I–I'm so sorry,' I said.

'No. We should go.'

The meaning of Henley's words took a few moments to dawn on me. I never thought he'd agree.

'You really don't have to. I was only—'

'We should go. It can't be that bad.' Henley cracked a smile.

'Are you sure?' This time it was Willie who asked.

Instead of giving a direct answer, Henley knocked on the side of the carriage, making the driver stop.

The servant came around and opened the door. He helped Henley down, then Willie. I saw Henley thank him. He didn't even have to think about it. It was second nature to Henley, but Willie looked right through the servant, as if he saw furniture in place of the man.

All of a sudden, I realized that Willie was nothing like Henley after all, and my respect for Henley only increased. I'd not had anybody to compare him to before.

As if reading my thoughts, Henley smiled up at me and helped me down from the carriage.

'Thank you.' I felt I was thanking him for more than just helping me down. And it felt like he understood when he squeezed my hand.

'Miss Dorothy Jones's Séance Parlour,' Willie said. 'It's right there.' He looked back at us as if to ask whether we were sure we wanted to do this.

Henley only nodded as he went ahead of Willie and pushed open the door.

'Good afternoon,' a female voice called out to us.

It took a while for our eyes to grow accustomed to the gloom within, but when they did, I saw a willowy woman approach us.

'Good afternoon,' Willie said.

'I am Miss Jones.' The woman gave her hand to Willie and Henley in turn. She only glared at me. 'You are here for a séance.'

Her sentence wasn't a question. It was a statement.

When Henley tried to say something, the woman hushed him.

'You are now in the house of the spirits. Be respectful.' She beckoned a younger girl from the shadows behind her. 'Clara, show these people to the parlour.' The older woman turned back to us. 'I will be with you shortly.'

Clara looked much like the older woman we left behind in the hallway. I decided they must be sisters.

Without a word, Clara led us deeper into the house. I noticed there wasn't a single source of light apart from the windows. I was beginning to think that coming here had been a mistake when Clara suddenly stopped in front of a door apparently chosen at random.

'Please wait in here.' Clara opened the door and paused just long enough for us to step inside before closing it behind us and walking away.

'I–I don't know what to say,' Willie said. I knew exactly what he meant.

The room Clara had left us in was as dark as the rest of the house we'd seen so far, despite the three lit candles standing in the middle of a circular table that had been placed in the centre of the room. The table and the chairs around it were the only furniture. The empty fireplace threw flickering shadows onto the wine-coloured wall-paper, making it look as if the room itself was engulfed in black smoke. The floor beneath me squeaked as I made my way over to one of the chairs.

'We might as well sit while we wait,' I said. My voice sounded braver than I felt.

Henley and Willie followed me to the table. Henley took his seat next to me and Willie next to him. Countless minutes passed before Miss Jones appeared. She took her time walking around the table and finally sat directly across from me.

'You.' The woman eyed me again. 'You are different. I know. *Tu scies numquam finem.*'

I felt a chill go through me though I had no idea what those words meant.

'I am ready, Dorothy,' Clara said as she entered the room. She took the remaining seat between Miss Jones and Willie.

'Let us talk to the ones who have passed,' Miss Jones said. She took Clara's hand, and Willie's, and motioned to me to do the same with Henley and Clara. 'Do not break the circle,' she warned and blew out one of the candles. 'Is there a spirit here among us?'

Almost a second later, the remaining two candles snuffed themselves out.

In the dark, Clara's hand felt small and lost in mine. I was surprised when she was the one who answered.

'Yes,' she said.

'Good, and who are you?' Miss Jones asked. 'Do you want to introduce yourself to us?'

'Yes,' Clara said again, but this time her voice came out stronger. 'I am Henley. Henley Beauford.'

I felt Henley's hand jerk in my own. My throat constricted and I struggled to breathe.

Miss Jones went on, 'Why are you here, Mr Beauford?'

'I am here to tell her something.'

In the dark I couldn't tell whether Clara was facing me or not, but somehow I knew she was talking about me.

'What do you want to tell her?'

'I want—' Clara's voice was like a child's again. 'I want to tell her that I know.'

'What do you know, Mr Beauford?'

There was a thud and I felt something hit the table.

'Clara? Clara!' It was Willie's voice. 'Someone, do something!'

Miss Jones lit the candles in a hurry. I saw her hands shaking, but couldn't make myself move to help her.

Clara's head was down on the table, her hair hiding her face. When Miss Jones gently raised her head, I saw blood on Clara's cheek.

'Call the physician.' Willie stood up in such a hurry that he knocked over his chair.

Clara giggled. 'Why would you do that? I feel fine.' She laughed again.

Miss Jones's face was pale in the candlelight.

'Out!' Miss Jones screamed. 'Get out!' She then glared directly at me. 'You do the Devil's work.'

Henley pulled me to my feet and dragged me from the room, along the hallway and then into the street. Once in the open air, I was able to breathe again.

'They're insane!' Willie said as we stumbled to our carriage. 'Absolute lunatics! And they thought you were dead.'

Henley grimaced at Willie's last sentence.

'You know, they probably just pulled that name out of the newspaper,' Willie said. 'Everyone knows your father, and everyone knows he has a son.' He patted Henley's back. 'Nothing to worry about.'

Henley agreed, but I knew he was still troubled.

We ended up giving up on boating.

On the ride back, Willie talked with Henley about Mary and his family, and about going home. It was obvious he missed his sister more than he would have liked to let on. I left them to reminisce about old times while I puzzled over what Miss Jones had said to me. I just couldn't get her words out of my head. *Tu scies numquam finem.*

'What did Miss Jones mean?' I asked them suddenly. I'd interrupted whatever Henley and Willie were talking about, but I couldn't help it. I had to know.

Willie waved me off. 'She just isn't the best reader. She probably thought she'd read Henley's name in the obituary section of the newspaper.'

Even Henley laughed at that.

'I mean before that. It was in another language. Latin, I think.'

'*Tu scies numquam finem*,' Henley said. 'You will never know the end.'

'God only knows what she meant,' Willie muttered, but soon he and Henley fell back into comfortable conversation.

You will never know the end. I shuddered at the thought that she might have known exactly what I was.

Chapter 12

'Miss?' I heard something murmuring near my face and my delayed hand reached up to swat at it. 'Miss?' This time it sounded more insistent and roused me from my half-sleep. 'Miss.'

I blinked open my eyes to see Nellie's face, close to mine.

'Good, you're finally awake,' she said. 'Mr Beauford just left for the country and you're running a bit late.'

'I'm late?' I exclaimed, suddenly fully awake. 'When are we leaving?'

'In a few minutes.'

'A few minutes?' I was now sitting up in bed. 'And you let me sleep in?'

'I'm sorry – it wasn't my place, I know, but you looked so tired last night, miss.' Her eyes were downcast, and I knew I couldn't be mad at her. It was my own fault anyway, given how I'd spent the night before.

I saw that Nellie had already laid out a dress for me. 'I hope you like it,' she said.

Nellie helped me dress, drawing the laces as tight as Miss Hatfield had. I rushed downstairs, grabbing the hat that Nellie threw at me. Henley was already waiting at the door.

'Took you long enough,' he said, his eyes gleaming. 'My father just left in the carriage with Father Gabriel. We'll be taking the automobile.'

It was hard not to laugh at someone as young as Henley calling a car an 'automobile', but then I wasn't in 1954 any more.

'And Willie?' I asked. 'Did he leave for home already?'

'I'm afraid so. He left last night.'

I felt a pang inside me when I realized I'd never see him again.

Henley led me outside to something that looked more like a carriage than any car I'd ever seen. It truly was a horseless carriage, and in its way, it was a wonder for both of us – to me because of its antiquity, and to Henley because of its modernity.

Henley helped me up into the passenger seat next to him. Then he took his seat behind the wheel and the engine roared to life, humming beneath us with the same excitement we felt.

'This will be my first time seeing the countryside in this area,' I mused aloud.

'Riding in an automobile really does open your eyes to new things, doesn't it?' Henley laughed. 'Here, wear these.' He passed me goggles then put on his own. I held my pair up uncertainly. 'You look suspicious,' Henley said.

'I think I have reason to be.' I waved the goggles at him.

'I guess I know one more thing about you now.' I looked up in surprise, wondering what secret I'd just revealed. 'You've never ridden in an automobile before, have you?'

I couldn't help but laugh. I nodded. It was true, I'd never ridden in an automobile before, but if he'd asked if I'd ever ridden in a car, I might have said yes.

'You're very mysterious,' Henley went on. 'You know so much about me already and I still know almost nothing about you.'

'Well, now you know I've never ridden in an automobile before,' I pointed out. He chuckled at that, but his voice grew downright serious.

'You know things that even people close to me don't,' he said. 'I–I told you about my mother … I don't talk about her, usually.'

I smiled politely as if I had no idea what he was talking about, but we both knew. I felt so comfortable with him near me. True, he knew almost nothing about me, yet at the same time he knew the most important thing about me. He didn't know my name, but he knew how I felt.

'So I think it's only fair that you tell me a little about yourself.'

I gulped inwardly, waiting for him to ask me my real name. Like Henley said, his request for information was only fair.

'Since I've told you about my parents and you've met my father, what are yours like?'

'They're like any ordinary parents, I guess.'

'No two sets of parents are ordinary. What's your mother like?' Henley's eyes flickered back and forth between me to the road.

'My mother …' I started. 'She fusses around with her hair, and when she's finally satisfied with it, she fusses around with mine.' I smiled at the image that brought up in my mind. Whenever I thought of my mother, I thought of her tucking me into bed with curlers in her hair. 'She has gentle hands – slightly cool to the touch. She stroked my hair as I fell asleep … when I was little,' I was quick to add. I hadn't realized I'd slipped into the past tense.

'And what about your father?' Henley looked genuinely curious.

'My father's a straightforward kind of man. He never beats around the bush. If he had something on his mind, he'd say it.' I laughed. 'Tact was never something he learned.' I thought back to the last time I'd seen him. He was dressed in my favourite suit – the light brown one with the matching hat that made his eyes look warmer – and he was off to work. I wish I'd got to say goodbye.

'He sounds like an honest man.'

'He was – *is*,' I corrected myself.

'Living apart from your family can't be easy,' Henley said. 'Were you staying with relatives? Siblings, maybe? Before you came to us, that is.' Henley's eyes were focused on me rather than the road, which I found a little disconcerting.

'I was living with a family friend,' I said, for I didn't know what to call Miss Hatfield. 'My parents live far away.' *In my time*, I wanted to add, but I bit my tongue firmly and kept the thought to myself.

'So you have parents?' There was a mischievous twinkle in Henley's eyes now. 'Finally, some more information about my mysterious "cousin".' He glanced at me again. 'You'd think I would know her well, her being my cousin and all.' Henley gave me one of those looks of his, which made me laugh so hard I almost lost my hat in the wind.

'Better tighten those ribbons on your hat,' he said, tugging at one of them with his spare hand.

As we drove out of the city in comfortable silence, I stared at Henley, trying to figure him out. He was busy driving and didn't appear to notice me puzzling over him. I studied every inch of his face, trying to memorize every feature. I wanted to know so many things – why he made me feel safe when I knew I wasn't, why he made me want to stay when I knew I couldn't, and why he drew me to him.

'You know, I can see you out of the corner of my eye.' Henley turned to face me with a huge grin on his face. 'Don't think I can't see you staring at me.'

127

I looked down, wishing the brim of my hat was large enough to cover my face and, more importantly, to hide my warm cheeks.

'Few people blush that easily, and you're just making it more entertaining.'

I almost stuck my tongue out at him. 'I doubt your father raised you to be this kind of gentleman.'

'And my mother would turn over in her grave to hear me talking in this way to a lady.' We both laughed, and for that moment we shook off all our responsibilities and duties and left them to the wind.

We'd been driving for some while already when a strange noise started under the low hum of the engine. The tall buildings of the city had long since given way to the rolling hills of the countryside. Henley and I began to open up to each other, regaling each other with stories of our earliest childhood memories. This was fortunate for me, since I then didn't need to lie about the gap in my life.

'... and then the farmhand came in and we realized he'd seen the entire thing!' Henley and I must have been red in the face from laughing so hard when I first became vaguely aware of the grinding sound of gear against gear.

'Do you hear that?'

'I was hoping I was just imagining it,' Henley said as he stopped the car in the middle of the road.

'You're not going to pull over to the side?'

'Why should I? No one uses these roads, and if someone does, it would be nice to have their help.'

Henley got out of the car and opened the hood of the car.

'Do you know what you're looking at?'

'To be honest, I have no idea what the inside of an automobile is supposed to look like, so I'm no help at all in this department, unfortunately.' Henley climbed back in. 'I suppose our best bet is to find somewhere to stop nearby.' With that, he revved the engine back to life.

We only drove a couple of miles further before the car stopped working altogether. It came to a screeching halt, and we had no choice but to get out and keep walking until we saw a house or a farm, or met somebody else. Dust from the road covered us within seconds, whisked up by a rising wind.

'Just our luck,' Henley muttered.

'No use crying over spilled milk,' I said, which made him laugh again for some reason. 'I'm glad one of us is finding this situation amusing.'

I gave him a look, to which he responded, 'I've just never heard that expression before. Is it common where you grew up?'

'My mother used to say it when I was whining over something useless – like you're doing now.' He only laughed again. 'Ouch!'

'What's wrong?' Henley was by my side immediately. He held my arm as I leaned on him to lift my heavy skirts.

'I just broke my heel,' I said, putting my skirts back in place. 'Now look what you've done. You've made me ruin a perfectly good pair of shoes.' Henley appeared to find that hilarious as well.

'You should take them off. There's no sense in staggering along on only one heel.'

'And go barefoot?' I thought about what my mother would say.

Henley appeared to read my mind. 'You don't have to worry about what other people will think.' He gestured to the empty landscape around us and a mischievous look came into his eyes. 'Tell you what – I'll do it with you.'

Without further ado, Henley bent down to take off his shoes. He tied the laces together and flung them over his shoulder, and then he was off and running. I stared at him for only a second before I took off my uncomfortable shoes and did the same, a matching grin on my face. I bunched up my skirts and ran after him.

We walked and ran in spurts like little children do, swinging our arms back and forth and laughing gleefully. Even though we couldn't see anything before or behind us through the dust, we were euphoric.

We went on like this for miles before we saw anything. Then, through the dust, we could barely make out the minute form of a man entering a house in the distance.

'Did you see that?' Henley asked me. 'There's a cottage up ahead on that hill.'

'How long do you think it'll take us to get there?'

'A few more minutes, I'd guess – but it's on our way.'

'So is anything in that general direction,' I quipped, pointing forwards. 'I suppose there's no harm trying that house.'

As we drew closer, we began to see flocks of sheep dotting the fields around us.

'A shepherd?' I wondered.

'Let's find out.'

Henley ran ahead and knocked on the cottage door. It wasn't long before the man we saw earlier opened it. I watched from a distance as he talked to Henley, then saw Henley point to me and the man nod some sort of consent.

The man's house looked cramped from the outside, as if it only had one room. It was crooked and stood taller on its left side, where its only window was missing a shutter.

When I caught up with Henley, he told me that the

man had agreed to let us stay the night in his house until his son came in the morning with a horse.

'You're taking their horse?' I hissed at Henley as I ducked under the arm he was using to prop open the door.

'No. *We're* taking their horse,' he said, removing his hat as he entered the house behind me.

'Can't you see it's everything they own?'

'Indeed, and I've already paid a good price for it.'

I glanced around and noticed a watch, glittering out of place on the only table in the room.

'You gave him your watch?' I whispered.

'What else could I do?'

'Couldn't you have given him money instead? Wasn't that watch a gift from your father?' I'd noticed the inscription on it the last time he wore it.

'My father … The watch doesn't mean that much to me. It's just a watch,' Henley said. 'Besides, I have no pocket money with me.'

'No pocket money? What do you mean, no pocket money? You have a house in the country, but no money with you?' I hissed again.

'I–I've never needed to carry money with me before.'

Then I remembered that in town, he'd put everything we bought on his tab. A perk of being from one of the richer families in town, I supposed.

The old shepherd motioned to the two chairs by the table and gestured for us to sit.

'Couldn't you have paid him and just borrowed the horse? Then they'd get the money without having to lose the horse. They need the money.'

'Everyone has pride,' Henley said. 'Even the poor.'

I opened my mouth to say something, but closed it as soon as I realized there was nothing to be said.

A loud clatter of cups on the table made Henley and I acutely aware of the shepherd's presence. While we were talking, I'd forgotten he was there and wondered how much he'd overheard. When I shot Henley a questioning look, he shook his head as if reading my mind. He looked certain that the shepherd hadn't heard anything.

The cups the shepherd had placed on the table were full of murky water. I could just about see my reflection on the surface of the brown liquid with flecks of grime deposited beneath, and I couldn't believe that the person I saw was me.

'We're fine, thank you,' Henley said, giving the cups back to the shepherd. 'If you don't mind, I think we'll retire to bed now.'

The shepherd pointed up and I saw there was a loft above us.

'Thank you,' Henley said again. He took me by the hand and began climbing up the ladder. 'Careful with your skirts.'

Henley pulled me up the last few rungs, and I saw that the loft contained little more than a mattress of straw and a window in the far corner.

Henley took off his jacket and put it at the foot of the makeshift bed along with his hat. He acted as if everything was perfectly normal and proceeded to spread blankets he'd found somewhere over the bed.

'You're not going to sleep in that, surely?' he asked when he saw me move towards the bed still fully dressed. 'At least take off that hat – that can't be comfortable to sleep in.'

I'd completely forgotten I was wearing a hat. I took it off and put it with Henley's things. Not wanting to wrinkle my dress, I took that off, too, and ended up going to bed in my petticoats. When I took off my dress, Henley drew back in shock. I informed him I intended to be comfortable and not get strangled in my corset. He offered to sleep on the floor, but I bluntly told him it was more important for both of us to get a good night's sleep, than it was to preserve his old-fashioned sense of propriety.

I was very aware of where my body ended and his began, but nothing felt out of place as I listened to Henley's breathing even out as he lay beside me. The warmth of his body against my side appeared to dissolve all my anxiety and fears about my impossible situation. I felt oddly complete – everything I'd wanted was fulfilled. The only thing that mattered was him; everything else vanished into the blackness of the night.

Chapter 13

The whistling of a kettle woke me, though my eyes remained tightly closed, determined to stay asleep. I prised them open to see sun already rising, reaching out to us through the window, and I rose as well.

I looked down at Henley's sleeping form, moulded around where I'd slept, and wondered if we'd shared the same dream. But try as I might, I couldn't recall exactly what my dream had been about. All I remembered was that it had been beautiful, almost glorious; something a person would suspend reality for, if they could.

The kettle continued whistling and I hurried as fast as I could down the ladder to stop it boiling over. The kettle hadn't woken Henley when it started whistling, and I was determined it wouldn't wake him up now. Sadly, my plan was short-lived.

There was a knock at the door, and before I could answer it, Henley had sprung out of bed, rushed down the ladder and run to answer it himself.

'I can get the door,' I said, and Henley looked bemused.

'In that?' He gave me a once-over with his glance, and I remembered I hadn't put my dress back on yet. 'It's a good thing people think we're cousins.'

I felt my cheeks and the rest of my face growing hot as I climbed back up the ladder. As I dressed, I could hear

Henley and another person's voice below. I couldn't quite make out their words and they soon fell silent. They were still sitting in silence when I went down again.

The shepherd sat wide-legged on a shaky bench with his arms around a young boy. The boy had a small knife in his hands and was carving a piece of wood. The shepherd's much larger hands enveloped the boy's, guiding his motions.

I understood the silence when I noticed Henley seated at the other side of the room, watching the pair intently. I saw something in his eyes, but it wasn't the envy I'd expected. What I saw was much closer to a deep and sinking sadness.

Seeing me, Henley stood up immediately. The boy followed suit.

'I left my watch on the counter,' Henley said. 'I don't have anything else of much value with me, but that should be enough for the horse.'

'That's most generous of you, sir.' Hearing the boy's voice, I realized he couldn't have been much more than twelve years old. 'My father and I can use the money to buy more sheep.'

The boy looked willowy – tall for his age – but his face still had the roundness of a child's and his freckles made him all the more lovable.

'Very well, then.' Henley nodded. 'Is that the horse outside?'

'Yes, sir, that's old Nancy-Ann. We've had her for as long as I can remember.' I heard a tinge of sadness in the boy's voice.

'We'll take good care of her,' I assured the boy, and he smiled gratefully.

After Henley checked the bit in the horse's mouth and the buckles in the bridle, he hoisted me up onto the horse's back and soon followed, sitting behind me and taking the reins around me. My skirts made sitting astride uncomfortable but I wasn't prepared to risk riding side-saddle.

As we rode away from the little cottage on its picturesque hill, I couldn't help but be reminded of the fairy tales I'd read when I was little. Was I the princess being whisked away by her prince to something better? Could I escape immortality? Or was it already a part of me I could never leave behind?

'Look behind us,' Henley said, and I was startled by how close his voice was to my ear. 'Doesn't the house look like a painting?'

'It does,' I murmured. 'I still feel bad for the shepherd and his son, though. They have nothing, and … look at us.'

'They have something I never had.' Henley's voice didn't sound bitter at all, nor did it reveal any hint of resentment. 'There wasn't any sense of obligation in their relationship,' he noted. 'It was all love; pure, confusing, and without need of a reason.'

'But what kind of obligation could the son have to his father? It's not as if he's the heir to his father's fortune and business.'

'He might have a much simpler obligation; one that most people, wrongly or rightly, feel towards the disabled.'

'The disabled?'

'Or the deaf, to be more precise.'

'I–I don't understand.'

'How can you *not* understand? We don't live in so different a world from them.'

'It's just that … the shepherd … he's deaf?'

'You didn't notice?' Henley asked. He sounded surprised. 'Why else did you think he wasn't comfortable talking?'

'But you spoke to him.'

'He reads lips well – he has to in order to communicate with his son.'

I wondered how many other things would have passed me by if Henley hadn't been there to tell me the obvious.

We rode on in silence for a while, then Henley pointed off to one side and said, 'Look – you can see the house in the distance. We'll be there soon.'

Though Henley simply called it 'the house', it was anything but. Henley's country 'house' was a grand confusion of buildings set amid a rolling green estate. It was gleaming white, and getting closer and closer.

'Are you ready?' Henley suddenly had a boyish grin on his face.

Before I could ask what I was supposed to be preparing for, Henley spurred the horse into a full gallop. We flew down the hill, and for a few seconds I couldn't feel the horse below me, as if we were afloat on the air itself. Then it was swiped from beneath us and we fell, crashing to the ground. The impact jolted me awake, throwing me into another world; one with country estates and horse riding on acres of green.

The house gleamed in the mid-morning sun, a startling white against the verdant landscape surrounding it. The pure, timeless elegance of the grand building took my breath away. I turned to Henley and found the same awestruck expression on his face that must have been on mine. His eyes held an unmistakable love for the house, and I was surprised that I understood what kind of love it was.

'Welcome to Maurrington, sir,' a severe-looking man said as he and the other servants filed out to line up in front of the house.

I counted eight servants in total but there might well have been more still working away behind the scenes.

The maids were dressed in starchy aprons and the valets looked equally pristine in their black coats.

'This is Wilchester, head valet.' Henley introduced him. Wilchester nodded towards me.

'I trust you had a good journey,' Wilchester said, and I noticed he had an English accent. 'I'm sorry the kitchen couldn't ready some food for your arrival – the staff in the city failed to send word of when you would be joining us.'

'Don't be too hard on Jim – he didn't know our automobile was going to break down.'

'Forgive me. I had no knowledge of your troubles. I was merely stating that he should have sent word you were on your way. When I was head of staff to the late Duke of Northumberland—'

'That will be all, Wilchester,' Henley said, dismissing him. I'd never heard him talk to a servant in such a distant and cold tone. It was as if he kept a barrier between himself and Wilchester. When Henley tired of him, he shut down and pulled the wall up higher.

Wilchester appeared accustomed to Henley's tone, however, and led the way past imposing double doors into the grand house. The foyer was an open space with a stately staircase that branched in two as it ascended. The room was filled with antiques and lavish furniture as well as paintings. The walls rose up and up to dizzying heights, and when I tilted my head back, my eyes were drawn to the spectacular gilded flowers adorning the golden ceiling.

'Miss Beauford, Hannah will escort you to your room.' Wilchester motioned to a slight girl standing near the stairs.

'Thank you, Wilchester. You may leave us,' Henley said, and all the servants except for Hannah disbanded and returned to their posts and duties.

'I'll be in the library if you need me, but if not, I'll see you at dinner, promptly at eight.' With that, Henley walked away, abruptly leaving Hannah and me alone in the foyer.

I felt that he had dismissed me in the same way that he had dismissed Wilchester, but I suspected Henley was just acting in a way that was deemed appropriate.

'If you will, miss,' Hannah said. I nodded and followed her up the stairs. Our footsteps echoed in the quiet hall and sounded lonely.

As Hannah was leading me to my room, I heard a bit of a commotion in the downstairs hall. When I peeked over the banister, I saw Wilchester carrying in Miss Hatfield's painting, and a couple of other servants I hadn't met yet toting boxes. I reached up to touch young Hannah's elbow. 'Just a moment, please, Hannah,' I said.

She nodded and paused on the stairway. She couldn't have been much older than I'd been when I was Cynthia, but that life was beginning to feel like a distant memory. No matter. I had to focus on what was going on at that moment.

I cleared my throat and called down the stairwell, 'Excuse me, Wilchester – could you please tell me where you're taking my uncle's painting?'

He glanced up, a brief look of curiosity flickering across his face which seemed to say *Why on earth should that matter to you?* But what he said aloud was, 'Why, it's going into Mr Beauford's study, Miss Margaret, as per his orders, along with these other items.'

'Ah, of course.' I began to feel conspicuous, knowing they thought it odd that I cared about an old painting. 'It's just that I've grown to admire that painting. It should look well in the study. Thank you.' I dismissed them with a slight wave of my hand. 'Let's go on now, Hannah, please.'

I did my best to act as though nothing was out of the ordinary, but my heart was pounding fast. The house was teeming with servants – how was I going to find time away from prying eyes to figure out the best way to snag the painting and get it out of this house? Furthermore, how would I find my way back to Miss Hatfield from this strange new location in the country? She hadn't told me how that was to be achieved.

At the top of the staircase, Hannah and I turned left and walked down a long hall. She stopped at the fourth or fifth door on the right. I was too distracted about the painting to notice exactly which one. But when she opened the door, the beauty of the room nearly took my breath away.

'Here we are, miss,' Hannah said softly.

Against one wall was a four-poster bed with a lovely ivory lacy bedspread and a canopy to match, artfully strewn with several huge fluffy pillows. Fresh roses in a blue vase sat on the dresser, along with a large bowl and a pitcher of water, which I knew – from Miss Hatfield's instructions – were for washing my face and hands. An ornate dressing screen, which looked as though it had come from the Orient, stood in one corner of the room, and I could see some of my new dresses hanging to one side of it. There was a small desk, or what I recalled Miss Hatfield referring to as a 'writing table', in one corner. On it was some crisp, fresh ivory stationary which somehow magically matched the bedspread; beside it, a fountain pen and an ornate ink bottle. A huge fireplace stood opposite the foot of the bed, a small fire within cheering the room with a nice glow and warming it slightly. I found it all beautiful, and at the same time very overwhelming. A nagging feeling in the back of my mind whispered that something wasn't quite right about me being here. How would I ever get the painting—

'Pardon me, miss. Will there be anything else?' Hannah's soft, young voice enquired as she looked at me inquisitively. She was probably wondering why I was so preoccupied with my thoughts and looking so concerned. As Nellie had pointed out, what would someone of my station possibly have to be worried about?

'No, that's all for now, Hannah. Thank you so very much.' I awkwardly patted the young girl's shoulder a couple of times. She was a sweet child, and obviously quite shy. I wanted to make her feel at ease, but didn't think I was doing a very good job so far.

'As you wish,' she said quietly, looking downwards as she made a curtsey and quietly departed. I found myself standing alone in the middle of this large room, slowly turning a complete circle and taking in all the tasteful, elegant decor. I should have felt grateful, I supposed, but something about the whole affair sent a cold shiver down my spine.

I slowly crossed over to the writing table and sat down on the fragile-looking blue-velvet-cushioned chair. I was tempted to journal my thoughts, but realized how foolish that would be. Someone might see them and either figure out who I really was, or decide I was stark raving mad and have me put away in an asylum. I sighed and glanced at the small clock on top of the mantle. Only 4.30? Almost four hours until dinner. I couldn't go wandering downstairs in search of the painting. My initial curiosity about it had already raised some suspicion. No, I would have to play this next part carefully. Suddenly I remembered Miss Hatfield saying she would contact me with further instructions. But how on earth could she do that, since I hadn't known the country estate's address to give her?

My head began to throb, so I carefully took off my dress and hung it up. Then I put on one of the soft nightgowns Miss Wetherby had made for me and stretched out on the bed. Hopefully a nap would make my headache subside, and possibly some clarity would come to me in a dream. I chuckled to myself. This *all* felt so much like a dream – would I be having a dream within a dream, then? I realized at that moment why Miss Hatfield often found odd things amusing. When you're a time traveller, even ordinary things take on completely different meanings. I closed my eyes and found it surprisingly easy to fall asleep on the big, comfortable bed.

'Miss. Wake up, miss.' My eyelids fluttered open and I saw Nellie's familiar face smiling down at me as she gently shook my shoulder.

'Nellie! You've arrived, I see. How was your trip?'

'Oh, fine, miss, thank you. I've never been so far outside the city. It's quite lovely here, isn't it?' She was taking in all the appointments of the room, much as I had done.

I sat up, squinting at the clock on top of the fireplace. It was 7.45!

'Yes, it's very nice, Nellie. I'm really glad to see you, but we have to move quickly now – dinner's in a quarter of an hour and I mustn't be late. I never thought I'd sleep so long.' I began bustling around, trying to decide which new dress would be most appropriate for dinner. Seeing my frustration, Nellie stepped in and made the perfect choice for me.

'This one will do nicely, Miss Margaret,' she said as she helped me off with my nightgown and, almost in one motion, pulled the dress down over my head. I was still wearing my corset and undergarments. They were beginning to feel almost like a second skin and hadn't bothered me in the least while I was sleeping, even though I'd slumbered far longer than I'd intended to.

I hurriedly crossed to the bowl on the dresser and splashed some water on my face, then pinched my cheeks as Miss Hatfield had instructed, in order to bring some healthy colour to the surface. Women of my station at this point in time seldom wore anything that was considered as vulgar as make-up, with the exception of perhaps some lip rouge (she'd told me they didn't call it lipstick back then because it was usually kept in a small jar, and wasn't really a 'stick' or in a tube yet).

I was about to dash out of the door, anxious not to keep the Beaufords waiting for me, especially not on my first night in the country, when Nellie burst out laughing. I wheeled around to see what was so funny. She was holding up my shoes.

'I think you might want these, Miss Margaret.'

I laughed along with her. 'That's an excellent idea, Nellie,' I agreed as I crossed the room and sat on the bed while she helped me on with them. 'A barefoot dinner guest isn't likely to make a good impression.' We giggled a bit more as I walked to the door. 'Why don't you go and get yourself some dinner, too, Nellie? Ask Hannah to show you around. She's very sweet, and quite helpful, you'll find.'

Nellie nodded, indicating she would do so. I took a deep breath and began making my way towards the stairs, knowing I needed to display the proper decorum as I was now not just under the Beaufords' scrutiny, but that of the entire household staff as well.

'My dear?'

I paused at the top of the staircase when I heard Mr Beauford call out.

'Yes, Uncle?'

'I believe you're forgetting something,' he said, when he reached the staircase.

I looked down at my feet, which were now in shoes. 'And what might that be?'

There was a glint in his eye, not unlike the one I so often saw in Henley's. 'An escort, of course!'

I smiled, lending him my arm.

'You see, my dear,' he said, patting my hand as we started down the stairs, 'a pretty young thing like you deserves to have someone on her arm, and anyone would be honoured to have you accompany them.'

I laughed. 'I'm glad you think so.'

'*Anyone* would think so.'

I was startled by the voice, as it didn't come from Mr Beauford.

Henley emerged from one of the rooms wearing a sophisticated-looking tuxedo, still tugging at his bow tie. His hair was swept back and his starched shirt lay flat against his chest. My eyes were drawn to just how sculpted he looked. I was reminded how broad his shoulders were, and his eyes looked even bluer in contrast with his white shirt.

'Oh, son.' Mr Beauford groaned. 'I thought I told you to do away with that dinner jacket. It looks dreadful – not to mention, it's *much* too informal for dinner with a lady in attendance. I just can't understand these latest styles that are growing in popularity.'

'I think it looks nice.'

There was a pause, and I didn't even realize what I'd said until I looked up to see Henley's cocky grin appearing.

'Y–you look … polished,' I said, for lack of a better word.

'Father, the lady has spoken,' Henley said.

Mr Beauford sighed in resignation. 'I suppose you're right ... but only because Margaret is too much of a lady to mind. You might as well escort her to dinner. I'm getting too old for this.' He chuckled.

Henley took my arm and wrapped it around his.

As we descended down the steps, I kept noticing the glances he was giving me out of the corner of his eye.

'I know – I look pretty good for someone who was running up hills barefoot and sleeping on a straw mattress just hours ago,' I joked once we were out of his father's earshot.

'You look stunning.'

I couldn't think of a clever response, so his words just hung there between us. Even during dinner, his words were the only thing I could think about. They lay unmoving in my mind, not letting me concentrate on anything else. His words made me feel something I'd never felt before. It might have been what Mother felt around my father.

It was the first time I'd felt more than just 'pretty'.

Chapter 14

The morning sun came streaming in through the curtains, gently awakening me. I slowly sat up on the edge of the bed and replayed the events from the night before as I returned to my body after slumber.

Dinner had actually been quite pleasant; the food was exquisite, the conversation less than riveting, but fine. I could tell that Mr Beauford appeared to prefer being here in the country; he was just a little more at ease. Henley, on the other hand, had grown a bit sullen since our arrival. I wasn't sure what was going on with him, although he'd intimated he would be spending an inordinate amount of time with his tutor while we were here. Mr Beauford was anxious for Henley to finish his education so that he could take over the family steel business soon.

'The old fellow's convinced he's on his last legs, and that I need to be ready to step in as head of the business any day now,' Henley had whispered to me as we left the dining room the evening before. 'Perhaps he's right. His memory appears to be slipping more with each passing day …' His voice drifted off on a note of sadness.

I touched his arm, not knowing the best way to comfort my new friend and confidant. He squeezed my hand and favoured me with a broad smile. 'I just remembered that my tutor will be off on a personal mission of some sort tomorrow, which means I'll have a rare day to myself. What say you and I go horse riding? Get some fresh air, do the whole gentry routine? I could show you all my favourite things about the estate.' He raised his eyebrows, trying to look snooty, and was using a false condescending tone, but when I started giggling at his antics he dissolved into laughter himself.

'I would be all too delighted to partake in equestrian pastimes with you on the morrow,' I replied with a curtsey. *Not bad impromptu chit-chat for a time traveller, if I do say so myself,* I thought, a secret smile flitting across my lips at my private joke.

'Hmm ... Thou art becoming all the more mysterious,' said Henley, playing along. Then he grabbed my hand and bowed, and when our eyes met, I saw something in his that both attracted and frightened me. I shivered slightly, because this game I was playing along with was suddenly becoming all too real, making me fearful it would be hard to detach myself from this captivating man when the time came.

'Very well, sir.' I nodded to him politely. 'At what time shall I meet you for breakfast followed by a jaunt around the estate on horseback?'

'Breakfast at eight, riding directly afterwards. Dress accordingly, dear cousin.'

I broke our eye contact because it was bordering on becoming far too intense for my liking. 'Yes, that will be fine,' I murmured. 'Do sleep well, Henley. I look forward to tomorrow.'

'As do I,' he said softly as his eyes followed me up the stairs. I'd gone straight to bed, not allowing myself to wonder too much about the feelings that appeared to be developing between us. I was most likely imagining them, anyway. What did I know? I had so recently been a child, although I could barely remember that time, and now here I was playing some odd grown-up game, and pretending to be someone I wasn't, on top of it all. And who *was* I now, really, anyway? I'd sighed and pulled the covers up over my head.

And now here was daybreak, and I wasn't one bit closer to figuring out how to remove the painting from the study, much less how I was going to somehow be transported – carrying it – back to Miss Hatfield. The whole business was making my head hurt.

'Nellie!' I called, and was startled when she popped her head inside my room right away.

'Yes, Miss Margaret?'

'Goodness, you gave me a turn! You must have been right outside the door.'

'Yes, miss.' It was only then that I noticed she was carrying a tea tray. 'Master Henley asked me to bring this bit of breakfast up to you.' She glanced at the clock on the mantle. I followed her gaze. It was already 8.15!

'Oh, I can't believe I overslept! I knew I was supposed to meet him for breakfast at eight—'

'It's all right, Miss Margaret. He's not upset. He laughed and actually made up this little tray for you himself. "The country air has relaxed her soul," is what he said, I do believe. I know I slept quite well myself, miss.'

'I'm glad, Nellie. And I'm so happy you were able to accompany us here. Could you please choose something for me to wear that would be suitable for horse riding while I eat my breakfast?'

She nodded and began picking through my new garments, oohing and ahing under her breath as she found each dress more beautiful than the last. I smiled. Before I left, I was determined to ask Henley to let her keep something. She deserved a little finery, for once in her life. I quickly finished my breakfast and washed my face. Then we hurriedly went about getting me dressed for the day.

Nellie had chosen the perfect outfit for me: a lovely tan flowing skirt with a rose-pink blouse, and a little weskit that matched the skirt. She helped me dress, and then we pulled on the new pair of boots Henley had obviously bought for me when I wasn't paying attention. He was so thoughtful, but I hated how he wasted money on me. And how had he guessed my size? Most odd.

Nellie pinned my hair up and put a smart little hat atop my head that crowned my outfit handsomely. 'Thanks for everything, Nellie,' I called over my shoulder as I hurried out into the hallway.' I'll see you later – probably sometime this afternoon.'

'Have a lovely day, Miss Margaret,' she called after me, a bit wistfully, I thought.

I dashed down the stairs but stopped dead in my tracks when I heard a familiar burst of laughter echoing up at me.

'You'd best be careful, Master Henley, or I shan't thank you for that delicious breakfast. Don't you know it's impolite to laugh at a lady, especially first thing in the morning?' I scolded, but my eyes were smiling back at him. 'What in heaven's name is so funny, anyway?'

'Just that you were moving at near breakneck speed, is all. I doubt any of our horses would be able to keep pace with you!'

'Hmmph!' My eyes were twinkling as I passed him, and he knew I was anything but angry. He quickly ran to walk by my side.

'Just a moment – you don't even know where the stables are. Wouldn't you like me to show you the way?'

I gave him a sidelong glance. 'I think my nose and ears could lead me there, even if my eyes failed me. But since you insist—' I took his proffered arm '—please, *do* lead on.'

He nodded. I sensed Henley was enjoying our silly little role-playing banter as much, if not more, as I was. I couldn't help but conclude that he'd had a pretty lonely childhood, especially after his mother passed away.

We were at the stables in no time, and the sight of all the horses stomping, whinnying and loudly exhaling was quite exhilarating. I'd always been enchanted by the idea of riding, but Cynthia had never had the opportunity. Strange. The few times a memory of my former life popped in to my head, I always found myself thinking of that existence in the third person. Miss Hatfield had intimated this would happen, but I hadn't truly understood what she meant until that moment.

Henley was busily talking with the stableman and pointing at a beautiful, spirited-looking black horse with a dazzling white splash exactly in the middle of its face. 'Saddle up Cedric for Miss Margaret, please, Wellesley,' he said. The stableman nodded and began to prepare Cedric for me to ride.

'Ah, wait a moment, please, Wellesley,' I intruded. 'I'd prefer to choose my own horse, if the two of you don't mind.' I felt silly insisting upon this, since I knew virtually nothing about the creatures, but a brownish-red mare had caught my attention, and she looked rather lonely in her stall. I felt an outing would be good for her, and somehow, I knew I could trust her. I pointed towards the mare. 'I'd much rather ride that one, if I may.' I looked at Henley for his assent. His face was inscrutable all of a sudden. *What's he hiding from me now?* I wondered.

'Oh, but, miss,' Wellesley interjected, 'you don't really want to ride—'

Henley held up his hand. 'Oh, I rather think she does, Wellesley. It's fine – saddle up the roan for her.'

Roan? Oh, so that was what a horse of that colouring was called. I smiled, pleased that I was going to get my way and had already learned a couple of 'horsey terms' I'd been unfamiliar with prior to our outing.

'Yes, sir,' said Wellesley, but he muttered to himself the entire time he was saddling up the roan. Her name was Bessie, I discerned from the plaque on the wall beside her stall. 'Can't understand why anyone would want to ride the oldest horse here, out of all the better choices—'

'Tut, tut, Wellesley,' Henley admonished. 'Bessie might be slow, but perhaps that will suit our Miss Margaret to a T.' He turned and favoured me with one of his wonderful smiles. 'Bessie's getting close to the end of her service here with us. Lately, we've been speaking of, ah ...' It was obvious he'd said more than he meant to.

My eyes widened with horror. 'Oh, don't tell me you're going to do something awful, like sell poor Bessie to a glue factory or some such barbaric thing?' I cried.

Henley smiled, but I could tell that he empathized with me to a degree. Doubtless he'd seen many a horse put out to pasture – or worse – when they'd outlived their usefulness.

'Bessie's an excellent choice, Margaret,' he assured me. 'And since you've decided to champion her cause, I'll ask Father not dispose of her, but allow her to live out her days in retirement here with us. In fact, you shall be her final rider, as long as you're here in the country with us. Then she'll just relax and get fatter and sassier. What do you think about that?' He grinned as he mounted his own horse, a beautiful white with an Egyptian motif on its halter.

'I think that's civilized, and so does Bessie, don't you, girl?' I patted her neck, and just before putting my foot into the stirrup, I whispered to her, 'I bought you some more time. The least you can do is return the favour and not let anyone know I don't have a clue about riding.' Wellesley gave me a boost up, and before I knew it, I was seated atop Bessie, feeling surprisingly safe and at ease. I was thankful that Henley had bought me a special skirt that allowed me to ride astride, rather than side-saddle, as I feared I'd otherwise break my neck. Henley had joked that this was the very latest fashion, and in wearing this, I would be one of the most modern young women around.

Bessie's broad back was steady as a rock beneath me, and she nickered very softly, as though she was agreeable to my secret request. I watched how Henley was holding the reins and copied him. How hard could this be, after all?

Henley clicked his tongue in a 'giddy-up' sort of way and gently tapped his heels to his horse's flanks. I leaned forwards and whispered to Bessie, 'Follow that horse, there's a good girl.' I patted her neck again and leaned forwards a bit. Surprisingly, she appeared to understand me and followed Henley and his horse out of the stables.

'All right back there, you two?' he called over his shoulder.

'Never better,' I responded cheerily, though keeping my balance while riding dear old Bessie was taking a bit more concentration than I'd expected. I had no clue why I wanted Henley to think I was an old hand at this; some bizarre feelings left over from school about having to be as good at things as boys probably had something to do with it. Cynthia had never played much with boys – or indeed with anyone other than her dolls, I faintly recollected – but she'd never allowed herself to feel intimidated in new situations, and neither would I. *There I go again,* I thought to myself, *acting as though I'm a totally separate person from her.* I snickered silently as I glanced down at my adult body and these strange Gibson Girl clothes, realizing that I truly was different from Cynthia in every way.

Henley gently called to his horse, 'Whoa, Jasper,' and they ambled to a stop to wait for me and Bessie to catch up. When we did, he looked me up and down. 'Well, you sit on a horse quite well, considering you've never ridden one before,' he said.

'What? How did you know ...' My voice trailed off. Why did I have such a hard time hiding things from this young man I was growing so fond of?

He grinned. 'Your right hand gives you away when you're nervous. You make a fist and open it again, about three times in rapid succession, and then you're fine. I've noticed it a couple of times before, but only figured out what it meant today. You do it when you're in new situations, am I right?'

I clucked my tongue at Bessie, and we rode along side by side in silence. All the while, Henley was observing me with a bemused smile. Well, he certainly was right about new situations – everything about this situation was new to me, including riding a horse. But I was disappointed I hadn't proved to be a better actress. How on earth was I going to fool him when it came to stealing the painting and getting back to Miss Hatfield?

Finally I broke my silence. 'Well, since you're so smart, give me some pointers about riding, please, sir,' I murmured demurely.

He laughed. 'I'll be happy to, but you're doing quite well, actually.' He reached over and patted old Bessie's neck. 'She's the perfect horse for you after all. May I?' he asked as he held out his hand for the reins. 'It'll probably be easier for you to get comfortable if you let me lead her for a while.'

I was grateful for his kindness and handed him the reins with a nod of thanks.

'So, where are we off to, then?'

He inclined his head towards a bend in the path just ahead. 'That path leads to an old abandoned sawmill on the property. I used to love to go there as a boy, just to think and play. It was a true source of comfort for me when we came here in my youth.' His eyes turned serious. 'It still is, at times. I'd like to show it to you.'

'That would be lovely,' I replied. How could I shake him out of his reverie and the sadness that had suddenly descended upon him? Ah, I had it. 'Henley, you were right after all.' I sighed.

'Right? Right about what, pray tell?' He raised an inquisitive eyebrow at me.

'Why, about my being able to run faster than our Miss Bessie here!' We both burst into gales of laughter at that and I felt uplifted, having been successful in shifting his mood, suspecting that his melancholy had something to do with the loss of his mother at such an early age.

When we arrived at the sawmill, Henley helped me down and then tied Bessie and Jasper to a hitching post in front of the old mill. The buildings were in great disrepair, nearly crumbling. I was astonished they'd been allowed to decompose to such a great extent rather than being torn down. Mr Beauford was normally so intent on everything looking just so. Henley read my mind, as he was becoming all too good at.

'You're wondering why Father didn't have this mill torn down completely a long time ago,' he stated, rather than questioning me. 'It was one of the few things I've ever begged him not to do, and he actually honoured my request.' He took my arm and gestured towards a small stream to the side of the mill. 'One of my favourite thinking spots is right there, under that old oak next to the stream. I believe there's plenty of room for two beneath it. Just for a little while – do you mind?'

I shook my head. 'Not at all.' I was touched that he wanted to share this special place with me.

We walked in comfortable silence until we reached the tree, and then he dusted off the ground a bit before helping me to sit. He plopped down beside me and stretched out, leaning back, propped up on his elbows.

'I used to love gazing into the stream and daydreaming, when I was a boy. The sound of its movement was mesmerizing. It made all my troubles fade into nothingness, if only for a few minutes.' He was getting that dreamy-eyed look again, but it wasn't quite sadness I read there this time. More like a wistfulness. 'It makes me remember that time is a river and will always go on. There's no turning back, so you might as well live life to the fullest.' I wondered what he might have said if I'd corrected him and told him the truth. Would he have believed me?

'Why was it so important to you that the mill remained standing? Were you ever tempted to ask your father to have it restored, make it a going concern again?'

'Oh, heaven forbid!' he exclaimed. 'That would have been the last thing I wanted. This old relic has always been one of the only places where time slowed down for me, where I could sort through my thoughts in solitude and quiet … There's far too much busy industry going on at the steel factory, noise and soot, smoke and grit.' He took a deep breath and indicated I should follow suit, which I did. 'There! Nothing like the fresh country air to clear the mind and the lungs, eh?'

'Yes, I quite agree.' I nodded. 'So, Henley, you prefer to let the mill just disintegrate naturally, rather than destroying it for progress's sake?'

'Something like that,' he replied. 'It felt like the kindest thing to do would be to let it return to dust in its own time, rather than knocking it down and forcing it.' He got up and foraged around on the bank of the stream. I followed to see what he was searching for.

'Here.' He handed me a smooth, flat rock, one of about six stones he'd found and was holding in his other hand. 'Have you ever skipped a rock before? Don't fib – I can tell if you do, you know.' His tone took on a chiding mock-schoolteacher tone.

'Yes, I'm learning that about you,' I said. 'No, actually, I've never skipped a rock. Please, kind sir, give me a demonstration.'

'Happy to oblige, as always,' he said, and took a mock bow before squatting down a bit to assess the best place to make his throw. He dropped all but one of his rock treasures onto the ground beside him, then cocked back his arm and smoothly let the stone fly with a flick of his wrist. I watched, enchanted, as the rock skipped one, two, three, four times before disappearing beneath the stream's surface.

'Oh, bravo, Henley!' I applauded, and nearly dropped my own rock in the process.

He bowed again, like a proud performer. 'It's all in the wrist, really. Just pick your spot on the water's surface, imagine the rock smoothly sailing across it, and then release the rock as you flick your wrist. Go on – give it a try,' he encouraged.

'All right,' I said, not feeling particularly confident. 'But if I can't learn how to do this, please don't put me out to pasture with Bessie, I beg you.'

A burst of laughter escaped from deep within Henley's core – a true belly laugh the like of which I'd never yet heard him utter. 'Oh, my – you *are* a card! Come on, then – show me what you're made of.' He'd returned to instructor mode.

Taking a deep breath, I did my best to emulate his every move and, to my surprise, my little rock skipped three times before diving down under the water.

Now it was Henley's turn to applaud. 'Quite the natural skipper, you are,' he said as he bent down to pick up two more rocks. 'Now, let's alternate and send these other little fellows skipping in after them.' He handed me my next small missile. 'Ready? Ladies first,' he said with a gallant half-bow.

This time my rock did four skips, and not to be outdone, Henley's managed six. 'Quite impressive!' I cheered.

He picked up the last two stones and handed one to me. 'No time to rest on our laurels – last round. Ready, *go!*' he commanded.

My last little rock was more of a skimmer than a skipper, barely managing two brief skips before sinking. Henley pretended not to notice and flung his own immediately after it, making it skip only once. I believed he'd purposely not done his best, so as not to make me feel bad.

We laughed and went back to sit under his oak. He talked for another hour or so, periodically picking up a stick to draw in the dirt, as though to illustrate a point. This intriguing young man had so many interesting philosophies about life. He told me how he'd always loved to write, and at one time had wanted to become a teacher. It soon became apparent that the last thing he wanted to do was take over the family steel business.

'We'd best be getting back, I suppose,' he said with a sigh. 'It's nearly lunchtime. Here, wait a moment.' He bent down and peered first at one of my ears, and then the other. 'Oh, good,' he said, as though to himself.

I looked at him, puzzled. 'What on earth is wrong with my ears, if you don't mind me asking?'

'Oh, I simply had to check and make sure I hadn't talked them off,' he teased. 'You let me go on and on about myself again, and I learned nothing about you. I hope I didn't bore you too terribly much.' He cast his eyes downwards as we approached the horses.

'Not even one little bit,' I assured him. 'I'm thoroughly enjoying getting to know you, Henley.'

He sent me a quick grateful smile. 'Yes, but you're still a woman of mystery. I must stop all this pontificating and coax you into telling me more about yourself!' He untied the horses, keeping hold of Bessie's reins to see if I'd let him help me mount. My stubborn pride prevented me, however.

'I quite like it when you pontificate,' I responded as I swung up onto Bessie's back. I was surprised how easy it was, and Henley looked surprised as well.

'Well done!' he said, mounting Jasper. 'Let's away to the house ... Father will be wondering what's become of us, I'm sure. I'll have Wilchester walk them back to the stables to save us a bit of time. Shall we?'

'Yes, let's! C'mon, Bessie, old girl!' I kicked her ever so slightly and, to my great surprise – and probably Henley's as well – she broke into a bit of a trot and easily kept pace with Jasper all the way back to the house.

'You're a good judge of horses, Margaret,' he said as we dismounted. 'The old girl obviously has life in her yet. Wilchester!' he called out, and the man was there

158

in what felt like an instant. How could he possibly intuit so quickly where and when he'd be needed? I wondered. 'Here, Wilchester.' Henley handed him both sets of reins. 'Take the horses back to the stable and ask Wellesley to give them a good rub-down and some extra hay and carrots, would you, old man?'

'I'll see to it, sir,' Wilchester replied, walking away with a horse following on either side.

Henley dusted himself off, and I did the same. What would Mr Beauford think of us, showing up for luncheon all dusty and a bit late? My question was answered almost immediately, as Henley's father met us at the door.

He looked us both up and down, shook his head slightly from side to side as though in confusion and sighed. 'Henley, my boy, why do you insist on neglecting your studies? You know I intend to introduce you to the board of directors next week, and I want you to feel prepared and comfortable.'

'Oh, Father, I'll be prepared, never fear.' Henley patted his father's shoulder with loving respect. 'How comfortable, on the other hand, I can't promise.' He winked at me behind the old man's back, and I knew there was more to his words than a mere jest. He really didn't want that to be his life path. 'Besides, someone must think about Cousin Margaret's interests, you know.'

Chapter 15

I wish I could say I came up with a plan to grab the painting and run that very night following our ride to the mill. Believe me, I wished many times after that day that I'd found the courage and ingenuity to pull it off. But there I still was, four days later, feeling in many ways more lost than ever and growing increasingly frustrated.

Despite Henley's protestations that he wanted to entertain me a bit and escape from his studies at the same time, the routine had been the same for the past three days. Meals would pass with the servants silently filling our plates, then removing them as we finished eating. The food was always delicious, but after the second day I gave up commenting on it, since neither Mr Beauford nor Henley appeared to be much concerned with conversation at mealtimes. In fact, Henley was retreating further into himself every time I saw him. His days were consumed with hour upon hour of study with his tutor; and although Mr Beauford's health seemed to be improving, he spent his days primarily in his study, so there was never much opportunity for me to look at the painting, much less abscond with it.

And what of my own days? Well, I walked the property and pondered many things, between breakfast and lunch, and again from lunch until dinnertime. No one appeared to notice – or care, for that matter. But as the days passed, the strange feeling I was experiencing only intensified. Being in this time for so long was beginning to make me feel uncomfortable, and with each passing day, the unease was evolving into a constant queasy nervousness in the pit of my stomach. It was as if my body was turned against me ... as if nature itself was turning against me.

I made sure to visit the stables each day, and to give Bessie a carrot or a cube of sugar. I confided quite a lot to that dear old horse, knowing she'd never betray my most peculiar confidences about being a time traveller who often felt about as much at home as a fish would out of water.

'You'd best be careful,' I heard Henley's voice behind me say one day. Startled, I turned around from Bessie's stall door to see him standing there, holding a small bouquet of wild flowers. He extended them to me, and I took them with a smile. I'd missed him terribly, but didn't dare let him know how much.

'Thank you, Henley. I'd best be careful about what, exactly?' I enquired.

He leaned over and examined Bessie's ears. 'Well, you certainly don't talk to me so freely, but I see Bessie has won your confidence,' he began, still carefully checking her ears. 'I simply must make sure you haven't succeeded in talking her ears off, the same way I was worried I might have done yours.' He grinned, satisfied that the horse's ears were still intact. 'And don't you know that horses gossip, too?'

'Yes, well, that's quite considerate of you. I'm sure Bessie appreciates your concern, but she actually appears to love our little chats,' I replied. 'In fact, many times, she nods her head in agreement, don't you, girl?' I asked my four-footed friend. As if on cue, she nodded twice. Henley and I both broke into laughter.

'For someone who'd never been on or around horses much until a few days ago, I do believe you've already learned how to train them, Miss Margaret,' he declared.

'Well, be that as it may,' I said, taking his arm and steering him towards the stable door, 'what presses upon my mind right now is how you've managed to escape your tutor's and your father's watchful eyes?' I added, softly, 'Not that I mind you paying Bessie and me a visit.'

He smiled, pleased to hear I was glad to see him. 'It wasn't easy, I assure you.' He lowered his voice to a conspiratorial tone. 'I asked Mr Lawrence a question that has absolutely nothing to do with the steel business, knowing he couldn't resist going off to research it. Then it was simply a matter of slipping out of the house through the kitchen, so as not to pass Father's study – easy as pie!' He snapped his fingers for emphasis and gave me a wink.

'What does that phrase mean, I wonder?' I mused, just to make small talk and extend our time together. 'How easy is pie compared to, say, cake, or your favourite – ice cream?'

He threw back his head and let out another of those belly laughs I'd first heard the other day at the mill. 'Oh, you're still quite the peculiar one, I see.' He wagged his finger at me. 'And don't ever change that about yourself. What goes on in that mind of yours while you have so much time on your hands?'

'Oh, nothing of great interest,' I mumbled. 'But I have another question for you – whatever did you ask poor Mr Lawrence to cause him to abandon his pupil in order to resolve it?'

'Ah, that.' Henley stroked his chin, as though he were a much older man with a full beard, replete with the wisdom that comes with a long life. 'I simply asked the old fellow if he knew anything about how the Egyptians had managed to erect those amazing pyramids, and if he felt their construction methods might have any bearing on the future of the steel industry.' He smiled, pleased with himself that he'd temporarily stumped his tutor.

'But that did have to do with the steel business, then,' I protested lightly.

'For argument's sake, yes, you have a point. But Mr Lawrence is so very focused on eating, breathing, sleeping and … Well, I won't be indelicate as you're a lady, but his every thought and action has revolved around steel since my father took him on as his protégé, long before I was even born. I believe he must have thought he'd be the heir apparent to the business until I showed up on the scene. Pity he can't live out that dream – we'd both be happier.'

I stopped in my tracks. 'Henley!' I startled him with my firm tone. 'You simply must tell them that you'd rather be a writer, or a teacher. Or a butcher, baker or candlestick maker – I don't care what you want to be, I just want you to be happy. But they won't know how unhappy you are unless you tell them.' I gazed up at him, wondering where the ringing passion I heard in my own words had come from.

'What a tirade! I didn't think I inspired such fire in you,' he said. 'Oh, please, won't you tell me your real name? I've – I've come to care for you so very much …' He grabbed me by the arms and pulled me towards him, but I resisted.

'This is neither the time nor the place for such things,' I replied, hoping he'd let it go. 'You simply must let your father know how you really feel.' I stomped one foot for emphasis, and Henley nervously laughed.

'I'd much rather let *you* know how I really feel,' he said softly, advancing towards me once again.

This was dangerous ground we were approaching, and I dared not do anything to encourage his behaviour, no matter how conflicted my heart was. So I turned my back on him, as it was the first thing that popped into my mind. I stood stiff and still, doing my best to surround myself with icy coldness to keep him at a safe distance. He felt it, I knew, because he remained behind me and said nothing, waiting for me to speak first.

'Henley,' I began, not daring to turn around and face him yet, 'I have feelings for you, too. I know you're aware of that. But this is a dicey game we've started, to say the least. I want to tell you more about myself, and I promise, when that's necessary, I'll do my best to tell you everything I can. I owe you that much for all your kindness. But can't you see that right now, the most important thing is for you to take charge of your own life before it's too late?' I turned to look at him then, knowing all too well what it felt like to have one's lifepath taken over and controlled by other people and situations. My memories of being Cynthia faded a little more each day.

Henley nodded and wiped his forehead with his sleeve. 'It suddenly got a bit warm, did you notice?'

I nodded, slightly amused by his awkwardness in changing the subject; something at which he was usually a master. At least I'd staved off his advances, for the time being. 'Will you promise me that you'll make every effort to tell your father what you really want to do with your life? Or if you're unsure about that, at least tell him you definitely don't imagine yourself as the new head of his steel business? Please, Henley – for your own sake, my friend.'

164

'All right – that's what a man would do, you're right. I'm no longer a silly schoolboy. I can stand up for myself and tell Father what I want. Or at least,' he said with a rueful smile, 'as you so eloquently pointed out, what I know I *don't* want. I'll endeavour to do that tomorrow evening.'

'Why wait?' I asked. 'Why not go to him right now, while your courage is up?'

'Well,' said Henley, 'that would be next to impossible as Father went into the city late this morning. He'll not be back until about noon tomorrow. But I give you my word, I shall approach him about this after dinner tomorrow evening.'

'I see,' I replied quietly as we headed back towards the house, but my mind was racing. If Mr Beauford was to be gone all night, perhaps I could finally get into the study and make off with the painting. After all, things with Henley were becoming rather intense, and I'd best extricate myself from this situation soon – the sooner, the better, in fact. We stopped on the porch, just in front of the house's main door.

'That's good, Henley. I'm proud of you,' I assured him with a steady smile. 'I'm sure that when he hears how you really feel, he'll work with you to see what the alternatives may be.'

'I wish I had your confidence.' He sighed. 'Well, I'd best go and look up poor old Lawrence and see what he's found out about those ingenious Egyptians. He's probably still rooting around in the library, looking for a book about them.' My friend tipped an invisible hat in my direction. 'Until dinner, madam,' he intoned.

I was too distracted to engage in our normal play-acting. 'Yes, see you then,' I said, and began to climb the stairs towards my room, but watched out of the corner of my eye to make sure Henley disappeared down the hall and into the library where he and Mr Lawrence always studied. Once I saw that he'd done so, I quietly backtracked down the hallway towards Mr Beauford's study, hoping that Mr Beauford had left the study door unlocked. Miss Hatfield must be quite anxious by now that we had been out of contact for so long and I had been unable to succeed in my quest. Something in the pit of my stomach lurched a bit at that thought, and I felt a strong foreboding that something wasn't quite right.

Glancing up and down the hallway to make sure no prying eyes were aimed in my direction, I swiftly closed my hand upon the doorknob to the study. I quietly turned it – or, rather, attempted to do so. It was locked! 'Drat,' I muttered to myself. This could only mean one thing. I was going to have to figure out how to pick a lock!

Chapter 16

The rest of the afternoon was spent concocting a plan which would allow me to get into the study, steal the painting and leave. I steeled my resolve, determined to do my level best to make this happen. I paced back and forth in front of the fireplace long after the flames had expired. Deep in thought as I was, nothing else mattered. The feelings between Henley and me were moving in a direction I knew I couldn't control much longer. I needed to complete my mission and move on before I hurt him even more deeply than I knew my inevitable disappearance was bound to do.

I heard a timid knock at the door and turned to see young Hannah standing there with some freshly folded linens in her arms. I smiled at her and waved her in. 'Hello, Hannah. I haven't seen you for a couple of days. Are you well?'

'Oh, yes, miss,' she replied. 'I've brought you some clean sheets and towels. I've been quite busy, doing laundry and putting things away. Nellie's been helping me.' She beamed.

'Ah, I see. So you and Nellie have become friends, then. That's good. You're both kind girls, and should be friends.' I noticed a glint of silver in her hair as she quietly went about making up my bed. That was it! A hairpin might be just the trick to pick the study door's lock! I had hairpins of my own, of course, but they were thicker than the one in Hannah's hair appeared to be. But how to ask her for it without causing suspicion?

'Where's Nellie?' I asked, just making small talk until I figured out how to get the pin from her.

'She's down helping the cook prepare dinner, miss. There are lamb chops tonight, and some roasted potatoes. Oh, but it all smells so lovely cooking!' she exclaimed. I wondered if the servants got to eat the same food we were served at the Beaufords' table, but realized they were most likely fed much simpler, cheaper fare. Perhaps the butler and the cook dined as we did, but I was sure the other staff weren't accorded such privileges.

'Hannah, have you ever had a lamb chop?' I asked, pretty sure I knew the answer.

'Ah, no, miss. But they look and smell … quite heavenly, I must say,' she replied shyly.

'Well, then, tonight you shall have your first. Tell Nellie that I specifically asked for you to serve me. It so happens that I don't particularly care for lamb chops myself, but I'd hate for mine to go to waste. When you bring me my plate, just slip my chop onto a plate for yourself, and put some extra potatoes and other vegetables on mine, so it doesn't look too bare when you place it in front of me. All right?'

Her eyes widened. 'Shan't I get in trouble, miss? I've never done anything like that before—'

'Oh, if anyone even notices, which I highly doubt they will, I'll just tell them my stomach's been a bit upset and I requested a lighter dinner, that's all. Besides, I don't know if you've ever witnessed a dinner at the Beaufords' table, but it's usually a pretty solemn affair. Not many pleasantries are exchanged, I'm afraid, with everyone focused on finishing up their meal and getting on with their evening.' I paused, knowing I'd given her something to look forward to – a new taste experience she might never have been able to afford herself. 'Hannah, would you come here, please? I see something in your hair I'd like to take a look at.'

She began brushing at her hair. 'What is it, miss? Not a spider, I hope!' She ran over to me, her voice very high-pitched, and I felt bad for having frightened her. Another tone in her voice reminded me of how Cynthia would squeal when she found a spider in her room. She wouldn't calm down until her father released it outside.

I found myself smiling at this sudden memory. I wondered if older people – those who aged naturally – thought of their younger selves as I now thought of Cynthia, as someone I'd known well, but a different person.

'What is it?' Hannah asked, seeing the look on my face. She still sounded distraught.

'Nothing,' I reassured her. 'You just reminded me of someone I used to know.' I soothed her as I swiftly removed the silver-coloured pin from her hair. 'It was only this. See?' I held the pin out for her to observe. 'I wonder if you know where I might get some pins such as this? I have hairpins—' I went to the bureau and held up a couple Henley had bought me to show her '—but I quite fancy these lighter weight, thinner ones. Could I trade you a few of mine for this one?' I held out a half-dozen of my bronze pins.

She walked over to where I stood and looked up at me, perhaps unsure whether I might be teasing her. 'Well, but, miss … These are much more costly than my simple pins—'

'Oh, that doesn't matter. I like your kind much better. Tell you what, you take these, and – if you have them

169

– bring me an equal number of the silver ones next time you come up. Don't make a special trip, just next time you need to bring something in here or tidy the upstairs rooms.' She took the bronze pins from my hand, staring at them as if they were made of gold.

'Thank you so much, miss. Yes, I will surely bring you five more silver pins and leave them right here on your dresser.' She headed excitedly towards the door with her treasure clutched in her hand, but stopped before she got there and turned towards me one last time. 'Miss, who was that person I reminded you of? Was it someone from home?'

When she saw that her question had caught me off guard, she blushed and apologized.

I shook my head. 'She was someone I knew of and about, but not someone I knew well – an acquaintance, if you will.'

She nodded sombrely and suddenly I wanted to see her smile again.

'And you won't forget about the lamb chop tonight, now, will you? You ask cook to give you some nice mint jelly to go with it – that really brings out the flavour. Say I asked for it especially.' I smiled at her.

'Oh, no, miss, I'll not forget, thank you.' She looked at me, gratitude brimming in her young eyes. 'Nellie told me you were very kind. Now I know what she means.' She curtsied and ran out of the room.

It was curious to me how such a young girl managed so well, doing the work of an adult, and in the capacity of a servant. On one hand, I felt sorry for her and Nellie; on the other, I rather envied that they knew what would be expected of them from one day to the next. In my current situation, I never had one whit of a clue as to

170

what might befall me in this strange world which was somehow becoming more familiar with each passing day. At that precise moment, all I knew for certain was that I'd acquired a helpful tool that might get me to the next phase of my plan. I straightened out the hairpin as best I could, and prayed it would be just what I needed when the time came. I looked through my clothes until I found a smart little weskit that had a pocket. Donning this over my blouse, I slipped the pin neatly into the pocket. At least that much of the plan was in place.

I returned to my pacing – it appeared to help me sort things out as I was thinking. I supposed I could grab the painting and borrow one of the faster horses. Then I'd ride back to the city and retrace my steps to return the painting to Miss Hatfield … I'd ridden Bessie now and again during the previous few days, but with Wellesley's help had also become more comfortable atop a couple of the younger, swifter horses. That had to be the solution; take a horse and ride back to the city, carefully holding on to the painting somehow. I wasn't sure I remembered the way, but it couldn't be that complicated, and I could always ask for directions. That was that – plan completed! Now all I had to do was pull it off.

Dinner was served promptly at eight, as usual. Henley, Mr Lawrence and I were the only diners, as Mr Beauford wouldn't return from his trip until the next day. The mood at the table was much lighter than when the old gentleman was present. I was glad Mr Lawrence had joined us, for I didn't trust myself to be alone too much with Henley right now.

Good girl that she was, Hannah brought me my vegetarian meal, and I winked at her quickly in thanks. I knew she'd enjoy that lamb chop, and they truly never had been a favourite of mine, so we'd both be happy with our food that night.

Henley was busy baiting Mr Lawrence and thankfully didn't pay me too much heed, although I suspected he would have liked to but was concerned about Mr Lawrence's impressions. They were discussing the Egyptians' building ingenuity, as well as the price of steel on the export side of things – topics I basically knew nothing about, and that was fine with me. It allowed me to think through my plan, step by step, over and over in my mind. Rather like an actor rehearses for a play, I realized. I found that amusing, recalling my – or rather, Cynthia's – father reciting something along the lines of 'all the world's a stage, and all the men and women merely players'. Funny that I could remember such trivial details of my past life while larger memories were already fading in chunks and pieces.

I heard Henley lightly tapping the side of his water glass with his spoon. 'I say, dear cousin, whatever is preoccupying your mind this evening? You've barely said two words. I dare say it's something amusing, considering that smile on your lips.' He looked at me expectantly and I knew some type of response was required.

'Oh, I was just remembering something my father said long ago.' I stood up and so did they, as gentlemen of the day always did when a lady entered or left a room. 'I'm sorry to say, however, that I'm feeling a bit under the weather and must retire early. Please forgive me, and do continue your conversation over dessert and coffee.' I nodded my head slightly and moved swiftly out of the dining room. I could feel Henley's eyes piercing my back as I exited. He was curious, I knew, but wouldn't want to pique Mr Lawrence's nosiness by being too solicitous of his 'cousin'. I was confident he wouldn't follow me and, thankfully, he didn't.

I quickly made my way along the hall towards Mr Beauford's study. The walls were adorned with several portraits of family members and an assortment of other people dressed in period clothing, most of which looked to date back to the 1600s; I felt them peering at me as I bustled past, some looking more disapproving than others. Glancing first to my left, then my right, I was convinced no one was watching. I removed the hairpin from my pocket and was about to commit my first crime when I realized the study door was slightly ajar. What luck!

One of the maids must have forgotten to lock it after cleaning. I slipped in and quietly closed the door behind me. I reached into my pocket for a packet of matches, as I'd known it would be dark in this room, were I fortunate enough to gain entry. I'd glimpsed a candle on the large desk when I walked by one day and peeked in, and saw Mr Beauford sitting there, poring over some papers. Now here I was, striking a match to light that very same candle. I did so quickly, and as my eyes adjusted to the soft light, I was quite astounded by what I beheld.

The room more closely resembled a laboratory than a library. To be sure, there were many books on the shelves, but what puzzled me were all the vials and test tubes piled upon several shelves and tables. Mr Beauford must be conducting some kind of experiments in his spare time, I thought to myself.

I remembered seeing Father Gabriel in this room with Mr Beauford. Whenever Mr Beauford called for him, Father Gabriel dropped everything and rushed from his residence in the local town to discuss anything Mr Beauford wanted to discuss. I imagined Mr Beauford talked to him about his illness and not wanting to die, while Father Gabriel consoled him with talk of a life after this one, filled with light and angels. Father Gabriel would pull up a chair near Mr Beauford's desk and they would talk for hours.

I thought back to Mr Beauford's antique-collecting obsession that Henley had mentioned. I heard Mr Beauford's voice inside my mind. *They are immortal. They were here long before us and will remain long after we're gone.* It was as if Mr Beauford was trying to escape death by collecting items he knew were from a time before he existed and would outlast him long after he ceased to be. Perhaps it was some deranged way of prolonging his own life. Father Gabriel probably saw Mr Beauford's fixation as irreligious – a superstition, almost. It was strange that he played along, but maybe he hoped to comfort the old man in what was the final period of his life. Even though he appeared to be a little stronger now, his overall frailty certainly gave the impression that he may not have long to live.

I snapped myself out of it. It didn't matter. None of it did. I had to complete my mission. I looked up at the wall behind the desk to find the painting Miss Hatfield so desired staring back at me. I glanced around for something to stand on and noticed a small footstool next to a chair. It would put me at exactly the right height to grab the painting, and then I'd be on to the next phase of my plan.

As I walked over to fetch the stool, I couldn't help but notice several old maps and some diaries or journals spread out on one of the many small tables in the room. What on earth could Mr Beauford be so fascinated about? I snatched up the footstool and headed back to the desk, but in my haste I knocked over a stack of papers.

Cursing myself, I scooped them up and put them back

on the table, hoping no one would notice they were out of order. Moving to place the footstool, I heard a crinkling sound and realized that I'd stepped on a piece of paper I'd missed. When I picked it up, I saw that it was a note from Ruth, Mr Beaufort's long-lost wife. It said, 'To my darling Charles. With all the love in the world, Ruth.' I put it back with the stack of paper. I felt uneasy, but refocused myself upon the task at hand. As I placed the footstool in front of the portrait, my eyes fell upon an open diary on Mr Beauford's desk. I squinted at the elegant, loopy and decidedly feminine penmanship. The candlelight illuminated the page just enough for me to make out three words that made my heart stand still. The entry read: 'I am immortal.'

What incredible coincidence was this? Was old Mr Beauford even crazier than I'd thought?

I moved the candle closer, trying to make out more of what was written, but watery splotches on the page made it difficult to decipher more than one word out of every few. I stuck a finger in the diary to mark the page Mr Beauford had it open to and flipped through the rest.

The handwriting grew more and more erratic, eventually devolving into illegible scribbles. I continued to flip through the diary and noticed the writer didn't finish it. After a while, even the incomprehensible scrawls gave way to blank pages.

Confused, I flipped back to the last page with legible writing on it. There were two sentences, written surprisingly clearly.

I have told James everything. They are going to come for me.

I felt a jolt run through me, and with trembling fingers I flipped to the first page of the diary.

Property of Miss Rebecca Hatfield.

I jumped as I heard footsteps in the corridor outside. Hurriedly, I flipped the pages of the diary back to the entry Mr Beauford had been reading and opened the door closest to me: a large cabinet that stood against one of the walls. Thankfully, there was just enough space within for me to squeeze inside and pull the door shut behind me. I kept the door cracked open just a sliver, as I wondered who else sought entry to the study this night.

It was Henley. He distractedly looked around the room for something, eventually glancing down at the diary and the entry I'd just read. I saw him read it for himself; whereas my reaction had been one of shock, his was to snort with derision. Obviously he thought his father slightly mad. He stopped and stared at the candle, and I could just make out enough of the look on his face to know he was wondering how that candle had come to be lit. A sudden knock at the study door drew his attention from the diary. It was Mr Lawrence.

'I say, Henley, did you find any of those excellent cigars of your father's?' his tutor asked.

'Afraid not, old boy. All that's in evidence here are the writings of an old man who's slipping out of touch with reality, it would appear.' He sighed and left the room with Mr Lawrence. Amazingly, he'd forgotten the lit candle on the table, so I could hopefully make my getaway without knocking anything else over. There was no way I could continue with my plan this evening, however. I was far too panicked; my heart felt as though it would pound right out of my chest, and my resolve had been weakened by my close call.

I slipped out of the cabinet, and when I turned to close its doors, I noticed a rack of small vials on the top shelf, just above where my head had been moments before. They all bore strange labels with unpronounceable names that were unfamiliar to me. All save one, that is: 'Islamorada'.

It couldn't be, yet there it was, staring back at me. I slammed the wardrobe door shut, and it sounded as though one of the vials went crashing to the floor inside. I didn't have time to investigate. I had to get out of there. But what did it mean, and what should I do about it? I blew the candle out, hoping to leave my confusion and dread behind in the dark. I ran wildly out of the room, pulling the study door closed behind me, and fairly flew up the stairs to my bedroom, but the feeling of utter fear was still with me when I slammed the door behind me.

Once I was safely inside the sanctuary of my quiet room, I leaned back against the closed door and slid slowly to the floor, allowing my heart to slow down and my breathing to return to normal. What I'd discovered this evening put everything in an even more precarious light. I closed my eyes and imagined Miss Hatfield standing in front of me. Silently, I asked her what I should do. I swear, it was as if she pointed to my little writing table, and I knew I had to write her a note, to bring her up to speed on everything I'd learned, and then wait for her advice. I dared not risk taking the painting just yet. There was more afoot here that she might need me to investigate before I could leave the Beauford Estate. I'd just have to be much more cautious around Mr Beauford now. He had appeared to be such an innocent, rather dotty old man. But I knew now that he was closing in on the dangerous secret that had altered my life.

I crossed to the writing table and sat down, gathering my thoughts. Dipping my pen in the inkwell, I carefully began to write. 'Dear Miss Hatfield, You won't believe what I have just discovered ...'

177

Chapter 17

I posted the letter first thing the next morning. Later that day, Mr Beauford returned from town, looking a little older and more stooped than the last time I'd seen him. Though he did not mention it, I knew Henley had noticed his father's frailty. Clearly, his father was no longer the man he'd been in his prime and was in no condition to receive difficult news. Henley was well aware that his decision not to take over the family business would break his father's heart, and feared that his father's illness made this the worst possible time to tell him. Seeing Mr Beauford for myself, I agreed with him, and we mutually decided it wasn't the right time to let him know.

I realized Mr Beauford was fading rather quickly now, and I felt sorry for him. I wondered how many years he'd chased the dream of immortality. He had to feel so very discouraged, and yet he'd come so incredibly close, even obtaining a vial of the Islamorada water! He must not have known what it was capable of doing, however, or he certainly wouldn't be in failing health. I couldn't dwell on it too much, as all my thinking did nothing but create one vicious circle after another, and a part of me feared I should go mad if I didn't find other activities.

I waited, none too patiently, for a response from Miss Hatfield. In handing my letter to Wilchester to post for me, I'd garnered Henley's attention. I remembered how he'd paused, looking up from his books, which he appeared to be studying without any obvious enjoyment or interest.

'A letter to your family?' he asked. 'Or maybe to a close family friend?'

'A family friend,' I was quick to reply, scrawling on the envelope the address Miss Hatfield had made me repeat dozens of times in case an emergency arose.

I remember seeing Henley's curious gaze as I handed my letter to Wilchester, but soon Mr Lawrence reminded him to focus on his studies, and so he turned away from me to resume his reading.

In an effort to distract myself, I began riding the horses every day, a bit further each time, and always in a different direction. These extended rides made me feel more alive, more in the moment. They also helped me keep my distance from Mr Beauford, and from his son. I could feel Henley looking at me with curiosity during our shared meals, but I pretended not to notice and chatted away merrily about some small-talk subject or another. That was unlike me, and I was aware that Henley knew that, but I thought it preferable to sitting there silently, which would have forced him into cornering me to ask what was wrong. I always made my way up to my room just a few minutes before he and his father were quite done with their meal. They always stood politely as I exited the dining room, but I could feel Henley's eyes following me.

Late on the fourth day, upon my return from a brisk ride, I was surprised to find a letter waiting for me in my room. My eyes fell upon the address. 'To Miss Margaret Beauford, in the care of Charles Beauford …' I made a mental note to thank Nellie for putting it in my room.

When I picked up the letter, I noticed my hands were trembling. I willed them to stop, but it was as if they belonged to someone else.

Hoping a walk would calm my nerves, I found myself in the stables again. I sucked in a breath and opened the letter.

Dear Rebecca, it began, *Thank you so much for sharing the details of your discovery. This confirms one of my most serious fears—*

The letter was snatched out of my hands.

'You're looking awfully grave …' Henley trailed off as he began to read the letter.

'Give it back!' I grabbed the letter from him. In his shock, I was able to easily pluck it out of his hands, but my fingers didn't appear to be working properly and the letter drifted to the ground between us.

'What do you care?' Henley snapped. 'You've virtually ignored my existence these past few days. You thwart my every attempt to engage you in anything other than trivial small talk.' He exhaled, exasperated. 'And now *this*.'

'Yes.' My voice was no louder than a whisper.

I wondered how much he'd read. How much had Miss Hatfield said? What if the letter said something important? What if Henley now knew everything?

'Who is it from?'

'I–I can't tell you that.'

Henley turned abruptly from me, as if trying to compose himself before speaking.

'Henley, I can explain—'

He turned back with his eyes narrowed into slits.

'Oh, can you?' he sneered. 'This should be rich. I bare my thoughts to you … my feelings, and yet you can't even bring yourself to share your real name with me. You use my cousin's name and refuse to tell me what's going on.'

He picked up the letter and flicked it with his forefinger. 'All right, then, "Cousin" –' the word dripped with sarcasm for the first time '– please do. Explain to your heart's content. I'm listening.'

'I … it's just that I …' My voice faltered into silence as I realized there was no way I could really explain without him thinking me stark raving mad. I turned away from him, trying desperately to think what to say next.

Undaunted, he was determined to have his say. 'Well, Miss Rebecca, or whatever your real name is, I'm not a man who enjoys being deceived. I know you have secrets, I've always known that. I was holding on to the tiniest modicum of hope that you might one day reveal at least a few of those secrets to me. You gained my trust. You made it easy for me to talk to you, and yet you withhold from me something I have the right to know …' He grabbed my arm and spun me around like a rag doll, dropping the letter in the process. 'Who the hell are you?'

He was breathing hard, and I felt a sob trapped in my throat. I couldn't speak and show him how frightened I was, nor how much I truly cared for him, for what point would there be, in the end? We could never be together – not really. I would outlive him and his – our – descendants. How in the world could I convey that strange fact to him? But then again, I didn't really have to leave. I could stay, but could I stand watching him grow old before my eyes? It would only be a few wrinkles around his eyes at first, but then his forehead would become lined, engraved with testaments to time that couldn't touch me. Maybe I could stand all that and stay by his side, but when the eyes with which he viewed me grew cloudy and blurred … Could he still love me? As much as I tried to lie to myself, I knew the answer to that question, so I just looked at the ground silently, knowing he would eventually leave me standing there. I could feel his eyes upon me for a few more moments, then he sighed heavily, turned on his heel and stalked off.

I stood for a moment, trying to collect the different parts of myself until I could function again. I picked up the letter from the ground and slowly walked over to an old bench that leaned against Bessie's stall. I sank down onto it and paused before opening the letter again.

… Mr Beauford has accumulated more than just the painting, and has more than a mere passing curiosity regarding immortality. I must tell you more about the painting, information I wasn't aware you might need before I received your letter.

The painting wasn't truly stolen from me; rather, Mr Beauford outbid me for it at an auction a short while before you and I met. The subject of the portrait is Juana Ruiz, and Ponce de León's diaries are what make it significant, along with some of the other artefacts Mr Beauford has accumulated. I wanted to retrieve the portrait before he could gain more insight into my secret, which is now your secret as well.

I paused. The intrigue that was interwoven throughout my very existence took my breath away. It all felt so incredibly surreal, and I couldn't understand the smallest part of it. I didn't even know who I was any more. I closed my eyes and breathed deeply until I felt my head was clear enough to continue.

Miss Hatfield went on to instruct me that I had to destroy all the records, diaries, vials – even the painting itself – everything I'd found in Mr Beauford's study that pertained to immortality. At all costs, I had to do this in order to protect both her and myself. However, she went on to warn me that I'd already stayed in this time for too long. She begged me to hurry, telling me that I'd be in danger if someone found out, or noticed something strange about me. She also said that our bodies couldn't remain in one time for long. My body wouldn't be comfortable staying put in the current time and place, and very soon I'd have to time-travel once again. I wouldn't feel pain, rather a queasy, almost nervous sensation that would make me feel strange and uneasy. Hearing Miss Hatfield's descriptions of the sensation, I realized the process had already begun. But Miss Hatfield warned that it would soon escalate if I ignored it and remained in the same time. I'd be driven to insanity before long.

Reading her words, I knew I had to accomplish what I'd been sent here to do before the uneasy feeling of displacement and unbelonging consumed me. *Remember, you are a visitor in all of time*, her letter said.

When I read that last sentence, I realized what was causing the gnawing feeling I'd been experiencing. Some part of me had started drifting away already. Now my mentor in time travel and immortality was telling me I'd experience this uncomfortable feeling even more acutely as the days went by. 'Perfect,' I said with a sigh. But I knew I had no choice but to do as she directed.

Chapter 18

I slept fitfully that night. I skipped dinner, not feeling up to facing Henley so soon after our confrontation over the letter. I asked Nellie to offer my apologies, but I needed to retire early and would see everyone in the morning. I tossed and turned, with dreams of my current location in time jumbled crazily with memories of Cynthia's life in the future. Planes were flying and cars were roaring along a highway in one segment, and then suddenly I was back in the days of horse-drawn carriages when the few automobiles – cars – on the road looked so very different from those Cynthia had grown up around. I felt very disorientated as I got up and went about my morning routine. Even Nellie noticed my distracted state as she helped me dress.

'What is it, Miss Margaret? I can tell you're worried about something,' she said softly.

I squeezed the hand she gently laid upon my shoulder. 'Oh, it's nothing, Nellie, really. Nothing to be concerned about. I'll be fine, honestly. Thank you for being so considerate.' I smiled to reassure her, but her eyes told me she didn't believe my cheeriness.

I headed downstairs, lost in my thoughts, but was stopped in my tracks about midway down.

'What in tarnation is going on around here?' Mr Beauford's voice bellowed up at me. 'And who in God's name are you, young woman?' He was staring at me angrily; his face was so red, I feared he'd have a heart attack and die right there at the foot of the stairs.

I rushed down to him, for he looked about to lose his balance. 'Mr Beauford, sir, please, let me help you sit down.' I guided him over to the nearest chair in the parlour. He allowed me to take his arm and walk him there, but then he jerked away from me and peered out from under his enormous bushy brows.

'No, I will not sit! Thank you, whoever you are, but let me be. All I want from you is an explanation.' He shook a letter in my general direction. Correspondence appeared to be a source of irritation for the men in this house, I noticed. 'This letter came yesterday but I only had a chance to open it this morning. It tells me my niece is still too ill to join us this summer, and apologizes for any inconvenience this may cause.' He stared at me. 'So what I need to know from you is, who are you, and what are you doing here? What are you playing at, young woman?'

I gulped, fearing that I was most assuredly about to be tossed out of the house into the deserted countryside – and that was the best-case scenario. Henley walked quickly around the corner to stand at his father's side. I thought he would surely betray everything he'd learned about me the day before, and I wouldn't have blamed him if he had. I steeled myself for the worst, trying to think what to do.

'Now, Father, you must calm yourself. You know what your physician said about getting too excited.' He turned and shouted down the hall, 'Wilchester! Please bring my father a glass of water.' Henley went to a cabinet along the parlour wall and took a small paper packet out of a box on the shelf. Wilchester hurried in with the water, which he handed to Mr Beauford, and Henley took a small pill

185

from the packet. 'Here you are, sir. Take your nitroglycerine tablet like a good chap, please.' He encouraged his father as though their roles had been temporarily reversed, and I felt my fondness for Henley rising again. He really was such a kind person at heart. I felt bad for confusing him, and waited patiently to see what he'd do next. He wouldn't look at me, so I was sure the axe was about to fall.

'Better now?' Henley asked his father, patting him gently on the shoulder. Mr Beauford nodded, but then turned to look at me with a mixture of disgust and suspicion.

'I'm fine, Henley. But this woman—'

Henley cut him off midstream. 'Yes, Father, I know all about this woman. This has all been a case of mistaken identity. There's nothing to be so suspicious about, really, Father. She showed up that day in the city and wanted to interview you. She's a journalist, you see, for one of the New York newspapers, and she hoped to write a story about the great Mr Beauford and his steel corporation. But you mistakenly decided she was your niece and accepted her as such immediately. Being a clever reporter, she saw an opportunity to learn about you from an insider's point of view and simply played along. She confided her secret in me immediately, so you see, in truth, we've both been deceiving you. I'm equally guilty. But I hope you can chalk it up to a proud son wanting the best story possible about his father to be written and published. Isn't that right?' He finally raised his eyes and met mine.

All of the anger and accusation I'd seen the day before had vanished, and I had the distinct feeling he actually relished concocting this fantastic story for his father's benefit. And his delivery was so good, I found myself almost believing him. I had no choice but to play along at this point, and nodded.

'And this young lady's name?' Mr Beauford asked Henley, as he gripped his water with a still-shaking hand.

'Miss Rebecca—' There was a glint of uncertainty and fear in Henley's eyes.

'Hatfield,' I finished for him. 'Miss Rebecca Hatfield.'

Henley had obviously read enough of the letter from Miss Hatfield to have gleaned my first name, at the very least.

'Mr Beauford, what your son's telling you – as fantastical as it sounds – is absolutely true. I apologize for pretending to be your niece, but it was a rare opportunity to get to know the real you, so that I can tell our readers that such an important businessman as yourself is truly a good soul, a kind man, and not just a wealthy bureaucrat who cares nothing for anyone other than himself.'

'Here, here,' agreed Henley. 'It's to be a five-part instalment piece, isn't that right, Miss Hatfield? To be published … When did you say? Starting next month?'

I nodded. 'Correct, Henley.' I knelt down at Mr Beauford's knee and looked up at him. 'Can you ever forgive me, sir? I truly meant no harm or disrespect. It was simply the chance of a lifetime, and I jumped at it, I'm afraid. I'm one of the few women journalists around, and I felt strongly compelled to do this, to prove myself to my superiors.'

Henley actually winked at me for that line, above his father's head. He and I were both quite skilled at telling whoppers, apparently! He effortlessly picked up the ball again. 'Yes, and I encouraged her the entire time, Father. She's interviewed me about my childhood, and what sort of father you've been to me. And when I learned a little while ago that Cousin Margaret couldn't make it this summer, well, why not continue with the charade? You appeared to be so happy to have *this* Cousin Margaret with us, and I didn't want you to be disappointed. We were actually going to tell you the whole story this very evening at dinner, weren't we, Miss Hatfield?'

'Yes, just so,' I said with a nod.

'I see,' mumbled Mr Beauford. He looked startled and disorientated, but what came out of his mouth next surprised me. 'Well, given these extraordinary circumstances, I feel I owe you an apology, Miss Hatfield. And please, stay with us as long as it takes to complete your assignment. I'm flattered you chose me as a subject, and I hope this assignment helps you make your mark in the journalism world.'

'Oh, you're too kind, sir – it should be me thanking you. And you have nothing to apologize for – it's the other way around.' I glanced over towards where Henley had just been standing. He'd somehow slipped out of the room while I was discoursing with his father, clever boy. I looked back at Mr Beauford, whose colour had returned to normal, although he still sounded quite winded. 'Sir, I believe it might be advisable for you to lie back down for a while this morning. I'm so sorry I caused such a shock to your system, Mr Beauford.'

He nodded and struggled to stand. I helped him to his feet and walked him towards the hallway. 'You're as wise as you are pretty,' he said quietly. 'These old bones will feel much better after a brief nap. I'll see you later on.' He nodded and ambled slowly down the hall towards his quarters.

Once I saw that his door had closed, I sat for a few moments, gathering my strength. The queasy feeling in my stomach had returned, and I couldn't tell if it was due to the morning's dramatic events or the time displacement Miss Hatfield had warned me about. After I'd recovered a little, I went to the kitchen with a dual purpose in mind. I sought out Nellie, who was happily slicing vegetables and laughing with the cook. It was the most animated I'd ever seen her. I was so glad that at least I'd been able to do something positive for *her*, if not for the Beaufords. 'Oh, Nellie, may I see you for a moment?' I called out.

Her head bobbed up and she put down what she was doing and came right over. We stood to one side, but I could feel and see the other servants' eyes watching us. I knew at least some of them must have heard Mr Beauford confront me earlier, but I really didn't care.

'Nellie, Mr Beauford isn't feeling at all well this morning. Could you make sure that Wilchester keeps an eye on him, please? He's retired to his room for the time being. If Wilchester could just check on him once in a while, make sure he's all right and so forth, that would be excellent. I believe he'll be most open to Wilchester looking in, rather than anyone else intruding upon his space.'

She nodded several times. 'Oh, yes, I'll be glad to tell Mr Wilchester, Miss Mar—' She looked down, and blushed.

'Oh, Nellie, it's all right. It was bound to get out eventually. You may call me Rebecca, and you needn't say "Miss" Rebecca … I'm a newspaper woman, and I was only posing as Miss Margaret to gain more detailed insight into Mr Beauford for the piece I'm writing about him. Did you hear all of that, or just that I had a different name?' I smiled to let her know I wasn't angry, and wasn't going to treat her any differently.

She looked up, flushed. 'Oh, Miss … ah, Miss Rebecca – I don't think I could call you by your name without saying "miss", miss,' she stuttered, and we both laughed, relieved that we were still friends.

'Whatever suits you, Nellie, is fine with me. Thank you for conveying the message to Wilchester – he probably already knows, but just in case. The second thing –' and at this point I raised my voice, addressing the whole staff '– has anyone seen Mr Henley lately? I must talk with him at once.'

Most of the servants shrugged or ignored my request, but the kindly old cook, Eloise, spoke up. 'Yes, mum, he'd be in his room, he would.' I detected an English accent, and then it dawned on me that this must be the same Eloise who had been like a nanny to Henley when he was a little boy, following his mother's death.

His words floated through my memory: 'She's a sweet old English gal, very kind. Took care of me when I was sick and Father had no clue what to do, played nurse when I scraped my leg. I think the world of Eloise.' Henley had told me about her when we sat under his thinking tree, and I'd made a mental note to thank her for her kindness if the moment ever arrived.

I smiled at her. 'Thank you, Eloise, ever so much.' I cleared my throat and addressed the entire staff again. I realized the cover story Henley had so cleverly cooked up would actually serve me well for the remainder of my stay at the estate, and that was a great relief. 'May I have your attention, please? I know you're all very aware of most things that go on around here, and I don't want any of you to feel awkward around me. My true name is Rebecca Hatfield, and I'm here writing a newspaper article – well, a series of articles, actually – about Mr Beauford and his business.'

Some of the servants nodded sagely, so I knew the gossip had already begun to spread. A few, however, looked up at me with renewed interest and curiosity. 'I'm telling you this so there'll be no confusion about what to call me, and so you don't have to wonder what I'm still doing here. Perhaps it was wrong of me to pose as Mr Beaufort's niece, but Mr Henley and I decided that subterfuge was permissible, given Mr Beauford's age and health. It's helped him to trust me more easily, and to open up more. In short, it'll help me write the best possible story about him. We should have told him the truth earlier, but I believe events happened as they were meant to. Everything's fine now, and I'll be staying on just a short while longer. I appreciate everything all of you have done for me during my visit, and just wanted to thank you. And there you have it.' I nodded at them ever so slightly and left, hearing the whispers beginning to buzz as I headed down the hallway and up the stairs to Henley's room.

Once there, I knocked lightly. 'Henley?' Dead silence. I knocked again, more forcefully. 'Oh, Henley, I know you're in there. Eloise has ratted you out, I'm afraid, but only because I pressed her. Please, won't you talk to me? I owe you my thanks—' At that, the door swung open slowly; I paused for a moment at the threshold to regain my poise.

When I entered Henley's room, I saw him sitting in a large brown leather armchair facing another chair and the window. His feet were propped up on an ottoman that matched the armchair. He silently indicated that I should take the seat opposite him, but to close the door behind me first.

I closed the door and made my way to the chair he'd offered me. 'I can't begin to thank you enough for—'

'For lying for you? For telling my poor old father perhaps the biggest whale of a tale I've ever made up?' His eyes narrowed, and then opened back up and twinkled. There was the Henley I'd grown so fond of. 'Actually, it was rather fun. You see, I'd been privately working on that story for a while, as I felt it was only a matter of time before we had to tell Father something.' He looked down and pretended to pick a piece of lint from his trousers, but I knew he was only buying time. He'd just revealed another wonderful trait of his – extreme loyalty in dire circumstances.

'You have no idea how grateful I am for your cleverness, and your incredible defence of me. I'm quite stunned, I must say. I thought you'd begun to hate me and would surely help your father throw me to the wolves.' It was true. I had believed I'd be going back to the real Miss Hatfield empty-handed, having failed miserably. The sinking feeling in the pit of my stomach had intensified during my confrontation with Mr Beauford, but it had dissipated as I listened to Henley spin his fantastic tale on my behalf. In fact, at this particular moment, I felt quite alive and present. My friend and I were talking again, and that made my heart rejoice.

Henley cleared his throat and sat up straighter, taking his feet off the ottoman and placing them flat on the ground. He leaned forwards, elbows resting upon his knees, and peered intently at me. 'Yes, well, not even wolves are deserving of such a mysterious personage as yourself, Miss Rebecca Hatfield. Do you trust me enough, at long last, to tell me more about why you're here, if not about yourself?' He wouldn't break his gaze, so I had to be the one to look away. I stood up and walked towards the window, speaking softly but at a volume I knew he would hear.

'I do trust you, indeed, dear Henley. No one has ever been kinder to me, or more protective of me, that I can recall. And such goodwill from someone who really knows nothing about me. I—'

192

He stopped me by touching my elbow, very gently. He'd followed me to the window so as not to miss anything I might at this point be willing to share with him. I still didn't turn around; I didn't trust myself to look at him just yet.

Continuing to stare out of the window, I decided to throw caution to the wind and tell him *almost* everything, with the exception of the part about me being immortal and from another age. If I threw that into the mix, he'd probably take me for a raving lunatic. I could only hope that he'd accept the rest of my story. 'The real reason I came to your house in the first place was to steal the painting – the painting that now hangs behind your father's desk in his study … And, Henley, my mission hasn't altered. I must still take the painting, but I need to accomplish even more now, I'm afraid.'

Finally, I turned to face him, since he hadn't interrupted me yet. I wasn't sure what to expect – would he now throw me out, or … ?

'Can you tell me who has commissioned you to steal that pitiful old painting? It's not as if you or they are likely to get much for it. It's not even by a famous artist.'

I nodded. 'Yes, I surely owe you that much. The painting belongs to a close friend of mine. She needs it back. She tried to outbid your father for it at an auction earlier this year, but she didn't have sufficient funds. It was taken away from her and mistakenly placed in that auction. That's all I can tell you about it, I'm afraid.'

'Mmm. I see. More and more curious, Miss Hatfield. I—'

'Henley?' I interrupted. 'Could you please call me Rebecca? "Miss Hatfield" makes me think you're addressing … well, my mother.' We both smiled at that, and I could feel our friendship slowly but surely rebuilding.

'All right then, Rebecca, but only in private. God knows what my father and the servants might think if they were to overhear us calling each other by our first names.' He took a second to wink at me, but soon his face turned grave again. 'And what's this other problem that's now compounded the complexity of your mission?'

I wasn't quite sure where to begin with the next part. I was astonished he was even still listening to me! But I knew I had to try, so I launched forward. 'You're aware that your father has become obsessed with learning about things such as the Fountain of Youth, the possibility of … immortality.'

His response confounded me further, for it was one of those rare, deep, genuine belly laughs of his. His eyes even teared up a bit, he laughed so hard; he had to wipe them before he could catch his breath and speak. 'Aware of that old man's fixation? Painfully aware, yes. He's disturbed. Deranged, even. You remember that chase we had in the park? Poor Willie, running after all of us.' He laughed more darkly then. 'I've even discussed it with a psychiatric doctor in town, for I feared Father was going insane when I first learned about all this. But after he met with Father a few times, he assured me he was simply deluded; that this had become a hobby, as the old gentleman – my father! – was winding down his life. The psychiatrist said it gave him something to think about and, in a sense, to live for. So while I believe it's utter nonsense and a complete waste of time, it gives Father something to look forward to. We simply have an agreement not to discuss it. I keep a close eye on him, as I'm sure you've noticed, or make sure the servants do when I'm unavailable.' He paused for a moment as another thought crossed his countenance. 'He's growing weaker physically, though. That's painfully apparent after his episode this morning.'

I felt horrible. 'I'm so sorry to have instigated that, Henley. If there's anything I can do—'

He held his hand up in a gesture of dismissal. 'You didn't make him ill, Rebecca. Old age has done that. Don't blame yourself in any way, I beg you. You and I should have talked all this through sooner, and simply presented the story to him earlier, so it wouldn't have come as such a shock.' He looked down at me, his eyes and smile warm and friendly. 'So, please continue – what's the other portion of this mission of yours?'

'Well, as strange as it sounds, I've been instructed to … do away with his curios, the ones that have to do with this delusional belief in immortality. His maps, diaries, some vials that he apparently has in the study …' I made the sentence more of a question than a statement, hoping he'd know what I was referring to.

He did. 'Ah, yes – the vials in his wardrobe. Incredibly strange collection of what looks to me to be nothing more than water of various shades – some dirty, some clean – but with strange names labelling each vial.' He looked down at me again, a question in those dark eyes of his now. 'Do away?' He repeated my words. 'You mean destroy?'

I nodded.

'But who wants you to do this, and to what end? As I told you, these things have kept him going, in a way. If he's deprived of them, I'm afraid he'll slide downhill even more quickly.'

I shook my head, for I really believed what I was about to say next. 'No, Henley, I think it could actually help him get better. The friend who has commissioned me to do this—'

'The same one who wants her painting back?' he enquired.

'Yes, the very same. Well, she's seen …' I caught myself before I made what would have been a huge error of judgement. 'She's heard tales of many of her ancestors going mad pursuing exactly the same path your father's on right now. He may be shocked at first, Henley, but in the long run, it'll probably be best for him not to dabble in matters that can never end well.'

'I see,' he said, and his tone told me he agreed with me. 'But wait – you just said "for *him*" – surely you don't believe that anyone can become immortal?' His voice was incredulous. Not wishing to lie to him any more, I thought of a response that wasn't exactly a lie – an honest answer, if a partial one.

I laughed very lightly. 'Oh, no, I don't believe immortality is possible for anyone,' I replied. I merely added in my mind the words *but it is for me.*

Henley looked sufficiently reassured and nodded to himself. 'Destroy his obsession and whisk away the painting.'

'Yes.'

He stood up and clapped his hands together, rubbing the palms against each other briskly. 'Very well, then. When do we begin?'

I felt my eyes grow wide and my jaw drop slightly in disbelief. 'Are you telling me that you plan to help me in this? After everything you've already done for me?'

'Mm-hmm. You are precisely correct in your deduction,' he responded, dropping his voice to a conspiratorial tone. 'Let us continue our planning later today, for the servants are sure to take note that a very beautiful young woman who isn't my relation – any more, at least – has been in my bedroom with the door closed for nearly an hour now. And they do talk, Lord love 'em.' He chuckled, having grown accustomed to servants' gossip from a lifetime of being around it. I was starting to understand why he was occasionally dismissive with some of the staff. There was a bit of a love-hate relationship going on, and it affected some more than others.

'Yes, you're quite right,' I agreed. 'Impropriety must not be our downfall. If we can meet by the mill this afternoon, say around three, we can cook up a plan, I'm sure. I must carry out this mission right away – in the next two or three days, if at all possible.'

He walked with me to the door. 'Good idea. I'll ride Jasper, and you take one of the faster horses – you've become quite the equestrian lately, so I hear.' His eyes twinkled as I blushed. 'You think I haven't asked Wellesley what you're up to when you're out there with the horses? He told me you have natural talent and you're learning fast. I'm pleased.' He squeezed my elbow to show me his approval.

As he opened the door, I curtsied, just in case the walls with ears and eyes might be observing. 'Very well, I'll see you then. I do believe I'll go for a ride now, and think through what I shall write next about Mr Beauford.'

We walked down the main stairs together. I continued towards the front door, but he kept pace with me, determined to be the one to open it.

'As you wish,' he said gallantly, and opened the door. Much to our mutual surprise, there were two young women standing right outside, the elder one poised to knock.

She started at the sight of Henley, then again when she registered my presence, looking me up and down thoroughly. 'Why, Mr Henley, I do declare, you gave me a fright.' She curtsied, and blushed, while her younger companion rolled her eyes slightly at this display.

197

Henley recovered his composure and extended his hand to the beautiful older girl. 'So nice to see you, Miss Christine,' he said politely. Then he turned to the younger, paler girl, who looked to be about eleven, but might have been older. 'Miss Eliza, how are you these days?' he enquired. I noticed Eliza was leaning on a walking stick held at her side. When I looked at her gentle face, I realized she had the steady, unfocused gaze of someone who was blind.

Eliza attempted a slight curtsey, but nearly lost her balance in the process. She looked very pale and weak, and I took her arm to lead her to the parlour. 'Why don't you come with me, Miss Eliza? I believe you might benefit from sitting down for a spell. My name is Rebecca, by the way.'

I heard Henley cough with embarrassment behind us as he escorted the older girl in. 'Oh, my goodness, where are my manners? Miss Rebecca Hatfield, this is Miss Christine Porter and her younger sister, Miss Eliza. They are long-time friends of my family. And I'm glad to see you both,' he added quickly. 'What an unexpected pleasure. To what do we owe this visit?' he politely asked.

Christine huffed, 'Didn't your father tell you? We've come to spend a fortnight with you, to try and build up poor Eliza's health. I do hope it won't be an inconvenience?' she asked, looking rather pointedly in my direction. I detected a slight Southern accent from this gorgeous blue-eyed, blonde-haired belle, although I was half sure she was putting it on.

Henley smoothed things over quickly, as he was wont to do. 'Good gracious, not at all, Christine, not in the least. I do hope our healthy country air gives you strength and fortifies your spirits, Miss Eliza,' he said, making a full bow to the younger girl regardless of her blindness, who was now seated in the same chair Mr Beauford had collapsed into earlier that morning. Henley took her hand and kissed it in a courtly manner, which embarrassed and delighted young Eliza at the same time. It was sweet how Henley treated her, I thought. Then I looked over just in time to see Christine's eyes burning two holes right through me. Obviously I'd upset some plan of hers, and I knew the arrival of the two sisters was undoubtedly going to complicate mine.

Chapter 19

When I returned from my ride, I managed to sneak up to my room without running into anyone, which had been my intention. Naturally, my plan to meet with Henley at the mill had been thwarted by the arrival of the Porter sisters, but I still wanted my ride. I jumped on Thunder, the fastest horse in the stable, clucked to him and gave him his head. We roared down the path for about three miles before he slowed down. The breeze rushing over me was exactly what I needed. It made me feel very present in my body and helped me release my worries about what was going to happen next, if only for a little while. When we returned, I rubbed him down myself, which always amused Wellesley.

'You're the first young lady I've ever known who enjoys tending to the horses so much,' he'd remarked a few days earlier.

'They deserve to be treated well for their service,' I replied as I brushed Thunder down carefully but thoroughly. I followed that up with a fresh bucket of oats. Logic had taught me that the first thing the horses needed after riding was a good long drink of water from the trough in front of the stables. Then I led them into their stall and wiped them down and brushed them, talking softly to them all the while. The routine ended with a bucket of oats, and a carrot or an apple for a special treat. I felt as if I'd been riding all my life, and in a sense, in this *new* life, which was mine now, I pretty much had.

Back in my room, as I allowed the warm water from the bowl on my dresser to cleanse and refresh me, I thought a bit more about Eliza – a pretty girl in her own way, but much plainer than her elder sister. She was pale as porcelain, but with an almost faded look to her skin, and her dark hair was rather severely pinned back. Her opaque, grey eyes still held a flicker of intelligence, and she could certainly roll them easily enough when she was fed up with her sister! She presented a complete contrast to Christine, with her radiant, flawless skin, her silky blonde curls and her bright azure eyes. She was a beauty, to be sure, and from the way she'd batted her eyelashes at Henley, I had a pretty good notion what her intentions towards him were.

It doesn't matter, I told myself firmly. *Henley and I can never be together in that way; we're friends, and he's helping me under extraordinary circumstances, far above and beyond the call of duty.* I was brushing my hair rather brusquely while having this little self-talk when in walked Nellie.

'Oh, begging your pardon, Miss Rebecca …' she faltered. 'I would have knocked, but I didn't know you'd returned from your ride.' She stood by the door, awaiting my permission to come in.

I beckoned her by crooking a finger towards her. 'Do come on in, Nellie, don't be shy. You've seen me in my undergarments many a time now, and just because my name's changed, nothing else has.' I smiled up at her as she took the brush from my hand. I was thankful to allow her to finish brushing my hair more gently than I'd begun, and she always did a better job of pinning it up than I could. She brought five silver-coloured pins out of her apron pocket.

'Hannah sent you these, miss,' she quietly informed me as she laid them on the bureau. 'Would you like me to use them to fix your hair today?'

'Oh, yes, please, Nellie. I rather prefer them to the bulkier bronze pins.' I couldn't tell her why I'd really wanted the thin ones. It didn't matter any more, since I'd enlisted Henley's help. Picking locks would no longer be necessary, and I was greatly relieved, for a potential life of crime didn't exactly suit me. It was one thing to fabricate stories, but quite another to steal. Yet I knew I must take the painting and destroy the other artefacts, according to Miss Hatfield's instructions. I would simply have to observe the Porter sisters for a day or so, and find a way to meet with Henley to plan our next move.

Once I was groomed and dressed to Nellie's satisfaction, I laughed and turned to thank her. 'I'm so grateful you're here with me, Nellie. You take such good care of me, helping me groom and dress. It's rather like what goes around, comes around.' I smiled.

'Beg pardon, Miss Rebecca?' she asked in confusion.

'Well, you see, I enjoy grooming and attending to the horses' needs, and then I come inside, and you return the favour.' She laughed as she caught my meaning. 'But what can I do for you in exchange, Nellie?' I really wanted to help improve her life in whatever way I could, at least for the brief time I was to be a part of it. I couldn't explain it, but I felt a strong connection to her, Hannah and Henley. The rest of the people there were nice enough, yet I didn't truly want to know more about them. Nellie had touched me in some way when we first met, and I cared about what might happen to her once I had to move on.

'Why, you've already done a tremendous amount for me, miss,' she replied. 'I'd never been allowed to come out here to the country before, and I far prefer it to the city, actually. I've made friends here, and I never felt that any of the staff in the city were my friends.' She looked wistful, then smiled brightly at me. 'So you see, you've done a great deal for me already, and I'm truly grateful. Thank you, Miss Rebecca.' She curtsied, and was about to leave.

'That's a small thing, Nellie, and I'm glad to have done it. One last question before you go – have you seen young Miss Eliza recently?'

'Oh, yes, miss. She's down in the parlour, listening to some music on the Victrola. She seems to love classical music. She's sitting there in the master's big old chair, with the most peaceful smile on her face as she listens ... I believe she said it was a recording of Mr Beethoven's Ninth Symphony. It's quite pretty,' she added.

'Thank you, Nellie.' I had a distant memory of Cynthia hearing someone whistling a tune they called 'Beethoven'. 'Yes, Beethoven's music is exquisite, I quite agree. I think I'll go and talk with Eliza for a while before dinner. And what of Mr Henley and Miss Christine? Do you happen to know their whereabouts?'

She nodded. 'I believe they went for a drive, miss. I think Miss Christine mentioned something about needing a few things from the dry-goods store.'

'I assume the c–automobile has been retrieved and fixed, then.'

'Yes, miss.'

'Excellent. Thank you, Nellie. I appreciate you keeping your eyes and ears open for me. I miss out on quite a lot when I'm off on my jaunts on horseback, but I do enjoy my rides so.' She smiled in understanding and vanished down the hallway.

I looked around my beautiful room until my eyes lit on a small bottle of rose water. It had a very light, pleasant scent, and I thought perhaps Eliza would enjoy it. I vaguely recalled Cynthia learning something about blind people's other senses being heightened, so on a whim I decided to take it with me and offer it to her.

I heard the final strains of what I assumed to be Beethoven's Ninth Symphony floating majestically up the stairway, and then the bumping of the Victrola's needle that indicated it had reached the end of the disc. I hurried in when I saw Eliza struggling to get up to turn it off. 'Allow me. Please, stay seated,' I said gently as I passed her. When she flounced back down, obviously irritated, it occurred to me that she'd probably been treated as an invalid for many years, and understandably had grown to resent it. I made a mental note to let her be as independent as possible in our future encounters.

I pulled up a chair to sit beside Eliza. 'Do you mind if I join you? Would I bore you too much if we chatted for a bit?' I asked politely. It was gratifying to see a nice smile brighten up her face.

'Why, no, not at all, Miss Rebecca. I should enjoy that immensely. What sorts of things do you enjoy conversing about?' she enquired. I could sense that not too many people sought out her company, and that she was excited at the prospect of a good talk.

'Whatever would suit you, Eliza,' I replied. 'And please drop the "Miss" – it's simply Rebecca, all right?'

She nodded, again appearing quite happy to be the centre of someone's attention, even a stranger's. My heart went out to her, but I was determined not to allow her to sense any pity from me. 'Well, let's see,' she said. 'I enjoy talking about philosophy, sometimes about politics, but not too much. I really love discussing literature!' she enthused.

'Is that so? Who are some of your favourite authors?' I wasn't about to be impolite and ask if someone read to her, or if she had read prior to losing her eyesight. Once she knew me better, perhaps I'd be able to gently find out those answers. But for now, I simply wished to befriend her, and let her have a confidante. I must admit, I also knew that learning more about Eliza and her sister would enable me to carry out my plan without raising their suspicions. But mainly, I already admired Eliza and instinctively knew she had virtually nothing in common with her sister Christine.

'Oh, I quite like Dickens, particularly *A Tale of Two Cities*,' she said. 'I found Sydney Carton *so* romantic. I'm also very fond of Jane Austen, Mark Twain and Ralph Waldo Emerson.'

'My goodness, your tastes are diverse, I must say! Those are all excellent authors.' I'd heard all the names before – or rather, Cynthia had – but I didn't recall her reading much, if anything, by those authors. After all, Cynthia was only … quite young when …

I took a deep breath, realizing I'd forgotten how old Cynthia was when all this happened. I remembered that she was young, but was she twelve, ten, or even younger? My failure to remember worried me a little, but by now I'd accepted my strange new life. Then that all faded away, and I refocused my full attention on Eliza. Since I didn't know much about the plots of any of the books she was so excited about, I asked her to tell me all about her favourites. I received quite an education in the parlour that afternoon, for once Eliza was off and running there was no stopping her.

This young woman was quite well educated, and I could tell she'd consciously worked to drop – or at least modify

– her Southern accent, whereas her sister capitalized on her dulcet tones to the maximum. I assumed Christine had made a study of how many men simply melted at the sound of a genteel accent from the South and worked it to her advantage. I doubted Henley would fall prey to it, but one could never tell. She was so very beautiful that I couldn't blame him if he found her attractive. What man wouldn't?

At any rate, without my needing to probe for the answers to some of my unanswered questions, Eliza disclosed that she was actually just a couple of years younger than Christine, though she was small for her age. She'd been sickly from the time she was born and had lost her eyesight completely when she was about nine years old.

'I don't mean to be indelicate, but what caused you to go blind?' I asked gently.

'Oh, I don't mind you asking. It feels to me like such a long time ago,' she replied. It was clear she was absolutely thrilled to have someone with whom to talk. 'I had scarlet fever and nearly died. I survived, happily, but my eyesight didn't. I'm grateful to the Lord above for sparing my life. My blindness has actually taught me quite a lot,' she added fervently. I saw that this young woman's faith was a large part of how she got through life.

Just then, the grandfather clock in the hall struck six. 'Where on earth did the day go?' I mused. 'Have you been told dinner is at eight? Is there anything you'd care to do for the next couple of hours? Perhaps take a short nap, or go for a walk—'

At that suggestion, she nearly jumped up out of the chair. 'Oh, Rebecca, would you take me for a little walk? I should love that. After all, I am supposed to breathe in as much of this countrified air as possible while we're here. And I quite enjoy talking with you,' she added shyly.

206

'We absolutely shall and must walk, then, I insist,' I replied. Determined to give her the independence I knew she so valued, I teased her just a bit, to see how she would respond. 'Up with you then, young lazy bones, and let us away to stroll the grounds!' I made my voice quite animated, and realized I was copying the way Henley did this sort of thing, to let her hear that I was joshing and actually in a good humour. She picked up on it right away, giggled slightly and easily got to her feet, grabbing her stick and heading towards the door before I could even take her arm.

I opened the door, asked her permission to take her free arm, and we made our way down the front steps. We walked towards the left, where the path led through a lovely grove of pine and evergreen trees. I thought Eliza would enjoy their scent, and she commented on it right away. We strolled and chatted for about an hour, fast becoming friends. This pleased me, as I noticed her features begin to light up the more we talked. She continued telling me about some of the wonderful books she treasured so much, which her tutor had read to her since she went blind. She talked about God's mercy, grace and love, and I didn't quite know how to respond. Her show of faith was admirable, but I couldn't exactly wrap my mind around how she'd cultivated it, given that her sight had been stolen from her. She was in such good humour, however, that I decided to save some of those heavier questions for another time.

Just as we completed the circle through the grove and were heading back to the house, Henley and Christine drove up and parked in the driveway. Henley jumped out immediately and rushed over to us, leaving Christine to sit impatiently in the car. It was obvious she was miffed that he hadn't helped her out before coming over to talk with us.

'Say, you two!' he enthusiastically greeted us. 'Out and about, walking the grounds – good for you, Eliza!' He patted her arm and she blushed. I realized that one didn't have to see Henley in order to feel the effects of his charms.

'Henley,' I said pointedly, and inclined my head in Christine's direction. 'Someone would appreciate your assistance.'

His eyes widened as he realized he'd quite forgotten about her. 'Oh, my goodness. I'm coming, Christine,' he called. As he helped her out of the car, she smiled at him with her mouth, but she was looking over his head at me as she got down. I knew there would be no making friends with this young woman, and that was fine by me. She seemed very shallow and phoney, from what I could already discern at this juncture. I much preferred getting to know Eliza.

Henley appeared to be oblivious to all this underlying tension, and gathered Christine's many packages in his arms as she daintily ascended the front stairs. I held Eliza back with me, allowing them time to make their entrance. Eliza snickered when she heard Christine trip over the hem of her dress on the top step and utter, 'Dear me!'

I leaned close to my new friend and whispered, 'Is she always so clumsy?'

Eliza nearly burst into laughter at that, but restrained herself so as not to embarrass her sister further in front of Henley. 'Only when she's around young men she wishes to impress, as a rule,' she whispered back.

Chapter 20

Dinner that evening was pretty interesting to behold. I decided to take the stance of an observer, for the most part, and spoke only when asked a direct question. Christine had obviously been holding court with the men around her for most of her life, and it was akin to watching a play, seeing her flutter those lashes and wave her small fan in front of her face from time to time. She virtually ignored me, which was fine as far as I was concerned. She only had eyes for Henley, and now and again for Mr Beauford, who looked delighted to have awakened and found these two young women were his house guests. I wondered if he'd want to rush me out of the way now that he had more company. I told myself it really didn't matter, since that's what had to happen anyway.

Now and again, Henley looked in my direction and shrugged just enough for me to notice, as if to say, *What can I do? I didn't see this coming.* In order to escape Christine's nearly non-stop chatter, he made it a point to include Eliza in the conversation, and as she was seated beside him, this was easily accomplished. Christine was directly across from Henley, to the left of Mr Beauford at the head of the table, with Henley on his right. I sat on the other side of Eliza, despite the fact Wilchester had indicated I should sit by Christine. I looked at him as if to say, *I think not!* and that was that. Poor Mr Lawrence got the dubious honour of sitting to Christine's left, and of being essentially ignored as a result.

Mr Beauford was laughing at one of Christine's inane stories about how life on their plantation in Virginia was idyllic yet, at the same time, dreadfully boring to her. 'I just long for the sophistication of city life.' She leaned towards him and patted his hand. Old as he was, I could see that Mr Beauford wasn't immune to a pretty woman's charms. He turned his hand palm upwards beneath hers and squeezed her hand in a fatherly way.

'Well, then, it's a good thing your family and I made the arrangement we did several years back. It won't be long now, son, eh?' He clapped Henley's shoulder with his other hand. It was obvious that the Porter sisters' arrival had cheered him up; so much so that he appeared to have forgotten the shock and unpleasantness that had passed between him and me that very morning. I was naturally relieved and grateful for that unexpected benefit of their presence. *But what's this 'arrangement' he's referring to?* I wondered.

Henley didn't reply, just smiled at his father, then Christine, then quickly looked at me over Eliza's head and had the audacity to cross his eyes! Ever the prankster, his boyish silliness endeared him to me all the more. I was pretty sure I understood Mr Beauford's statement, but would wait and ask Eliza about it later, as I had absolutely won her confidence. I knew I'd rather hear it from her than from Henley's lips.

Christine was already on to her next point. 'Yes, and once we're settled with all of that, it will be ever so wonderful, I know.' She leaned even closer to the older man and had the brazenness to ask, 'How much money did your steel business make this year, Uncle Charles?'

I'd figured out that she addressed him as 'uncle' out of respect, as a long-term friend of the family, but that they weren't blood relations. I focused on my meal of pheasant and fresh vegetables, and only periodically made a brief response when Eliza asked me a question. I could tell that she felt special, seated between Henley and me, and I was glad for her to have some extra attention. I instinctively knew that when she was at home, she was definitely not in the spotlight. That was the place Christine had carved out for herself with her family, and indeed wherever she went.

Unobtrusively, I took note of Mr Beauford's response to Christine's materialistic enquiry. It wasn't really like eavesdropping, since it was nearly impossible not to over-hear every word that was said at the dining room table.

'Oh, my dear, it has been a banner year in many ways. Isn't that right, Lawrence?' He asked for his protégé's 'yes man' response, which he promptly received.

'That's quite right, Mr Beauford, sir. Best year we've had to date, as a matter of fact,' he added to no one in particular, since no one but me was looking in his direction. He sighed and went back to savouring his meal.

'That must be a lot of money, then,' Christine persisted.

Wanting to take part in the conversation again, Eliza chimed in. 'God is always watching, and he will always reward the good.'

Christine didn't miss a beat in scoffing rather loudly, 'If God's always watching, he'd have given me a new fur coat by now.' She cocked her head coyly and looked around the table to see if anyone agreed. 'Mink, to be exact.'

I leaned towards Eliza who, like me, had finished eating. Eliza certainly heard her sister's comment but didn't respond, choosing instead to use the back of her fork to push her leftover food around her plate.

'Do you feel up to sitting on the back porch and talking for a bit after dinner?' I asked her. 'Maybe we could enjoy a cup of tea, if you like? I understand if you're too tired from your trip today, and all, and would rather retire for the evening.'

Her face lit up once again. 'Oh, that would be wonderful,' she responded. Then she sat up straight and raised her voice to address all those at the table. 'This has been a wonderful dinner, and I thank you so much for having us here, Mr Beauford, Henley, but when you've all finished your food, I'd like to excuse myself and retire outside to have Rebecca all to myself.' She giggled.

Mr Beauford was quick to excuse both Eliza and me with a wave of his hand. I suspected he was even fonder of Eliza than he let on. 'No, no. You mustn't wait for us. You girls run along now, if you've finished.'

Henley, Mr Beauford and Mr Lawrence all stood up to excuse us womenfolk. Christine looked greatly relieved that she would now be the only female left, surrounded by males – her favourite audience.

I asked Nellie to go and fetch a shawl to wrap around Eliza's shoulders, and to please bring us both a nice hot cup of tea with some honey and lemon on a tray. She nodded quickly and bustled off, while I gently guided Eliza along the back hall and out onto the house's rear porch. The moon was full this night and the stars quite beautiful. I almost commented upon it, but realized it might be cruel to talk of something Eliza couldn't enjoy. However, it was almost as though she'd read my mind.

'Describe the night sky to me, please, Rebecca,' she entreated.

'Very well,' I agreed. 'The moon is waxing full and bright. Every star of the Big Dipper is easy to see, and Orion's Belt is clearly defined.' I was somewhat surprised to find that I could name all the constellations. Must have been something Cynthia had learned, long ago, that had somehow stayed imprinted in my memory. It was fascinating to me what bits and pieces surfaced now and again, like my recollection earlier that day of Cynthia hearing someone whistle one of Beethoven's tunes.

'Oh, it must be lovely.' Eliza sighed. 'You describe it so well. Have you always had a great interest in astronomy?' she enquired.

'I suppose so, yes,' I answered truthfully. I really couldn't recall that for a fact, so I figured supposing was the most accurate way to describe it. I decided to elaborate a bit more, since Eliza appeared to enjoy it so much. 'Um, the light breeze you feel ruffling through your hair is causing the leaves to dance slowly on the limbs of the trees. Not quite strong enough to force them to abandon ship, but just to wave at us a bit.'

This brought a smile to Eliza's lips, and I knew she was visualizing the scene in her mind's eye. I could only imagine what it must be like to have to live without sight. I admired this young woman greatly, more determined than ever to enhance her stay in any way possible.

Nellie brought our tea, and we drank in companionable silence for a while before Eliza spoke again. 'I often wonder about travelling into space,' she murmured, more to herself than to me. 'And ever since I read Jules Verne, I wonder about the possibility of time travel ...'

I coughed to cover the quick exhalation that the shock of her statement had forced out of me. Of everything Eliza could have possibly brought up, her choice of time travel was almost more than I could handle. I decided to excuse myself, lest my trembling voice tip my hand or cause her any distress.

'Eliza, dear, I'm feeling a bit tired all of a sudden. I must excuse myself, I fear. Will you be all right out here for a bit longer on your own? I can ask Nellie to attend to you, should you need another cup of tea, or—'

She gently waved me away. 'I'll be fine, Rebecca. Take care of yourself. I'm quite used to being on my own, and in fact, I rather enjoy it. I know the servants here will keep an eye on me, and that's nice.' She turned to look up towards my face, and I swore for a moment that we could really see one another, and even more than that, into each other's souls, somehow. 'I'll see you tomorrow. Sleep well, my new friend.' She extended her hand to me, and I pressed it between my own.

'Thank you, and you rest well, too. I've truly enjoyed meeting you, and look forward to talking more with you tomorrow.' I meant what I said, but for now I had to get to my room to collect my thoughts and emotions.

I hurried down the hall and was just rounding the banister at the top of the stairs when Henley stepped out of the shadows from the doorway next to mine. I nearly shrieked with fright, given that I was already shaken up, but I coughed again to cover my surprise.

'I'm sorry to have alarmed you,' he said. 'You look as though you've seen a ghost!'

'You have no idea,' I mumbled, and continued walking towards my own doorway. 'Have a good night, Henley. I'm quite exhausted, I'm afraid. I don't mean to be rude, but can we talk tomorrow, please? That is, if you can tear yourself away from Miss Christine's charms …' I batted my eyelashes at him, mimicking her, and he nearly chortled aloud. He shushed himself, though, for Christine's room was just on the opposite side of the stairway from mine.

214

'I hope you know, Rebecca, that I'd far rather be spending time with you than with her. I truly didn't expect their arrival …' He was at a bit of a loss, for once. I felt sorry for him and quickly squeezed his hand.

'I know you didn't. I read the surprise on your face. I know you well enough by now to at least be able to do that,' I assured him. 'It will all be fine, and things will look brighter in the morning. Do get some sleep and I shall do the same. Good night,' I said softly and closed my door behind me.

As I sat on the edge of my bed, pulling off my shoes and then my clothes, I wondered where Eliza found her faith in God. I wasn't even sure if I believed in a Higher Power of any kind now, or remember how much I'd believed in one before. *If such a thing truly exists, why has he abandoned me, and left me in such strange circumstances?* I wondered.

I splashed some water on my face and then went into the bathroom to brush my teeth. I pulled on the nightgown Nellie had laid out for me over the top of the trunk at the foot of my bed, as was her routine. When I stretched out, lay back and closed my eyes, the last thing I remember thinking was, *If someone is watching over Eliza, is anyone watching over me?*

Chapter 21

The days blended into a week, and soon we were into the second week of the Porter sisters' visit. The nagging feeling I'd been experiencing for a while now had escalated from a vague sense of uneasiness to an ever-present reminder that I was an unwelcome stranger here. My body knew things weren't right, that I needed to travel in time again, and Miss Hatfield's warning played constantly in my mind. If I hadn't known better, I'd have thought I was going insane. Maybe I was. Whatever the case, I knew I had to finish my assignment, and soon.

Henley and I barely had a moment to exchange pleasantries, let alone hatch a plan for disposing of Mr Beauford's immortality artefacts and securing the painting. Henley's time was spent either with his father, Mr Lawrence or, mostly, Christine, and I knew the hours he tolerated with her were an attempt to placate his father's desire to push them together.

One day shortly after lunchtime, I was visiting Eliza in her room. She'd confided in me that, as I'd suspected, Henley and Christine had been all but betrothed since they were both about thirteen years old. The 'arrangement' Mr Beauford had mentioned that first night at dinner didn't exactly require a brain surgeon's intellect to figure out. When Eliza told me this, she said, 'Oh, yes, it's been an understanding between our families for a while. Mr Beauford borrowed some money from my father many years ago, before his steel business really took off. When it did, he paid Father back with interest, and they've been fast friends ever since. Now our fortune's a bit down on its luck, and Henley's marriage to Christine will keep both families … well, able to live in the style to which they've become accustomed.'

It was interesting that she spoke about the whole affair as if she wasn't really a part of it, and I understood why she probably felt that way. She was speaking in a relatively detached manner as she sat there, periodically moving her rocking chair back and forth as though to comfort herself a bit. I decided to ask her a question that had been pressing upon my mind since we'd first become friends.

'Eliza, how is it that you still have such a strong faith in God after all you've been through? I can't help but notice that your sister doesn't appear to share that belief … Just an observation I made when listening to Christine at dinner a few nights ago,' I added quickly, so as not to sound rude, but I needn't have worried.

Eliza laughed lightly. 'I'm afraid my sister's God is her own beauty and what money can do for her. I've always pitied her, really, because neither of those things will last for ever. Only the soul does that.' She paused to reflect a bit before addressing the first part of my query. 'Rebecca, I would have to say that my faith in God is so strong because I've always believed that my time here on earth will most likely be short. I feel that I'll be gone before I'm twenty, and in many ways I rather relish that thought.' She smiled peacefully, and I knew she was speaking her truth.

'But won't your family miss you terribly?' I blurted out, already knowing the answer.

She laughed again, and reached out to take my hand in hers. 'Rebecca, they barely notice I'm here now. How much more convenient it will be for them when I'm no longer around for them to worry about in any way, shape or form.' She squeezed my hand, but continued to hold it for a while. 'That's the way it is. I've known for many years now that no one loves me more than God the Father, Jesus the Son and the beloved Holy Ghost. Many angels have ministered to me since my sight disappeared. Even though I get lonely at times for physical company, I'm never really alone.' She released my hand, with one final comforting squeeze. 'Please don't misunderstand me – I'm very grateful to be able to call you my friend. I don't shun earthly companionship; it's simply that so little of it has been available to me for so long, I find I believe more in what lies on the other side of the veil than in this world.' She sighed contentedly, and rocked in her chair again.

'Eliza, I have tremendous respect for you,' I said honestly. 'You're an inspiration, and anyone who doesn't take the time to know and understand you is a fool, plain and simple.' I was shocked a bit by the vehemence of my statement, but it came from deep within me, and I meant every word.

She blushed, just a little. 'Why, Rebecca, that's one of the nicest things anyone has ever said to me. Thank you so very much.' She smiled as though she'd just been given an amazing gift.

'Well, it's true,' I added, as a way to wrap up that conversation. The odd feeling in the pit of my stomach was back suddenly, more persistent than ever. I must be very close to the point where I needed to time-travel again. I'd never felt so ... so *unnatural* before, as if I didn't belong here, or any place in the world.

I had to excuse myself from Eliza's presence and find some way for me to reground. Henley and I still hadn't made any plans, so I determined right then and there that I must find a way to do Miss Hatfield's bidding on my own. 'I have some writing I must do,' I fibbed, in an attempt to leave graciously. 'I'll see you tonight at dinner, all right?'

'Thank you, dear Rebecca,' she called after me. 'Enjoy your writing, and I look forward to seeing you at dinner.' She waved and I waved back, knowing that even though she couldn't see it, she somehow felt it. I gently pulled her door closed and went upstairs to ponder and plan.

Back in my room I began my pacing routine, which really did appear to help me focus and calm down more than just about anything else I'd tried. It relaxed me nearly as much as that day spent by the mill stream, skipping rocks with Henley. That was the most openly relaxed I'd been since my arrival at the estate. Pacing wasn't quite the same, but it appeared to help my heart beat normally, and to clear my head.

'Very well, if Henley can't help me, I understand,' I told myself. 'He's got his hands full with this obligation of marriage to Christine, poor boy.' I felt a pang of something like jealousy about that, but ... jealousy didn't quite describe the feeling. I knew Henley and I could never be together in a romantic way; if I'd been foolish enough to give in to his advances prior to the Porter girls' arrival, well, that would have been a sticky situation indeed. And I couldn't bear to think about breaking his heart when I told him the truth, or just disappeared from his life altogether when the pressing need in my stomach became too much to bear. So my feelings towards their engagement weren't so much jealousy as anger and a certain sadness at being deprived of any sense of normalcy in the crazy immortal life I'd been swept up in.

I felt sorry for him, truth be told, having to marry that chatterbox Christine. Yes, she was beautiful, but her head was full of air, vanity and nonsensical small talk. She and her sister were so opposite in character and temperament. I believed in many ways it was Christine who couldn't see the real side of life. Anyone who could ignore their own sister, not to mention the brilliant mind Eliza so clearly possessed ... Christine was the one who was truly blind. That was the most appropriate word for it. Strangely, I found myself pitying Christine a bit as well, even though I knew she'd find it next to impossible to understand why anyone could possibly pity her.

But despite all my rationalizations, were I truly honest with myself, it wouldn't be the persistent discomfort in my stomach that would drive me away. At least that wasn't painful, just a dull, nagging ache. It was nothing compared to what I felt when I saw Henley laughing together with Christine on his arm. Henley looked so happy ... and it hurt.

I'd endured that agony because I knew Henley's rightful place was at Christine's side. But in that instant, a part of me broke. I just couldn't take it any more. I decided I would have to act that night.

As soon as I was sure everyone had gone to bed, I planned to sneak into the study, destroy everything in Mr Beauford's archive pertaining to immortality and make away with the painting. I hadn't been riding Thunder so much just because I loved him. I cared for the horse, to be sure, and was grateful he'd allowed me to become comfortable riding him at a good gallop, but all along we'd actually been rehearsing my getaway. Unbeknown to Wellesley, Henley or anyone else, I'd ridden Thunder at least three times at night during the past week, to get him used to being out with me. It was easier than I'd anticipated to creep out of the house through the back entrance when everyone, including the servants, was asleep. All I had to do was slip out without making a noise loud enough to wake anyone. I'd even taken a painting from my own room with me a couple of times, to make sure I could control the reins with one hand and hold the painting with the other while we made haste into the city. I could and I did – more comfortably than I'd dared think possible, as a matter of fact. We'd be travelling tonight with only the moon and stars to light our path, but the sky was clear, and I believed it would be absolutely safe.

I felt confident I'd be successful tonight. Once I reached the city, I was going to leave Thunder somewhere safe with a note I'd already composed in his saddlebag, stating that he belonged to the Beaufords and needed to be returned to their country house immediately; that a family friend had borrowed him due to an emergency in order to catch the first train out of the city. I was proud of myself for having created this scheme without Henley's help. I wished I could tell him the details, but I knew it would distract him from what he really needed to do, which was to get on with his own life.

Suddenly I heard running in the downstairs hallway, clearly several people moving all at once. I heard Henley's voice call, 'I'm coming, Father – hold on!' and then the running stopped. Concerned, I made my way downstairs and towards Mr Beauford's room as quickly as my feet could fly.

Chapter 22

When I arrived at the old gentleman's door, it was closed but not completely shut. This meant I couldn't see everyone who was in there with Mr Beauford and Henley, but I could hear much of what was said without intruding too much on their privacy.

'What were you thinking, overdoing it like that? You know you can't do everything you once were able to do.'

'Son, I'm dying.' I winced at Mr Beauford's raspy voice and the bluntness of his words. 'I'm dying. I know it.' He paused, trying to catch his breath. 'Henley, send for the chaplain again.'

'Hold on, Father, the physician should be here within the hour.'

'No.' Mr Beauford's voice was suddenly surprisingly strong. 'My chaplain,' he demanded. 'A physician can't help me now.' He wheezed out a breath and said more softly, 'All I can do now is prepare to meet my creator.'

'Wilchester's already driven the automobile into town to bring the physician back here,' Henley said, talking over his father as if he couldn't hear what he said. His voice was low and calm to reassure him, but I could hear just the trace of a quaver in it.

I felt torn; part of me wanted to rush in to be at their side, but I knew that wasn't my place. It was mainly Henley

I wanted to comfort, but, in a strange way, I did care about Mr Beauford, too. I certainly didn't want him to die, not while Henley still appeared to need his support so much.

I heard Eloise's voice say soothingly, 'Now, now, Mr B, you need some chicken broth to keep your strength up. I'll go and fetch a nice cup of that for you, and you must drink a lot of water, too.' She clucked her tongue on her way towards the door, as though she knew her advice was likely to be ignored. I quickly stepped aside to stand more within the hallway so as not to appear to be eavesdropping.

'Miss.' Eloise nodded as she passed me and headed towards the kitchen. I nodded back at her, then followed her to see if I could locate Nellie or young Hannah. Neither of them was to be found, so I asked Eloise if she knew their whereabouts.

'No, mum, I don't, to be sure,' she replied. 'But I have a feeling that perhaps Miss Christine has enlisted their services in some way. If I had to guess, that is,' she added as she began preparing Mr Beauford's chicken broth.

'Thank you, Eloise,' I said as I hurried out of the kitchen, unsure where to go next. *Eliza!* I thought, and headed towards her room. I knew she'd have heard the commotion and would probably be worried. I knocked lightly and said her name, and she called out for me to enter.

I went in and sat down by her side and quickly brought her up to speed regarding Mr Beauford's health. Once I'd told her what little I'd been able to deduce, I added, 'I'm afraid he's taken a turn for the worse, Eliza. He's asked for his chaplain and the doctor's on his way. I knew you'd be wondering what the hubbub was all about.'

'Thank you for coming to tell me, Rebecca, but I guessed what was going on. I've been up here saying prayers for Mr Beauford ever since I heard the first steps running down the hallway.' Her face was radiant, as though her prayers had pulled some Divine Illumination down from the heavens and filled her up. I stood to leave, but she called out to me. 'You should know that Christine can't bear to be around people who are ill. When I had scarlet fever, our parents shipped her away to stay with relatives because she gets so upset whenever anyone's sick. I think she may have taken one or two of the servants with her and headed out in the carriage. I'm sure I heard it leave, and I don't know who else might have taken it. I don't know where she might have gone, but I'd suspect to a rooming house in the local town somewhere. She's quite a coward.' She almost smirked.

I realized that not only did Eliza pity her sister in some ways, she was also repulsed by her in others. 'Thank you for telling me that, Eliza – I'll let the others know where she's likely to have gone, just so they don't worry about her.'

'Oh, people would be wasting their time worrying about her,' she muttered. 'She always lands on her feet.' Then she looked right at me and raised the volume of her voice to make sure I heard every word that followed. 'I've only told you this so you can comfort Henley in her absence. I know she's kept the two of you apart. I can't see how he looks at you, but I can feel it and hear it in his voice when he talks to you. He needs support now more than ever, and she runs away. Truly a coward,' she added with disgust.

'Thanks, Eliza,' I called over my shoulder as I headed out, running nearly headlong into Henley, who was obviously looking for me.

'There you are,' he said, and without thinking, we embraced.

'I'm so sorry, Henley,' I said. 'I know your father's ill—'

'Yes, I assumed you did. Would you like to take a walk with me? I could use some fresh air.' He stepped back, but I could tell he was a bit calmer after having connected with me.

'Of course – just let me grab my cloak, as it's nearly sundown.' I darted into my room, snatched up my cloak and closed the door behind me as I exited. 'Let's go.'

As we walked, Henley's demeanour grew noticeably more peaceful. I thought he would want to speak about his father's condition, but he was more focused on convincing me how much he'd missed me the past few days. I didn't want to hear this; I was still determined to make my getaway that evening, and becoming all worked up emotionally was not going to make that any easier. The sensation in my stomach pulsed and throbbed, making me feel unnatural and strange. I knew I couldn't delay much longer.

'Henley, please, can we simply talk about your father? This isn't easy for me, and I know it's hard for you on so many levels. I must leave tonight, my friend.' I looked up into his eyes. 'I have it all planned out. You'd be proud of me, putting it all together on my own—'

I was startled to see his knees buckle beneath him as he fell to the ground, holding his head in his hands and openly sobbing. I immediately sat down beside him, putting my arms around him and rocking him like a small child. 'There, there,' I said, 'shh, shh, now, it's going to be all right.'

He was sobbing less, but still finding it hard to catch his breath as we rocked slowly back and forth. 'I … I simply couldn't bear it if you left tonight, Rebecca. That would be the cruellest blow of all. Not tonight, I beg you.' His soft sobs began again, and I couldn't stand to think of hurting him any more, not with his father's death so imminent. He must have been taken more severely ill than I'd guessed.

'Of course I won't leave you now,' I consoled him. 'I don't know what I was thinking. Very, very selfish of me. I cooked up the scheme earlier, before your father fell ill. I was just determined to carry it out tonight, no matter what. I'm so sorry. I give you my word that I'll not leave until you feel stronger.' I wasn't sure how long I could last before I absolutely had to go, but surely I could withstand the pain for one more night, at least.

Henley's sobs had stopped and he sat up. I pulled out my handkerchief from my sleeve and dabbed at his tear-stained face. He grabbed my hand, and before I knew it, we were kissing passionately, seated right there on the ground. I wanted to stop, but I wanted to continue more. I'd never been kissed like this before, so I didn't have anything to compare it to. It was as if the kiss itself was made of fire and it burned right through to my very core. For that moment in time, there was no one and nothing but me and my beloved Henley. Inexperienced as I was in matters of the heart, something told me this kiss was extraordinary, and that was why I had to pull away.

I was totally lost in the moment, lost in my love for him, but still aware I mustn't make any promises I knew I couldn't keep, and this kiss was one of them. Something within me snapped and I realized I had to stop him – stop *us* – from making a grievous error. I pulled away, disengaging myself from his arms. It was the hardest thing I'd ever had to do.

'What's wrong?' he asked, reaching to pull me back to him. 'Oh, my sweetheart, my dearest – I'm mad about you. I love you, Rebecca, and I know you love me. I've never been kissed that way before. And I never want to be kissed by anyone other than you ever again.'

I knew I loved him, too – in fact my body fairly ached for him; but things had already progressed much further into the danger zone than I'd ever wished or intended to allow. I got up and held out both hands towards him, keeping him at arm's length.

'We must stop, Henley. This is getting out of control,' I warned.

Standing and moving closer to me once again, he smiled his devilish grin. 'That's how I want it – don't you, Rebecca? We've had to be in control so much of our lives. Let's say hang it all and just do what we want, and everyone else be damned.' His eyes were flashing with excitement, and I knew I could give in to his wishes all too easily unless I put some distance between us, and quickly. He began to come closer and I felt my knees go weak, but my elbows somehow got the springs back in them and pushed him away, hard. I decided if he believed I was angry, he'd respect my wishes.

'Stop it now!' I commanded and pushed him again, this time so hard that he lost his balance and sat down on the ground. He was obviously shocked.

'Rebecca, love, how have I offended you?' he asked, hanging his head in shame. 'I've hurt you, and I'm–I'm so sorry.'

'You're going to marry Christine! Isn't that your inten-tion? She's gorgeous, wealthy, your father approves … That's who you're betrothed to, and that's who you shall marry. You'll always belong to her.' I hoped my angry act had fooled him. He did look bewildered at first, but then he burst into laughter.

'You think Christine's perfect? Her head is full of nothing but air; she drives me insane with the continual drivel that spouts from that so-called perfect rouged mouth of hers. She babbles incessantly and I detest that. I no more intend to marry her than I would marry Wilchester!' he declared. 'I've just been placating Father, to make him happy. But I assure you, there's no way I shall ever walk down the aisle with that creature who you appear to think is the epitome of perfection.'

While he was talking, I started walking back towards the house, knowing he wouldn't dare show physical affection to me once we were within sight of the servants. 'Well, that's all well and good for you to say now,' I threw back over my shoulder, 'but you and I don't belong together, no matter what. It simply can never be.'

At that, he ran around and blocked my progress, making eye contact with me but this time respectfully keeping his hands to himself. 'You can't fool me, Rebecca,' he said softly. 'I meant it when I told you I've never been kissed like that before. I felt it surging from the tips of my toes, all the way up my body until my hair felt like it was standing on end. And I know you felt it, too. It's impossible you couldn't have. I don't love Christine. Even if I'd never met you, that would still be God's honest truth. But from the first moment I laid eyes upon you, my darling, darling Rebecca, my heart has belonged to no other. How could you not know that?'

I took a deep breath. I was afraid I might start crying and lose my resolve, so I quickly pushed my way around him and began running towards the house.

'Tell me you love me, too, Rebecca. I know you do. Please, please say it …' Standing helplessly on the path some thirty yards from the house, he called after me desperately. I ran up the stairs to the porch, shaking my head and sobbing angry tears, determined not to stop until I'd reached the relative safety of my bedroom and locked the door; feeling ashamed that I'd broken my promise to myself never to let our relationship get to this point, and terrified at what I'd have to do next.

Chapter 23

The following morning, I took my breakfast in my room. Nellie, who had at least temporarily escaped from Christine's demands, brought me my tray when I told her I was ill and didn't want to intrude upon everyone else. I don't know whether she believed that or not, but I didn't really care. I wasn't ready to see Henley yet, and didn't know if I ever would be. The only time I ventured out was to go down the hallway to Eliza's room, just to let her know I hadn't abandoned her. She asked about Henley, but I found ways to change the subject pretty quickly, only commenting that I'd heard Mr Beauford was holding his own. Nellie had told me that, since Mr Beauford had taken a turn for the worst last night, Father Gabriel barely left his side. She said the family physician floated in and out of the old man's room several times a day, usually shaking his head from side to side as though he didn't know what else he could do, and that Mr Beauford might depart at any moment.

'Then I shall continue to pray for him, I swear,' Eliza said, 'and for Henley, of course. I pray for you, too, Rebecca,' she said softly, 'even though I don't think you believe in the power of prayer. Or maybe even in God.' She paused. 'I've come to love you as a sister, Rebecca, and God loves you, too, more than you know. You've brought me much

230

comfort, and I'll be forever grateful for having met you. I'll see you in heaven someday, I know it. It doesn't matter whether you believe or not, you see,' she added. 'God loves you either way.' Then she fell silent, and I could see her lips moving in inaudible prayer. I left her room quietly.

If she only knew that I was the one thing God didn't intend to create. I was coming to believe that my very existence went against nature itself, and for that I knew I would not be welcome anywhere.

I had no sooner returned to my room when I heard a gentle knock at the door. It was Henley. His voice held such a tone of entreaty that I couldn't help but lean against the inside of the door as I imagined he was leaning up against the outside. 'Rebecca, please. Rebecca, won't you please come out? I need you. I promise not to touch you. Please? Father has asked to see me, and the doctor says it's most urgent. I must go to him now, and I'd like to have you by my side.' His voice caught in his throat. 'If I ask nothing of you ever again, would you please come downstairs with me now?'

How could I not open the door after that? I took a deep breath and very slowly looked outside. He looked dishevelled in a way I'd never expected to see my handsome Henley. He had what Cynthia's father used to call a dark five o'clock shadow, and I knew he hadn't shaved for at least two days. His clothes were all rumpled, and I could swear he must have slept in them. I didn't care. He was still my Henley, and he needed me. I reached up and smoothed down his hair a bit.

'We can't have you going in to see your father looking this rough.' I clucked my tongue. 'I'll go with you, yes, of course.' And though I'd promised myself I wouldn't say it to him, I knew it was the only thing that would give him the strength to go and see his father upon his deathbed. I took a deep breath and said, 'And yes, Henley, you're right.'

He looked at me with a puzzled expression. 'Right about what?'

'That I love you, Henley,' I said very softly. 'But we must away to your father now. We'll talk about that later.' I took his hand, more like a playmate than a lover. 'Come along, now.'

We descended the stairs like that. There was no passion flying between us as there had been the last time we were together, only the familiar comfort of being in the company of a good friend, as it had been at the beginning of our acquaintance.

When we arrived at Mr Beauford's door, Henley motioned that I should come inside. I'd have preferred to stay in the hallway, but his eyes implored me. I sat upon a small chair close to the door where Henley could see me, but Mr Beauford would be unaware of my presence. Father Gabriel gave Henley a nod in my direction, as if to question why I was in the room, but Henley merely held a finger to his lips to tell him not to let his father know I was present. Father Gabriel nodded to me as he left the room, so now it was only Henley and his father, with me watching from a distance.

'Henley, my dear boy,' Mr Beauford began in a quaking voice.

'I'm here, Father,' Henley said, taking his father's trembling hand.

'Please sit down, son,' the old man continued. 'There are things you must know before I die. Things I've withheld from you for far too long.'

Henley's face creased with concern as he pulled a chair close to his father's bedside.

struggled, but soon agreed when I swore on my life that I would raise you as my own.' He looked up at the ceiling again, as if to let whoever he'd spoken with just before know he'd be joining them very shortly. 'When morning came she was gone, leaving you behind. She'd written me a note, asking me to keep true to my promise if I'd ever loved her. I sent the police looking for her – I didn't know what she was going to do and I was scared at the possibilities, but they never found her. She was presumed dead, although they never found a body. They thought it might have been suicide, but that's not Ruth. Not her. But you see, Henley, I'd promised your mother that I would take care of you for the rest of your life. I said I'd make sure you didn't go without anything, but I know I haven't provided the emotional support you needed. I know that now, son.'

Henley visibly jerked back upon hearing the word 'son', as though it was a dagger in his heart. He hadn't said a word this entire time, and I knew he'd forgotten I was witnessing the whole thing as well. Now he only asked one simple question. 'What was my real father's name?'

'Benton,' answered Mr Beauford. 'Your parents were George and Ruth Benton.' He paused for a moment, because his voice was growing steadily weaker and softer. 'I have to tell you, Henley, that though I've done my best to provide everything you've needed in the way of food, clothes, shelter and education, when Ruth … went away, I became obsessed with finding the secret to escaping death, so that I could keep on looking for her. I know she's still alive, still looks exactly the same as she did that first night I met you. It's as if she's managed to stop time. And I know your mother's waiting for me – I've seen her. I've seen her right there!' Mr Beauford feebly pointed towards the window, but Henley didn't even glance in that direction.

Henley's lips turned pale as he saw Mr Beauford get riled up, but the old man was blind to everything but the vision only he could see. He continued as Henley shut his eyes.

'Ruth's waiting for me. I just had to beat death. That was all I had to do.' Mr Beauford's hands started to shake as they clasped each other, as if hoping to find comfort. 'Son, I'm dying. And only now do I realize I've wasted my entire life in the pursuit of this folly.' I saw Henley cringe again at the word 'son'. 'All I want is your forgiveness. I should have been focusing my attention on you, since you were the only part of Ruth that remained here on this earth. You, my son—'

Henley angrily jumped to his feet. 'I am *not* your son! You … you old *hypocrite*!' he screamed. Mr Beauford shook his head as if he didn't understand the words Henley was using. 'You're nothing but a liar. You just use everyone around you … If you see my mother in the afterlife, tell her she should be happy that she left when she did.' He stormed out of the room, not even seeing me. The force of his anger nearly pushed me off my chair in his wake.

'Son – Henley!'

I glanced back to see Mr Beauford sink into his pillows. Buried in a mound of comforters, he looked like a small child; vulnerable and afraid of something he didn't know and couldn't understand. I shut my eyes, trying to rid myself of that image. So this was death.

Chapter 24

Dazed by everything Mr Beauford had just revealed, I went outside to take some deep breaths of fresh air. I could only imagine the intense shock Henley was experiencing. He'd fled to his room and bolted the door behind him. I knew because I'd tried to follow him after telling the doctor to go in and tend to Mr Beauford. When I tapped at Henley's door, I heard the bolt slide shut.

Knowing Henley needed time to process everything he'd just heard, I went to the stables and had a chat with Bessie. Wellesley wasn't around, so I could talk freely rather than whispering to her as I had many times before. I told her all about Mr Beauford's deception of Henley, about Henley's disillusionment now that his entire world had been turned upside down. I told her that I'd fallen deeply in love with Henley, but that it was an utterly hopeless situation from which I must extricate myself, and the sooner, the better. She snorted at that, as if agreeing with me. I fed her a carrot and stroked her soft nose for a couple of minutes before heading back to the main house.

I walked slowly, wondering how Henley was feeling now. Nearly an hour had passed, but I knew this was something that might take him a lifetime to get over. I wanted to help him, but had absolutely no idea how. Once inside the house, I aimlessly wandered from the parlour to the kitchen, unsure of where I was going or what I would do. I found myself once again outside Henley's door. I was about to knock when I thought better of it and started to step away, but then I heard the sound of muffled sobs coming from within. I knocked on the door and called softly, 'Henley, dearest, please open the door. Is there anything at all I can do to help you?'

I stood there, praying he would open up and let me see him, though I had no clue what I could possibly say that might make his hurt any less. 'Henley, darling … please just let me see you. I'm not going away until you open the door.'

I heard him blow his nose and knew he was trying to make himself a bit more presentable. I couldn't have cared less what he looked like at that moment. I just wanted to hold him and comfort him. But when he opened the door, his eyes were red and bloodshot from crying, and he had the look of a defeated man about him. His shoulders were slumped, so unlike his usual sharp posture.

Regardless, I took a step towards him, thinking to give him a sisterly hug to reassure him, but he recoiled from me the same way he had from his father when Mr Beauford had last called him 'son'.

'What do you want? I don't want your pity, for God's sake,' he growled. His voice sounded like gravel. He flung the door open wider. 'Come in, if you're that reckless. I'm not a pretty sight, and I won't be for some time to come.' He crossed to his writing table, where two snifters and a carafe of brandy stood. 'Would you join me in a drink?' he asked with false gaiety, waving me towards a chair.

I shook my head no. 'I'm afraid I'm not a drinker,' I said softly. 'But I completely understand if you need to drown your sorrow—'

A guttural laugh escaped him; unlike his carefree belly laugh that he favoured me with sometimes, this laugh had an air of danger about it, and it frightened me. 'Drown? What a cruel choice of words, considering my dear daddy drowned at sea.' He began pouring himself a snifter of the brown liquid, then thought better of it and took a deep swig directly from the carafe. He ambled over to sit on the bed, dangling his legs over the edge of the mattress as he faced me, holding the carafe at calf-level in both hands. I'd never expected to see him like this. I had no idea what to say next, for fear that anything I came up with would set him off again.

He took another long pull from the carafe. 'You know, "Rebecca"—' and now his voice dripped with sarcasm '—if that's even truly your name, because something tells me it's not ...' He smacked his lips and had another drink. 'You know, Miss Righteous Honour— Are you afraid you'll be disgraced by kissing me and having me marry another?' He laughed at his own wit. 'That's a fine name for you, let's change it to that, what do you say? Miss Whoever You Are, I don't expect you to understand this at all, because I surely do not, but I have absolutely no idea who I am right now. Which really makes us perfect for one another, my sweet, because I don't know who the hell you are, either. And neither do you, I suspect.' He was getting drunk rapidly, and hitting closer to the truth than he could possibly know. I wanted to leave, but was frozen there in my chair.

'You needn't worry about me disgracing your reputation,' he mumbled as he set the carafe on the floor and began to unbutton his shirt. 'I can't even stand right now, much less do anything to a delicate flower such as you. All that's left is for me to sleep this off.' He fell back on his bed, then turned onto his side and looked at me with a terrible sadness in his beautiful eyes. 'Go on, get out of here, before I embarrass myself further. I must look a sight.' With that, he rolled onto his back and almost at once fell into a deep, if troubled, sleep. I crossed over to him, pulled his shoes off and covered him up with a blanket.

'Yes, you are a sorry sight at the moment, Henley,' I said as I gently kissed his forehead, 'but I still love you.' I quietly made my way out of his room, hoping he would fall asleep to numb his pain, though I was certain he'd be hung over whenever he did awake.

Chapter 25

The next morning, I chose to have breakfast in my room once again. I knew Henley's head would be throbbing from his hangover and didn't want to cause him more pain on any level; he needed time to sort things out for himself. As was my wont these past few days, I saddled up Thunder and went for a ride, but took my time about it. I breathed deeply, and when we got close to the old mill, I dropped the reins and let Thunder walk wherever he chose. This wonderful horse and I had formed a mutual admiration society now. We trusted one another. I extended my arms straight out to either side and did my best to embrace the day. I was desperately attempting to feel alive in this moment, focused, even if only for a short while. The pangs in my stomach had increased throughout the night, and I knew this was a signal that I didn't have long left in this reality.

'There, Thunder, good boy,' I murmured as we stopped under the spreading branches of one of the trees. I dismounted and let the horse help himself to some grass. I knew he wouldn't take off, and even if he did, a long walk back to the estate wouldn't hurt me. However, I was loath to return for other reasons. I'd been awakened by a dream that Mr Beauford had died in the night. Yet when I descended the stairs to slip out for my ride, no one was astir in the house. The intuitive feeling only grew stronger, though, and I knew at the core of my being that when I got back, the old gentleman would have passed on.

I skipped a couple of rocks over the water, going over my memories of my short time with Henley. I knew I was procrastinating, delaying my inevitable return to the house. Growing bored after a while, I sat down where Henley and I had sat when we visited this lovely spot. Closing my eyes, I tried to relive that innocent day, but I kept feeling waves of desire pulse through me as the scene of our kiss a few nights ago washed over my memory and sent shivers through my body. The pain in my stomach was slightly muffled by these pangs, but it remained ever present, ever growing.

'Now, Rebecca,' I told myself out loud, 'or whatever my name is these days, you *must* relinquish such feelings for Henley. They'll only frustrate you more, and cloud your judgement. Besides, his mind is certainly not on what happened between us. His father is gone, and he's still in shock after learning that the man who raised him wasn't truly his father at all. You must go back and be strong for him, like a good friend. No, like a *sister*. He needs support. You can do this!' I finished my pep talk, took a few more deep breaths and stood up.

To my surprise, Thunder had crept up silently behind me, and now he gently put his head over my shoulder, nuzzling me.

'Aw, what's the matter, Thunder?' I teased softly. 'I've been ignoring you, haven't I? Well, I apologize, sir.' I gave him a curtsey and he gently pawed the ground with a front hoof. 'Oh, ready to go, are you? Very well, let's be on our way.'

Reluctantly, I mounted the horse and turned his head homewards. He wasn't in a big hurry, either, he just seemed to feel that we needed to get on with the day. *Animals are amazingly intuitive at times*, I thought. *Why can't people be like that more often?*

As we approached the stables, gently trotting down the path towards the house, my feelings were confirmed. There was a very early-model hearse parked out front, and as it drove off, I saw the coffin inside. Many of the servants were standing on the porch, watching as it disappeared. But Henley wasn't there. I handed the reins to a servant and made my way into the house. The remaining servants filtered back inside, all except Nellie, who walked over to meet me.

'Oh, Miss Rebecca,' she said sadly. 'I'm not sure what to think. Mr Beauford hadn't been happy for many years, and I know he'll be better off where he's gone, but ...' She paused, as if not quite sure what to say next.

I had a pretty good idea what she was thinking. 'But you're wondering what will become of your job, as well as those of all the other servants?' I offered.

She nodded nervously. 'I feel horrible, being so selfish at a time like this, worried about my own well-being ...' She began to cry, and I knew it was partly worry, but also because she'd been fond of Mr Beauford and would miss him. I gathered her to me and patted her gently on the back, letting her release some of that pent-up emotion. It felt like comforting a sister or a cousin, and came very naturally. I'd grown so fond of Nellie, and she'd certainly taken wonderful care of my needs ever since I'd met her. The least I could do was let her have a cry and support her for a few minutes.

After a minute or so she stepped back, looking

242

embarrassed. I pretended not to notice and simply offered her my handkerchief. 'There you are, Nellie, you keep this, all right? Better now?'

'Yes, miss. Thank you so much.' She paused to blow her nose and to regain her composure before we walked up to the house.

'You're fine, Nellie,' I whispered as I squeezed her arm, walking side by side with her. 'Henley won't throw anyone out in the cold, believe me. He has a heart of gold. If for some reason he sees fit to let anyone go, he'll find them another station first, rest assured of that.' I patted her arm again and then we walked up the front steps. She took her more familiar place a couple of steps behind me. The decorum that had been drilled into these servants from the time they could walk both fascinated and repelled me. Yet they weren't slaves. They received a decent wage from the Beaufords and, in some ways, were treated almost like extended family. I sighed, knowing I couldn't fix everything for everyone. As we walked through the doorway, I looked about, but Henley still wasn't in evidence.

I turned to my friend. 'Nellie, have you seen Henley this morning?'

Her face was almost back to its normal colour now and her eyes were brighter, having been washed with her tears. 'No, miss. From what Eloise says, he was nowhere to be found in the house when the mortician arrived.'

Curious, I thought. Henley was no coward, but he was obviously still very emotional from what he'd learned about his birth, and doubtless had a headache to boot. Perhaps he hadn't wanted the staff to see him that way and had slipped out. I knew he'd resurface soon. 'Thank you …' I began to say to Nellie, but she'd already left me standing there, deep in my thoughts.

The rest of the day passed in a blur. I barricaded myself in my room and renewed my resolve to complete my task as soon as things settled down – destroy Mr Beauford's collection of immortality artefacts, take the painting and go. The old man's funeral was scheduled for the next morning, and it was dusk now. I'd seen neither hide nor hair of Henley, having decided to let him come to me when he needed to talk. I wasn't hurt so much as surprised that he didn't appear to feel any need to seek me out. I hoped he wasn't on another bender somewhere, or in danger, but instead was finding some clarity – or at least some peace – about his upbringing.

I heard a gentle rap at my door, and when I opened it I found Eliza and Hannah standing there. 'Oh, do come in, both of you,' I invited, opening the door wide. Eliza was holding on to young Hannah's arm, and I smiled to myself, happy to see they'd befriended one another. That was good, for both their sakes. 'Do sit down,' I offered, silently gesturing Hannah towards the chair I felt Eliza would be most comfortable in. The girl nodded and led her charge to it, then turned to exit the room.

'Thank you, Hannah, but you may stay if you wish,' I told her.

'Oh, no, miss, I must go and help in the kitchen. They're preparing things for Mr Beauford's wake tomorrow, following the funeral.' She glanced up at me, for she'd been looking down at her feet while speaking, as most of the servants did. I wanted to change that if I could, before I left, so that all of them felt comfortable looking anyone in the eye, anytime, anyplace. I knew that would have been impossible in most households, or at least risky if they wanted to keep their jobs, but in Henley's house I believed it would be accepted. 'Will you be attending the funeral, Miss Rebecca?' she asked quietly. 'Eloise wanted me to ask you, as Wilchester's arranging carriages to take people to the church, and then the cemetery.'

'Why, yes, of course I'll go, out of respect for Mr Beauford,' I replied. 'And please thank everyone for all they're doing to keep things flowing smoothly here.'

Hannah nodded and quietly left the room, closing the door behind her. I turned back to see a beatific look on Eliza's face.

'He's with the angels now,' she said, and I heard a slight tinge of envy in her voice. 'Dear Mr Beauford ... I look forward to joining you there before too many more years go by.'

'I'm sure he's free from his suffering now,' I said, feeling a bit awkward in the presence of this somewhat saintly girl who had become my friend, but was still something of an enigma to me. 'Did you wish to speak to me about anything in particular, Eliza?'

She started, as if I'd shaken her from a dream. 'What? Oh, I just wanted to ask if it would be all right if I rode in the same carriage as you to the service tomorrow. Henley and Christine—'

'Will be riding together, I'm sure,' I interjected. 'Of course – I shall be honoured to be your companion, Eliza.'

'That'll be lovely,' she responded, 'but what I was going to say was, Henley and Christine haven't really made any plans yet about when or how they'll get there. He's been in absentia quite a lot these past couple of days.' She turned her sightless gaze in my direction. 'As have you, my friend. Every time I've asked about you at the dining table, they've told me you've been holed up here in your room.' She paused, her expression one of sympathy. 'You'd grown quite close to Mr Beauford, had you not? I'm sure you miss him, as I do.'

245

I blushed, and was glad she couldn't see me doing so. I decided to be as forthright with her as I dared, as I had learned from our talks that she was quite intuitive. 'Well, I enjoyed interviewing Mr Beauford, and hope I can write something that will do him justice. However, it's Henley I'm closest to, and I felt he needed some space to work through his grief over the loss of his father.' I wasn't quite sure how much anyone else knew, if anything, about Mr Beauford's final disclosure to Henley regarding the truth of his parentage, so I left it at that.

Eliza nodded understandingly. 'Yes, well, hopefully the poor boy will pull through. Christine's been incredibly frustrated that he won't really talk to her.' She'd lowered her voice to a conspiratorial whisper, and I caught a trace of mischievousness in it; I knew she'd never approved of her sister marrying Henley to combine their family fortunes, and I suspected that Eliza was secretly hoping their marriage would never take place. I felt the same way, of course – for Henley's sake, not for mine. I wasn't a player in this … at least not for much longer. I stood up.

'I don't mean to be rude, Eliza, but I'm quite tired, and want to be refreshed for the service tomorrow. Shall I come to your room at the appointed time, so we can go downstairs together to board our carriage?'

'Yes, please,' she replied. 'I need to rest, too, so you're anything but rude in taking care of your needs, Rebecca. If you could come by my room around nine, I've been told the carriages will be leaving promptly at nine-thirty. That'll give us time to get organized and so forth. Is that all right?' She stood up and I took her arm, as she hadn't brought her walking stick along.

'Yes, perfectly all right, dear friend.' I escorted her to the door, and then along the hallway to her room. 'Would

his nose and said, 'Too drab and dreary – next!' I smiled at that memory, and hoped my dear Henley would someday soon recover his humour and usually happy outlook.

In my riding togs, with my boots in my hand so as not to make too much noise, I crept down the stairs and slipped out of the front door. Sitting down upon the steps, I pulled on my boots, then headed to the stables. I decided to ride dear old Bessie this morning. Though I always talked to her when I went to the stables and gave her a treat of some sort, I seldom rode her any more. It felt fitting to take her out this morning, as I had plenty of time to pick the flowers, return, dress for the funeral and then further refine the details of my mission.

She nickered softly as I entered the stables, as though she knew I was there to take her out. 'Hello, old girl,' I greeted her softly. 'Yes, it's your turn again at last.' I got her saddled up and we slowly made our way down the lane and out onto the bridle path. Something about the fresh air made the feeling that I'd spent too long in this time fade away a little. It was a lovely morning; I'd seen the flowers about three days previously, so I knew they'd still be in beautiful bloom. Sure enough, as we approached the meadow the sun had completely risen and its light made the beautiful colours of the wild flowers stand out like some celebrated landscape painting. 'Painting,' I muttered to myself as I picked myself a bunch. 'Yes, Miss Hatfield, I'm going to bring you the painting.' It was as if I could hear her in my head as soon as I'd had the thought about the flowers resembling a painting. I could have sworn I heard her say, 'Paintings are beautiful, but the one you need to focus on is still in the study.' I wouldn't blame her if she thought I'd forgotten – I'd tarried much longer than I'd ever thought possible, and she must have known from personal experience how bad the uneasiness in my stomach was becoming by now.

After giving Bessie a quick rub-down and a gentle thank-you pat on her soft nose, I headed to the house with my posy of flowers. I went to the kitchen, as I could hear servants moving about and talking in respectfully hushed tones. As I pushed open the door, I saw Eloise's kind face.

'Good morning, miss,' she said with a nod, raising her eyebrows at the flowers. 'How lovely those are. Will you be taking them to Mr Beauford's service?'

'Yes, exactly, Eloise,' I answered. 'Would you know where I might find some wrapping paper to protect them during the carriage ride into town?'

She nodded and went into the pantry, returning with a large piece of butcher's paper. Not fancy, but it would do the trick. She took them from me, and I could see she'd done a bit of flower arranging in her day. Her deft fingers arranged them into a more balanced spray than I ever could have managed. She pulled from her apron pocket a pretty bit of blue ribbon, which she tied around the stems, then wrapped them with the paper. She smiled and handed them back to me. It had taken her less than five minutes to turn my humble offering into a thing of true beauty. I was impressed, and told her so.

'Aw, go on with ye, Miss Rebecca,' she mumbled, but I could tell she was pleased. 'Me mum an' her sister had a little flower shop when I was a girl, and they taught me a thing or two, that's all.' She turned back to her food preparation, embarrassed, it appeared, to have disclosed something personal about herself to someone who was 'above her station'.

'Well, they taught you well, and you've retained the knowledge beautifully,' I complimented her. 'Thank you again, Eloise. I know Mr Beauford will see these from heaven,' I added quickly. I remembered Eliza telling me that she and Eloise had often fervently discussed the Divine and heaven.

'Thank you, miss,' she said as she stirred whatever was in the pot on the stove. 'He was a lovely old gentleman, in his own eccentric way,' she added, more to herself than to me. As I turned to leave her to her cooking, I saw her quickly wipe a tear from the corner of her eye. My heart went out to her – she'd been with the family for a very long time.

I carefully laid the bouquet of flowers on the marble table in the hallway, just outside the parlour. I fairly flew up the stairs to my room and quickly made myself ready for the funeral, hair pulled back neatly, dress smoothed so that not a wrinkle was in evidence. I'd been enjoying getting myself ready the past few days, and knew what Eliza meant when she said she liked doing things on her own. I knew that Nellie and Hannah often laid her clothes out for her, then told her exactly where she'd find them before she went to bed. 'Shoes beside the chair at the window, Miss Eliza; petticoat and other undergarments on top of the dresser,' I'd heard Nellie tell her one day, and then Eliza finished the litany.

'And dress laid neatly on the trunk at the foot of my bed as usual, I assume?' She'd sounded amused, but I could tell she'd grown fond of Nellie and Hannah both, just as I had.

'Yes, miss,' Nellie said with a curtsey. She always curt-sied to Eliza, out of habit, mostly, but also I think because she knew Eliza would hear the curtsey even if she couldn't see it. Nellie did her best to treat everyone with the proper respect.

I glanced at the mantle clock in my room. Ten minutes to nine – right on time. As I walked the short distance to Eliza's door, I felt a strange sense of calm, almost as though Mr Beauford was there observing me somehow; the feeling was not so much happiness as peace. For his sake, I hoped he'd found his Ruth, waiting to welcome him into the 'Great Beyond', whatever that meant. I wished him no ill. He'd lived a long life deprived of the woman he adored, and I knew I would soon move on myself, leaving my own love behind for ever. *Living a solitary existence without the partner you longed for creates a loneliness like no other*, I heard his voice say in my head. It sounded much stronger than I'd ever heard it, and I felt he'd already become younger, somehow, in his new existence. I was glad for him, wherever he was.

I tapped on Eliza's door. 'Eliza? I'm a bit early – are you ready?' I slowly pushed the door open so as not to startle her, but she was already determinedly headed towards me, dressed flawlessly, her hair pinned up beautifully.

'Do I look all right, Rebecca?' she asked with concern. 'Hannah did my hair for me, but I dressed myself.'

'You look perfect,' I assured her.

'I really wish Mother and Father could have come for the funeral,' she said. 'But Father broke his leg in a hunting accident recently and Mother just couldn't bear to leave him alone and travel without him.'

'You and Christine are here, and that's what counts,' I said. 'Let's go downstairs, since you're ready, and find our carriage.' As an afterthought, I added, 'Have you talked to Christine this morning?'

She smiled the quirky smile that often appeared on her face when discussing her sister. 'No, and that's completely fine with me.' She picked up her walking stick with one hand and squeezed my arm with her other, trusting me to guide her down the stairs. 'I much prefer your company,' she whispered.

'Yes, somehow I've gathered that,' I whispered back, and we exchanged a very quiet little giggle. I asked her to wait a moment while I collected my flowers and settled them in one crooked elbow, then took her arm once again.

Once we were outside, Wilchester came up to me and gestured sombrely towards the second carriage in a line of four standing ready to take passengers to the local town. Christine was sitting alone in the front coach, looking beautiful despite her pouting expression. I nodded at her, but as I expected, she ignored me. She was in her own little world. *Poor Henley*, I thought to myself.

We were seated in our carriage and waiting for our driver when Eliza echoed my last thought aloud. 'Poor Henley,' she said, and sighed. 'All alone in the world now. That is—' she leaned towards me '—except for good friends like you.'

'And like you, too,' I rejoined. I looked around, but there was still no sign of Henley.

So this is what turn-of-the-century funeral processions were like, I found myself thinking. Very different from the few Cynthia had witnessed, where a motorcycle rider led the procession, blocking traffic as the line of cars drove along the street. At least Mr Beauford merited four carriages' worth of people. Glancing around, I imagined most of them were business associates rather than close friends. The old fellow hadn't been particularly sociable, from what I'd observed and Henley had told me.

The lead driver slapped the reins gently to get his two horses going, and we were off. Still no Henley, and I began to worry about his well-being. His state of mind had been so disjointed the last time I'd seen him; yet somehow I felt he was all right, and would undoubtedly join us at the church. *Perhaps he'll prefer to ride Jasper and be alone with his thoughts*, I mused.

Once we got to town, I unwrapped my flowers while the others disembarked from the carriages and entered the simple church. As Eliza and I walked side by side down the aisle towards the altar, I saw Mr Beauford's mahogany casket at the very front of the church. The casket was closed. I thought this might be at Henley's request, but couldn't know for sure. I helped Eliza settle in the second pew, then quietly excused myself and took my spray of flowers to lay them with several other bouquets already on the chancel steps. As I set them down, I gazed upwards, hoping Mr Beauford could somehow see and hear me, and silently told him, 'These are from Henley. I'm simply the messenger.'

Shockingly, Henley never did make an appearance at Mr Beauford's funeral, and I heard many mutterings and whisperings about how disrespectful, selfish and ungrateful a son he was. Only I knew the true depth of Henley's pain, but even so, I'd expected him to show his face, at least for a while. But this was not the case.

The service was pleasant enough, though the eulogy sounded a bit forced. Mr Beauford hadn't been a regular churchgoer, either here in the country or in the city. But he'd apparently contributed generously, probably at the suggestion of Father Gabriel, in order to make his funeral a good show. I gleaned as much from two plaques I saw hanging on the walls – 'Courtesy of Mr Charles F. Beauford' and 'Charles F. Beauford Memorial Chapel'. No wonder the old boy had wanted his funeral here – he was keen for people to see he'd at least done his best to buy his way into heaven! 'Good for you,' I found myself saying to him. I had to give him credit – he'd been as generous as he could be in the only way he knew how, even if these nameplates were what he'd really been investing in.

The cemetery was adjacent to the church so we all walked over to it, the six pall-bearers hefting the elegant coffin, marching slowly in perfect synchronicity. They all looked too young to have been Mr Beauford's associates, so I assumed that perhaps their services, too, had been prepaid.

Father Gabriel stood tall in front of the congregation and began the final prayer. His youthful features contrasted with his dark, serious eyes, hollowed out with grief. As he spoke, he captivated everyone with his strong voice.

'We commend to Almighty God our brother Charles Fitzpatrick Beauford, and we commit his body to the ground.'

I wondered if Mr Beauford was watching from some place on high. If he was, did he like how his funeral had turned out, with his chaplain leading it? Or was he sad that so few people had turned up?

'In the midst of life, we are in death.'

I looked down at the dirt beneath my feet.

'Earth to earth.'

Christine sniffed audibly and dramatically patted her eyes with her handkerchief as she leaned on anyone she could around her.

'Ashes to ashes.'

Eliza squeezed my hand in a show of solidarity.

'Dust to dust.'

I looked at the faces of the people around me who had bothered to turn up for the funeral. Most of them were dry-eyed. To them, Mr Beauford wasn't a man you cried over, but they were respectful. They'd come to show their regard and admiration for him.

'The Lord bless him and keep him, the Lord make his face to shine upon him, and be gracious unto him, and give him peace. Amen.'

I felt Henley's absence sharply at that moment. I couldn't necessarily blame him for not showing up after Mr Beauford's recent revelations, but I did feel he needed to pay his respects.

'Amen.'

Once the coffin had been lowered into the ground, Christine made a bit of a spectacle of herself, openly crying as she tossed a few pieces of earth into the grave. I later saw her loudly thanking Father Gabriel between sobs for his prayer. She glanced around as if trying to make sure everyone saw her very public show of thanks.

Eliza, ever at my side during the entire service, said nothing disparaging, but when she heard her sister's snivels, she cleared her throat as if to send Christine the message: *Have some decorum, for goodness' sake!* I could only assume Christine felt she must put on a good show as the future daughter-in-law of the deceased. That whole title sounded odd as it went through my thoughts. How could anyone be the 'future' anything of someone who was dead?

I jerked to a ramrod-straight posture as I heard Miss Hatfield's unmistakable voice say, 'And how exactly do you explain your own presence in a time where everyone is already dead? Explanations are not always simple.' I heard her voice so clearly that I turned around quickly to see if she was standing behind me. I blinked to clear my vision, but she wasn't there and, sadly, neither was Henley. Not even for the burial of the man who'd raised him and provided for him in the best way he knew.

I wondered if I'd be hearing Miss Hatfield's voice more frequently and more prominently the longer I stayed here, a weird aural accompaniment to the uneasy feeling in my stomach that grew more painful with each passing day. It was quite unsettling. I wondered if she could hear my thoughts, too.

Of course I can't, you silly girl. She sighed impatiently. *Haven't you heard of something called imagination? I hear most people have it.*

I shook my head to try and get her out of there, but her tinkling, sarcastic laugh indicated that wouldn't work. *Oh, this is maddening!* I thought, and heard her retort, *Well, this is you going mad, isn't it? How else would you explain my voice in your head?*

I looked down to see Eliza gazing up at me with a concerned look on her face. 'You're squirming a lot, Rebecca. Are you uncomfortable?' she asked kindly.

'Yes, yes, I'm afraid standing for this long has made me feel a bit faint. Would you mind terribly if we make haste back to the carriage now?' Flustered, I hoped that talking with someone who was physically present with me would shut out Miss Hatfield. When she remained silent, I hoped it was working.

'Of course, dear,' Eliza soothed. 'The service is over, anyway, is it not?'

I looked around and was surprised to find that nearly everyone had already wandered back towards their carriages. The disruptive mental conversation with Miss Hatfield had made me lose touch with what was going on around me. I felt trapped between dimensions and times.

All I wanted now was to take the painting and go back to Miss Hatfield – back to normal, or however close to it I could get – but everything was going wrong. It wasn't supposed to be like this, and I found myself in no state of mind to concentrate on anything other than worrying about Henley.

'Come, let's hurry, then,' I urged Eliza. I grabbed her walking stick and took firm hold of her arm, and we were back aboard our carriage and on our way to the estate in a matter of minutes. The air on my face helped to calm me a little, but I was still feeling a bit hollow, as though part of me was beginning to disappear.

Chapter 26

The next day, Henley came ambling into the house as though nothing was out of the ordinary. I was coming down the stairs when our eyes met. He tossed his riding crop onto the small flower-patterned chair beside the parlour door and made one of his mock bows to me, as he'd done so many times in all our early play-acting and flirtations.

'Charmed, Miss Rebecca; you look excellent well.' He didn't sound drunk, so that was something, I thought.

I couldn't quite get into the role-playing again, though. 'I'm fine, thank you, Henley. But how are you? And—' I lowered my voice as I walked to his side '—the more salient question is, where have you been?'

His face clouded over. 'Why the hell should you care? Or anyone, for that matter? I may be the heir apparent as far as everyone else is concerned, but it's been made clear as day to me, and to you as my witness, that I no more belong here than … well, than a stranger such as yourself.' His tone had been snarling at first, but as he expressed his innermost thoughts, he grew pensive. I knew he wasn't really angry with me, at any rate, and just let it slide.

'How long has it been since you've eaten a decent meal?' I changed the subject and, crooking my finger at him, led him down the hallway towards the kitchen. 'Let's see what Eloise can cook up for you. You look famished.'

I glanced back over my shoulder at him. Good! He was following me. I smiled at him, but he didn't appear to notice. That was fine – it was easier to take inventory of his appearance if he was unaware I was doing so. His clothing was wrinkled and his beard had grown quite a bit since I'd seen him last, but at least his hair was combed. I decided to make no mention of his absence from the funeral. He appeared to be on the road to a recovery of sorts. At least he was making an effort, albeit a feeble one, to look somewhat presentable.

He begrudgingly followed me into the kitchen. When Eloise saw him, she nearly shouted in alarm. 'Mr Henley! Child, where on earth have ye been keeping yourself?' she exclaimed.

'I believe he needs the fortification of one of your excellent meals, Eloise,' I answered for him as he stared at the floor like a naughty child who'd been caught with his hand in the cookie jar. 'Could you please whip up something for him? He needs his strength rebuilt.'

'Ay, that's plain to see,' she agreed, and immediately set about slicing some of the roast beef left over from the previous night's dinner, and in no time had set before him an overstuffed sandwich of roast beef, cheese, lettuce, tomatoes and onions – obviously one of his favourites going by the way his face lit up before he bit into it.

I enjoyed seeing him relish it, but decided to slip out quietly, thinking perhaps he would open up a bit more easily to his old friend without me present.

I was feeling more antsy than I had a week before, but thankfully I hadn't heard Miss Hatfield's voice since the funeral, for which I was grateful. It was extremely disconcerting when she popped into my head. I knew I'd conversed with imaginary friends when I was Cynthia, but that sort of imagination wasn't something that scared me or drove me to a point where I couldn't trust myself to be alone.

Over the course of the day, I kept myself busy working on my plan to carry out my mission. With each passing hour, more and more of the many staff members were quietly leaving, usually with a single suitcase in hand. Clearly they all had relatively few personal belongings. This was exactly what I'd promised Nellie and Hannah would *not* happen, so I decided I needed to confront Henley about it.

I sought him out and found him in the garden with Eliza. They were sitting comfortably together in silence, and his countenance looked more peaceful than it had earlier. He'd trimmed his stubble nicely, and it was obvious he was planning on keeping it, at least for a while. It suited him, actually. I nodded to him, and when our eyes locked, I signalled that I needed to talk with him privately.

He excused himself from Eliza and walked over to the side yard of the house, where I joined him. Here we'd be out of earshot of Eliza and the remaining servants. Christine didn't appear to be in evidence, which suited me just fine.

'Are you quite well, Rebecca?' he asked with some concern. 'You look peaked.' He kept a respectful distance from me, and I felt a mixture of relief and something else – a deep love for the young man in front of me – but the feeling of relief was more powerful. The fewer complications I created before I left, the better.

'Yes, thank you, Henley. I'm fine,' I replied. 'I'm just worried about the servants … several of them have left already. Do you intend to dismiss them all?' I tried not to sound indignant, but I couldn't believe that Mr Beauford would have wanted his loyal staff to be let go.

'Why, no, not at all. All who have left have done so

by their own choice. Obviously you didn't know that.' He was reading the reactions on my face. 'I helped the ones who wanted to leave after Father …' His voice faltered and he dropped his gaze. 'After Mr Beauford passed away, several who had been with us for a long time just wanted to move on. Two were at retirement age and have returned home to live near their children, and I found stations for the rest at neighbouring estates.' He looked back up at me, just the faintest hint of a smile in his eyes. 'You have such a sense of justice, don't you? I admire that. But I should hope you'd know I would never throw anyone out into the street. We can afford to keep most of them on; some just decided to leave of their own volition, that's all.' He shook his head, then added, 'No one was more surprised than me. Except perhaps yourself.'

I felt embarrassed. How could I have suspected him of such a thoughtless act? I knew him better than that, or liked to think I did. I lowered my voice a bit; I knew Eliza's hearing was quite keen. 'Please forgive me for insinuating that, Henley. I was just distraught because Hannah and Nellie are worried about their jobs.'

He gently waved a hand from side to side, as if to erase the mere thought. 'They're both welcome to stay on as long as they like. In fact, with some of the older ones gone, I expect they'll be promoted a bit faster. It's a new start for all of us.' He tentatively reached out and touched my shoulder, as a friend would. 'But what of you and your circumstance – are you still determined to take your leave of us?'

I nodded. 'I must, Henley. I don't belong here …' I nearly told him more about the truth of my situation, but he'd already been through so much of late, the last thing he needed was the burden of my full story; and the odds were he wouldn't believe most of it, anyway. 'I do still need your assistance to destroy those artefacts we've talked of …' I remembered Henley's comments regarding gossiping servants. 'And it must be done as inconspicuously as possible.'

I saw a glint spark in his eyes and wondered if he might actually take great pleasure in helping me get rid of something that had been a source of such destructive fascination to Mr Beauford. 'That can be arranged,' he assured me. 'What exactly must you do away with in the study?'

I sighed. 'Virtually everything, to be safe. There's more at stake here than you or I can possibly fathom. Those records could be quite dangerous were they to fall into the wrong hands.'

Henley nodded, showing that he believed me even if he didn't understand. 'So everything save the painting you need to take with you, then?'

'Yes, and the sooner, the better.' I felt I owed him at least something of an explanation. 'You see, Henley, I'm living a double life in many ways, and it's not merely my own welfare I'm concerned with here—'

My dear friend looked grim, but held up his hand to let me know I need say no more. It was probably wise not to burden him with any more details, at any rate; and it was obvious he'd decided to help me, no questions asked. He really was a remarkable young man. Christine didn't deserve him, not by any stretch of the imagination. But that was their problem to sort out, not mine. He was concocting a plan, and was deep in thought. As he stroked his new beard, he looked older and perhaps a little wiser than before. It was obvious that Mr Beauford's death had touched his life in many ways and he had suddenly become a man.

'All right, then. Here's how it shall be played out. You're

to do nothing. Leave it all to me.' He paused, but when I opened my mouth to object, he held up his hand to silence me and said, 'Remember, servants do more than just listen. They talk. I don't want any suspicions cast upon you, and we can't risk your mission being delayed any longer by unwelcome meddlers.' He sounded firm on this, but I couldn't let him take on all the responsibility.

'Oh, you needn't go that far on my account,' I protested. 'Surely we can work out a plan whereby—'

He interrupted me. 'I already have it all worked out, and it's a dilly of a plan, if I do say so myself. But you'll just have to trust me. You're welcome to take Thunder to go wherever you need to when the time comes, but I insist you allow me to pursue this in my own way, Rebecca.' He extended his hand. 'Agreed?'

Reluctantly, I shook his hand and nodded. 'Very well, agreed. I can't thank you enough, Henley.'

'Think nothing of it.' He motioned that I should go and sit with Eliza while he headed off in another direction. 'You have touched my life profoundly,' he whispered. 'I shall never forget you, and I wish you nothing but happiness.' He briefly took my hand and silently touched my fingertips to his lips, but it was a true friend's kiss, and nothing more. I couldn't believe he was so agreeable to helping me, with really no explanation whatsoever. I went to sit beside Eliza, and when I turned back to thank him again, he was gone.

'Well, Eliza, there's been a slight changing of the guard, I'm afraid. You're stuck with me, dear, as Henley had to take off on some errand.' I patted her hand and she smiled.

'Oh, I'm glad, Rebecca,' she said. 'I've missed talking with you these past few days. Are you planning to leave us soon, in order to finish writing your feature about Mr Beauford and get back to your busy life as a newspaperwoman?'

'Yes, that's right, Eliza. Sometime during the next few days, that's exactly what I must do. I shall miss you all.' I squeezed her hand, knowing it was Henley and herself I'd miss the most.

Eliza laughed. 'We'll come and visit you in the city. You must have an office. How exciting! To have your very own desk in your room—'

'Indeed you must.' I didn't want to lie to my young friend, but had no choice.

Eliza paused and I sensed that she knew that something was wrong, but she didn't say a word.

I tried to think what would happen after I left. Eliza, Henley and all the others would grow old. Henley would marry Christine and their hair would become speckled with silver as the years went by. Even Christine's face would lose its youthful beauty, and maybe Henley would wind up with a walking stick like his father, but I ... I would have to live for ever without the one thing I wanted more than life itself, and knew I couldn't have. I closed my eyes, thankful that Eliza couldn't see the pain in my face.

She nodded and rocked herself gently to and fro; we remained just so in the garden for a while, comfortable together in the silence.

Chapter 27

A few uneventful days passed. I was quickly losing touch with this present reality as I prepared to leave it behind. I felt the detachment and sense of unrest growing within me more and more, and knew it was good that I'd be leaving soon. However, there was still no sign from Henley, so I had no idea when he'd decide the perfect moment had come to enact his plan – whatever it was. I hoped it would be soon – it was becoming harder and harder to disguise the pain and unease I felt.

I began taking meals regularly in the dining room with the group again. Henley genuinely looked merry when sitting by Christine, politely laughing at her feeble attempts at jokes, while Eliza's eye-rolling betrayed her weariness after enduring too many years of her sister's charade and brainless prattling.

I couldn't help but notice a faraway, haunted look in Henley's eyes from time to time, when he glanced away from Christine and in the direction of the study. I hoped I hadn't burdened him too much, soliciting his assistance with my mission at this difficult time. No one else appeared to be aware of this unease within him, however, and it was only for fleeting moments that I could detect it. Surprisingly, he actually looked quite happy and at ease with Christine. The more I saw them together, the clearer it became that he'd made his decision. While I knew this must continue to play out, it was still somewhat disconcerting to witness the man I couldn't deny I was still in love with carefree and smiling in the company of another woman.

I became more of a wallflower than I'd thought possible; keeping my comments to myself and usually just talking quietly with Eliza, and sometimes, of course, to Hannah and Nellie. I didn't want anyone to realize how difficult I was finding it to remain in this time. One day, after nearly a week had passed since the funeral, the two maids were in my room, changing the linens as I sat at my writing desk, pretending to be busy, but really wondering when Henley was going to make his move so that I could leave. I knew my days were numbered with Christine here, and with Mr Beauford – the subject of my supposed article – now dead. Even if I could have borne the ever-intensifying pain, it would have been impossible for Henley to allow me to stay.

I heard Hannah clear her throat. 'Miss Rebecca?' she asked expectantly. 'Will you be staying for the wedding, ma'am?' I could tell by her voice she hoped that I would, and I knew I must hide the nausea churning in the pit of my stomach from these girls.

'Oh, alas, I'm afraid not, Hannah. I'd like to,' I lied through my teeth, 'but I have to be getting back to my life as a journalist, you see.' I made a show of straightening some papers on my desk. For some unknown reason, this appeared to give Nellie a cue to offer some opinions and gossip of her own.

'Oh, but it's bound to be a grand affair, Miss Rebecca,' she enthused. 'They've been betrothed for many years, you know, and when the two family fortunes are united by their marriage,' and here she nodded knowingly at Hannah, 'I believe our positions in their household will definitely be secure for as long as we want them.'

I smiled politely. 'Yes, it's been common knowledge for quite a while now that Christine and Henley will be married, isn't that right?' It was a rhetorical question, but I felt some comment was required of me. The girls simply nodded, and kept on with their tidying and chores.

Even though I felt more and more ill at the thought of Henley being with that air-headed heiress, I knew there was nothing I could or should do to stop it. I had to return to Miss Hatfield, and Henley had to get on with his life in his time. I knew the only other choice would be to stay with him and watch him slowly die; something I knew I couldn't do, even if I found a way to stay – and I was becoming more and more convinced that Miss Hatfield had been right, and the universe was refusing to allow my existence in the wrong time to continue. I said a silent prayer to anyone who might be listening to please light a fire under Henley soon, to get the show on the road so I could move forward with my plans as well. I was beginning to feel like an insufferable inconvenience here, and I knew the servants, while fond of me, were also wondering why I hadn't already taken my leave now that Mr Beauford had passed away.

That night at dinner, even though Henley and I hadn't really spoken since that day in the garden over a week ago, he gave me a meaningful look and took out his pocket watch. I instinctively knew he was signalling me that the time was nigh, and wondered if it might be this very evening. I felt a rush of excitement at the thought. At last I could get back to someplace in the time continuum where my life was less complicated, with fewer emotional ups and downs hindering me.

Henley displayed his usual charm and made pleasant small talk with Christine and Eliza, but didn't talk directly

267

to me. When Christine excused herself to the ladies' room, he got up from his seat, and as he walked by Eliza and myself he said, 'Ladies, I bid you good evening. Rest well.' And with another significant glance at me, he placed a small piece of folded paper beside my plate. I made sure Christine was still out of the room before opening it, and unfolded it slowly so as not to alert Eliza to anything unusual, but she was on the opposite side of the table, engaged in conversation.. It said: *Everything is ready behind Thunder's feed bin, under a blanket. H.*

My heart fluttered in my chest. The time was finally at hand. 'Excuse me, Eliza,' I hurriedly said. 'I need to go up to my room – I'm not feeling too well at the moment.'

She clucked her tongue in concern. 'Tch, tch, Rebecca – I'm so sorry. Do go and have a good night's sleep then, dear, and I'll see you in the morning. You haven't been sounding very well of late – perhaps you should see a doctor.'

I touched her shoulder. She was so kind, so bright and so brave. I knew I would miss her. 'Thank you for understanding. I have been a little under the weather, but I was hoping nobody had noticed. I'm sure I'll be fine. I hope you sleep well, too,' I offered as I quickly exited and went upstairs. Nothing looked unusual in the hallway leading to the study, and I wasn't sure what to expect next. All I knew was that the game was afoot, and I needed to be ready.

I quickly packed a small bag with the bare essentials I'd need for the ride back to the city, and placed it along with my cloak by the door where I could grab it at a moment's notice. I lay down upon my bed, still fully dressed so that I could flee quickly whenever Henley's master plan was set in motion. I closed my eyes, thinking I would only take a quick nap, and almost instantly went into a deep sleep.

Chapter 28

The smell of smoke had only just begun wafting into my room when I heard the screaming start. Confused, I coughed as I sat up in bed, taking a moment to try and orientate myself to what was going on. Then Nellie burst into my room.

'Oh, come quickly, Miss Rebecca!' she cried. 'The whole house is ablaze – we must get out!'

'Eliza!' I screamed and started towards my friend's door, but Nellie just kept dragging me along the hall and down the stairs. I barely had time to grab my little bag and cloak.

'Hannah's helped Miss Eliza out already, Miss Rebecca. Come now, we must hurry!'

Everything was red and smoky, and it all felt so surreal. Events were unfolding in slow motion and, in some ways, I was sure I must be dreaming. But when the cold night air hit my face at the bottom of the stairs and I flung one last look over my shoulder, I knew it was truly happening.

The ceiling moaned as the chandelier in the hallway swayed and detached, crashing to the floor and shattering into a million tiny pieces. Then the ceiling itself fell in on top of it. A piece of burned paper fluttered through the air, almost hitting my face, but I automatically opened my free hand and caught it, sticking it in my pocket to remember this night. That was the last thing I recall before Nellie finally got me outside, and we were somehow standing with all the other residents of the Beauford Estate, huddled into a few small groups a safe distance away from the blazing mansion.

As I watched from afar, as the flames engulfed the beautiful old house, a montage of my time with the Beaufords was playing in my memory like an old black-and-white picture show in a different time. But that memory was from another lifetime and had no bearing here. I was immortal. Time had no relevance for me any more. I had to get away, and in the next couple of hours, before anyone had a chance to give me a reason to stay, or notice that I was taking a painting with me. I had to assume that Henley's plan to destroy the artefacts had been to burn them, and that things had got out of hand.

My attention snapped back to the present. I hoped Henley had retained the presence of mind to ready food in the barn alongside the painting on my behalf. Thinking of Henley, I looked around the huddled groups of people, but I didn't see him. In my reverie, I hadn't even noticed he wasn't standing in his rightful place beside Christine.

I had no words to describe the feeling that ripped through me the instant I realized he wasn't there. I felt paralysed, yet there I was, running towards the flame-engulfed house. I knew that what I was doing didn't make sense. It was hardly the logical thing to do, but somehow I couldn't find it in me to care. Henley was still in the house, and I was going to get him out. I didn't care what I risked. I just needed him to be safe.

My legs ran as if they weren't my own. It was as though my eyes were seeing what my body was doing a few seconds after it actually moved.

Out of nowhere, I felt arms grab me and I tried to break free. I almost succeeded, but the arms only gripped me tighter, and I knew the rough embrace would have hurt if I'd had the capacity to feel anything in that moment.

'Miss. Miss!' The arms shook me when I didn't respond. 'You can't do that. You can't run into the burning house, miss.'

The arms held me still when I struggled against them, pinning my fists to my sides. I felt my cheeks grow wet, and my hair, now loose and flying madly across my face, stuck to my skin.

'Think of the young master.' My arms went limp at the mention of Henley. 'He wouldn't want you to do this. He'd want you to trust him. He'll get out. Trust him.'

I looked up to see Wilchester's face inches above mine. His expression was fierce, determined not to cry out or shed tears.

My body gave in and all my limbs went slack. Without his arms supporting me, I would have dropped to the ground in a heap. It was all I could do to squint towards the house. Hoping. Just hoping that maybe, through luck or divine will, Henley had made it out alive.

Those seconds and minutes felt like the longest I'd ever endured. All I could hear was my heart in my ears and my eyes burned from the smoke. My vision blurred – whether from the acrid fumes or my tears, I knew not – but when at long last I saw movement in the flames, I thought I must be imagining it.

My grimy hands wiped frantically at my eyes, trying to clear my vision enough to see through the hazy smoke. A man was running towards us, covering his mouth with a handkerchief and coughing. It was Henley.

I was so thankful to see him, I thought I would go insane with joy. I took a step towards him, but stopped as I saw his eyes scan the crowd for any missing faces. I knew he had a role to play, and watched him take his rightful

271

place beside Christine. Surprisingly, Christine had her arm around Eliza in their little group, and Eliza actually looked happy. Perhaps, in times of great crisis, even Christine could rally to Eliza's defence and be a decent person. I certainly hoped so, both for Eliza's sake and Henley's. As Henley made his rounds, double-checking to be sure everyone had got out, he gave me a quick glance and a nod. There was a shadow of guilt in his eyes; we both knew it was he who had started the fire, but no one else would ever suspect the new young master of destroying his own home, intentionally or not. I remembered Henley saying that the house reminded him of his father in ways the city house did not. I found it strange, since they were both family houses, but I supposed that the house in the country was where Henley had spent most of his time when he was home from school. Perhaps this had been his plan all along – to wipe out every physical reminder of his painful memories so he could start again.

The flames were in their full glory now, and it was plain to everyone that nothing left inside could be saved. All we could do was stand there, awestruck, as we watched the destruction of the place that had once been home to us all; witnessing the rising flames devour what had been a gorgeous old mansion as it went up in smoke. I hadn't expected Henley's plan to have quite such a dramatic conclusion – but it had certainly been effective in achieving what I needed to accomplish. Not only were the study and all its contents now ash, but the whole house as well.

I looked up at the sky. The moon shone down coldly upon the devastating scene, utterly unbothered by the tragedy playing out beneath it.

Chapter 29

Henley assumed his full responsibilities as the master of the situation, since there was no longer a house to be master of.

'I'm so pleased everyone escaped without any harm. I'm sorry about your things, of course, but things can be replaced and there will be a new house. This is a time to start over for all of us.' He rubbed his hands together as though searching for his next words, but perhaps he'd rehearsed this speech a few times prior to setting his plan in motion this evening.

Whose plan? I heard Miss Hatfield's voice enquire, and I shuddered, trying to make her go away. I hadn't heard from her in several days, and her presence here felt like a true invasion of privacy. I silently sent her a request: *Please be patient just a little while longer. I'll be back with you less than twenty-four hours from now.*

Hearing no reply, I felt she must be satisfied that I was finally going to carry out my mission. I was startled back into the present reality when I heard Henley giving directions.

'All right, since it's so late – and we won't really be able to assess what's to be done until daylight anyway – rather than waking up our neighbours, I propose we set up temporary sleeping accommodations in the lofts above the two stables.' He paused, looking at me, and I knew we

273

were both thinking of the painting and supplies hidden in one of the stables. 'We won't use the third stable. It's too close to the house. The other two are far enough away from the main house that they should be safe, but one of us will stay awake at all times to make sure that no stray spark reaches us. One stable will be for the womenfolk, and we men will be in the other.' He grinned wearily. 'Hay can actually be quite comfortable to sleep on, if you aren't allergic to it.' He turned to the male servants. 'Come along, fellows, I'll show you where there are some nice clean horse blankets, and we can fashion some makeshift mattresses for the women. The men shall rough it and sleep right on the hay.'

The servants agreed and set to work immediately, although everyone was already exhausted from the ordeal. I was impressed by how quickly the men created sleeping spaces for the women in the first loft, but Christine could bring herself to do nothing other than complain. What a surprise!

'I simply *must* have my own mattress.' Christine flounced down on the hay near where Wilchester and another servant were busily creating the best beds possible for us. 'I can't tolerate having someone else so close to me while I'm sleeping – it's suffocating!'

Eliza and I were already stretching out on the bed we'd agreed to share, and it was surprisingly soft and comfortable. A wicked grin spread across Eliza's face as she heard this last comment from her sister. 'Lucky Henley. Perhaps they won't ever have to share a bed, then!' she whispered, and giggled like a schoolgirl.

I chuckled quietly, but kept my gaze on the rafters so as not to allow Christine to see our little joke was at her expense. She appeared oblivious, however, and went right on spouting her negativity even after the men created an extra high and wide bed for her. She sat on it tentatively.

'Oh, this is going to be so lumpy,' she whined. 'I wonder if my back will ever recover.'

Eliza could be silent no more at that. 'Christine!' she reprimanded, her tone uncharacteristically sharp. 'You are *so* ungrateful! We all might have died, but everyone got out alive. Henley has lost his home, and you're complaining about where you'll be sleeping for a few short hours. You should thank the good Lord above you're alive, and consider being a better helpmate to your intended husband. Now, I don't want to hear another word.' She rolled over, turning her back to her older sister, who was stunned into silence.

I wanted to applaud and say, 'Bravo, Eliza!' but I held my tongue. I was simply happy for my friend that she'd finally found a way to honestly voice her feelings to her sibling.

Wilchester and another servant stood at the top of the loft ladder, preparing to climb down and head over to the other stable to join the rest of the men. There was a delighted smile on Wilchester's face, which made him nearly unrecognizable. I'd never seen a smile light up his countenance before, and had wondered at times if the dour old fellow's face might break if he ever did smile, but that obviously wasn't the case. It looked a bit odd sitting there on his lips, but I smiled back at him as I realized he had little patience for Christine, either, and had thoroughly enjoyed the tongue-lashing Eliza had just delivered. He bobbed his head in our direction.

'Goodnight, Miss Rebecca, Miss Eliza. Some of us will be taking a carriage into town in the morning, bright and early, to fetch some breakfast back for everyone. I trust you'll all sleep well, now.'

'Our bed is very comfortable – thank you so much, gentlemen,' I said, and nodded back. Christine huffed and turned over first on one side, then the other, as the men descended the ladder. I decided to ignore her and got one of the best night's sleep I'd had in some time. I knew my mission was finally on its way to being realized and this was probably the last night I would spend with Eliza and Henley, or even in this time. I couldn't leave right then, although I knew I should – but I needed to say goodbye to Henley first.

Chapter 30

As sunlight streamed through a few chinks in the loft's log walls, I awoke feeling strangely refreshed. I could hear the sounds of people bustling outside, but it was muted, as they were trying to be considerate towards those of us who were still sleeping. I was grateful that I'd had the presence of mind to grab my bag last night, and slept fully clothed. Looking back at Eliza and Christine, I realized they'd at least have to start their day in their nightgowns, until Henley could see to getting them some new clothes in town. He'd still been fully dressed when he exited the inferno that he'd started, of course, and some of the male servants also had on their clothes from the day before. Obviously they were not normally early to bed.

As I walked outside, I observed Hannah, Nellie and the other female staff creating a picnic of sorts on a makeshift table with benches pulled up alongside it. I noticed that all the servingwomen were fully dressed, too, and mused that they must be accustomed to working from sunrise well into the evening. In this case, their long hours had been advantageous to them for once, and saved their dignity. I was sure Henley was aware of that, too, and had made every effort not to create total devastation and embarrassment for his loyal staff by staging the fire at a time when his servants would be still fully dressed, and therefore at least have one set of clothes.

My stomach growled as I smelled the bacon, potatoes and fresh bread that were being laid out for our morning repast. I wondered where Henley was and, as if reading my mind, Wilchester walked over to me and said, 'Mr Henley's gone to the nearest neighbours to borrow some extra carriages to take everyone into town. He's going to put us all up at a couple of boarding houses there until we can figure out the next step.' He paused, as though exhausted from making such a long speech. I'd never heard him say so much in one breath, certainly not to me.

I believed he'd decided it was all right to befriend me in the eleventh hour. I wondered if he'd worked out that I wouldn't be going into town and joining the rest of them at a boarding house. Little got past this observant man, after all. Our little bonding over Christine's fussiness had helped him lighten up a lot towards me, and it struck me that he really was a nice man, even if normally a stiff and formal one. That morning, he almost appeared reborn.

'Thank you for letting me know, Wilchester,' I said. 'I'll go and rouse Eliza and Christine for breakfast.'

'Oh, no need, miss.' He smiled and glanced in the direction of the women's stable. 'I've sent Hannah and Nellie to do that.' He graciously pulled a bench back from the table so that I might be seated more easily. 'Go on and eat your breakfast now, while it's still a bit warm, at least,' he encouraged.

I was touched; it did smell quite delicious. I fell upon it ravenously, and everything tasted so wonderful, so scrumptious! I didn't know if my increased appetite was the result of knowing that everything was finally heading in the right direction for me, or if the exertions of the night before and relief of surviving the fire had anything to do with it.

278

I saw Eliza walking impatiently away from her sister, using her stick to guide her, which someone had obviously thoughtfully grabbed as we exited the burning house. Most likely Hannah, I supposed. She was such a clever young girl.

Christine was showing no signs of the momentary compassion she'd offered her sister in the wee hours of the morning, outside the blazing house. Once again, the world revolved only around her.

'Rude impertinence, not to wait for us to arrive before eating,' she reproved me. I simply smiled and waved a piece of bacon in her direction, and went right on eating. 'Hmph!' she snorted.

Hannah and Nellie helped Eliza get seated and got her a heaped plate of food. They ignored Christine, which amused me greatly. It finally appeared to dawn upon her that no one else shared her high opinion of herself, and she grumpily began to fill her own plate.

'What a sight!' I heard Henley's voice call from a carriage that had rolled up behind us. 'It looks like everyone has a good appetite this morning, and that's marvellous,' he enthused as he jumped down from the buckboard. He hardly looked like someone who'd just burned down his own beautiful home – the majority of his heritage. There was a sense of … well, I'd have to say great relief emanating from him. He, too, ignored Christine, who seemed totally preoccupied with grousing to herself and everyone around her about the fact that her breakfast was cold. Henley leaned down next to my ear. 'Could you spare a moment for an old friend?' he whispered.

I nodded, indicating I was quite full, and followed as he led me back towards the stables. 'Wilchester!' he called over his shoulder. 'Once the ladies, and I mean *all* of the ladies –' he made a sweeping gesture that included Eloise, Hannah, Nellie and the other servants, as well as Eliza and Christine '– have eaten their fill, let's help get them into the carriages that will be showing up shortly and head on into town.'

'Yes, sir,' Wilchester replied. 'As soon as they're done and the carriages roll up, Mr Henley.'

Henley and I kept walking until we were standing just inside the door of the now empty women's stable. The horses softly nickered and whinnied, having just eaten their breakfast, too, content now to watch us as though they were the audience of some play. Henley glanced about furtively then closed the door, leaving it just slightly ajar to avoid any concerns about impropriety should anyone be watching. He needn't have bothered. Christine was far too absorbed in eating and complaining to have even noticed our exit from the breakfast table. I guessed that the shock of the fire had made her so preoccupied with her own comfort that she even forgot Henley.

'Was everything executed as you'd have liked?' he asked breathlessly as he made his way over to a lump on the ground covered with a blanket. He lifted the blanket to reveal the painting, as well as some food. Thunder observed us from a nearby stall and pawed the ground, as though he approved.

I reassured him that the whole plan had been executed perfectly, even though I found it hard to believe he'd intended the destruction to go as far as it had. I tried to thank him, but I felt quite tongue-tied. I cleared my throat as I sought the right words. 'I can't believe you burned the whole house down—'

'Shush, now, there, there,' he said quietly. 'It was actually a very cathartic thing to do, to be honest. I'll rebuild a house that's even better in many ways, and it won't have the old man's memory in it, either, so please don't concern yourself with that. I'm more interested in you and your plans. Once you've taken the news and the painting to your friend, won't you consider rejoining us, helping to oversee the new mansion being built?' There was the slightest hint of pleading in his voice. So he hadn't forsaken all his feelings for me after all! My heart leapt in my chest at this confirmation that I hadn't dreamed up this love all on my own. The way he'd been acting towards me over the previous few days and his increasingly obvious admiration of Christine had half-convinced me that I'd made it all up. I'd known that was the best possible solution, but the realization that I'd been wrong still stunned me. But just as quickly, my heart fell when I remembered that this love could never be, and I dared not encourage him now.

'You know I can't,' I replied softly, turning my back to him. I crossed over to Thunder's stall and began saddling him up. 'I have to go—'

'Go where?' he entreated. 'Home?'

I nodded thoughtfully, wondering where exactly my home was now. 'Yes, in a way, I suppose,' I said, and continued preparing Thunder for our trip. I knew I'd have to wait until the carriages had taken everyone off to town before I left, but I couldn't trust myself to look directly at Henley as we were talking. Better to busy myself with grooming and saddling Thunder, to keep me focused on what must happen very soon.

'What if you didn't have to leave to go home, Rebecca?' he asked quietly. At this, I turned to see him shyly looking down at his own feet. What could he be thinking? 'Do you remember the best gift I ever gave you?' he continued.

I watched him, feeling helpless to stop whatever it was he had in mind, but totally confused as to where these questions were leading. 'You've given me numerous lovely, kind gifts, Henley,' I replied. 'I can never thank you enough. But the greatest gift I shall always treasure is your friendship.' I quickly clasped my hand over the back of his, as a friend would do, then tried to pull away. But he held on to it and forced me to look at him.

'Well, I should think you'd remember telling me that the best gift anyone ever gave you was me *not* buying you a ring in a store window.' His eyes twinkled as he gently teased me. I suddenly felt queasy, as that urgency to leave this place and time resurfaced inside me.

The roiling discomfort in my stomach reminded me that I couldn't stay with Henley. I could lie to myself and remain in his time, but that indescribable feeling – that nagging ache in the pit of my stomach – would always be there, and eventually it would destroy me. My nature would always come between us. We were two different beings entirely, Henley and I. Was I even human any more, now that I couldn't die?

'Does that ring a bell?' Henley was oblivious to the thoughts that were surfacing in my mind. And he had every right to be. We were different. Not meant to be together.

I remembered quick flashes of our shopping day in town, when he'd purchased all that lovely clothing for me, the beauty of the ring's sparkle, the way his hair gently fell across his forehead. With some surprise, I realized I'd begun falling in love with Henley at the moment he'd agreed not to purchase that ring for me. But he was talking again now, and his voice startled me out of my memories.

I turned to look at him and felt paralysed as I watched him pull a small box out of his pocket. He then began to kneel in front of me. My voice was frozen – I couldn't think of anything to say, and no sound came out. I wanted to jump onto Thunder and ride away, never to look back. I couldn't stay. That much was clear and the only constant I could cling to. But for the universe to taunt me with what I knew I could never have? I shut my eyes, willing the scene in front of me to go away, but Henley wasn't done yet. I was sure that everyone but Henley knew the answer I had to give him.

'Well, I broke that promise a few days later,' he continued. 'I went back to the shop and purchased it for you, knowing that one day, the timing would be right to do what I do now.' When I opened my eyes, he was fully down on one knee, the ring box open. His eyes shone brilliantly – even brighter than the ring – as he extended it towards me. 'Rebecca Hatfield, will you do me the honour of—'

'Stop!' I cried. 'Henley, for God's sake, please get up, and I beg of you, don't continue with your proposal. This can never be.'

'But why?' he asked, earnestly watching my face. 'Why should I not propose to the woman I love more than anything else in the world?' He slowly stood up and approached me. 'Rebecca, I plan to make you happy beyond your wildest dreams.' He paused and pocketed the ring box. 'You're different. Different from all the other girls I've met, different from all the other people I've met. I don't have to play a role when I'm with you. I don't have to be a Beauford when I'm with you. God, Rebecca – look at me.' His arms were outstretched now. 'Forget Henley Beauford. I'm not him any more. I'm just Henley. *Your* Henley. And I don't care about anything or anyone else. It's as simple as that. We won't have to answer to anyone. No expectations.

We can live however we want to live. We can build our own future.' He took my hands and engulfed them in his own. 'Don't you see? We can be happy together. We'll start over. We're young. We can do it. As long as I have you beside me, nothing can go wrong, because whatever the world throws at us, we have what really matters.'

I unclasped his hands as gently as I could and withdrew my own. I hoped he hadn't noticed the shaky breath I took and how my hands trembled. He almost had me there. Almost. If only it were really that simple. I would be his girl. And he would be my boy.

It would be wonderful. But it would only be a dream.

Henley only knew a part of what was happening. He didn't know what he was getting himself into. I had to make the decision for both of us.

'You can't give up on what we have,' Henley said. 'This is different. My feelings towards you … Most people spend a lifetime searching for what we have and some don't even find it in that time. Some people, like my … father … find it but then lose it. What we have is pure magic, something that surpasses love. It's a once-in-a-lifetime thing.' He fell silent, for I'd turned away from him and was tightening the girth on Thunder's saddle.

'You're serious.' His voice sounded incredulous. 'I can't believe you're willing to throw away what we have. I thought this was what you wanted. I had to play the silly game of making it look as though I was planning to go through with the marriage to Christine because that's what everyone was expecting. But now, you see, with the old man gone, his house gone – it's a chance for a fresh start, Rebecca. And I want to start over with you. Christine won't want to start over with me from scratch; she's full of tradition and stupidity. And I certainly don't want her – I never have. I'm so sorry if you ever believed I'd go through with that—'

I turned to face him, finally, tears burning my eyes and streaming down my cheeks. I wiped at them with my sleeve. 'Henley, that's a nice daydream, but that's all it is. You'll wake up and realize I'm not for you. I could never make you happy—'

Henley grabbed my face in his hands, so we were only inches apart. His brow was furrowed, but he still smiled. 'God, Rebecca, you stupid girl. You've already made me happy – you always have, from the moment I met you. None of the past matters now, only that we'll be together for ever.' He moved his face towards mine to kiss me, but I turned away from him. As his cool lips brushed my cheek, I was again reminded of the life we could have had.

Even if I fought the urge inside me to leave, I knew I couldn't watch him slowly die in front of me. And what of Henley? How could he possibly still love me, never ageing, stuck in the form I was currently in for eternity, while his hands grew gnarled and his skin leathery? Miss Hatfield had never mentioned an immortal dying of love, but I felt it might well be possible, right there in that stable.

I rebuffed him by climbing atop Thunder's back. 'I care for you, Henley, I can't deny it. But a marriage between us would be disastrous – for more reasons than I can say. If you really do love me at all, you'll go ahead and marry Christine, and merge your two family businesses, fulfilling your father's wish for you. Now, if you'll kindly hand me the painting and the food, I'd best be off. I'll take the back road so as not to alert the people waiting for the carriages. I've ridden the route a few times before now. Come now, please do as I ask.' I was begging. It was so hard being cruel to him in this way.

'But what of *my* happiness, Rebecca? I don't give a fig for the merging of family fortunes. Christine would make me miserable in no time. In fact, she already has. Please, Rebecca, is there anything I can say to make you change your mind, love?' He was back on one knee, the ring extended up towards me. I felt so sorry for him, and my own heart was breaking, too, but I couldn't let on that I was having even a moment of doubt, for he would surely notice it.

Heartbreak. It was real. I wished I could tell Cynthia that those songs she used to hear her mother playing in the kitchen were right. Fairy tales didn't happen. You can break your own heart, and when you do, it's far worse than any physical pain.

'Get up.' I willed my voice not to tremble. 'I don't love you, Henley, but I do believe that what's best for you must come first. You'll be happy somehow, I know you will. You can be happy if you allow yourself to be. Now, please hand me my bag.' I was taking slow, deep breaths, trying not to start crying again. Resigned to the fact I was not going to give in, he turned away and slowly picked up the bag, put the food into it and collected the painting. But when he walked over to me with it, he held the ring towards me first.

'We both know you told a great untruth in saying you don't love me. I know the truth, Rebecca, and so do you. I have no idea why you're insisting on breaking my heart, but I would never force you to do anything against your will. Please – take this ring. It's meant for you and no one else should wear it.' He put down his burden, took my left hand and placed his gift on my ring finger.

'I–I can't …' I said. 'You really must go, Henley, they're waiting for you …' But he was resolved. He turned the ring around so that its beautiful blue stone was facing my palm.

'It's not an engagement ring any more. Don't think of

it that way, I beg you. Perhaps when you wear it, you will think of me now and again, and remember how much I love you, and always shall. You'll always hold my heart.' A tear fell from the corner of his eye as he handed everything up to me, then he turned on his heel and was gone.

I sat there, stunned, frozen all over again. I heard his retreating footsteps, then the snap of a carriage door and the rumble of wheels heading away from the rubble that had once been Mr Beauford's estate. I felt the cold morning air on my face, and I couldn't help but wish fervently that I didn't have to leave.

I would go back to Miss Hatfield and the world I left behind would continue as if I'd never existed. Henley would, in time, forget these past few weeks. There would come a morning when Henley would wake to find that he didn't remember that strange girl's name any more. He'd sit there in bed for a few minutes longer, trying to retrace his steps into the dream he'd shared with her. But try as he might, he wouldn't be able to recall even the first letter of her name. Already the conversations they'd shared together would have started slipping from his mind. It wouldn't be his fault, no. Quite the contrary – it was a natural process, time claiming its children again, returning them to that ignorant bliss they'd once enjoyed. Soon the last shadow of that girl would disappear from his memory, and he'd be happy again.

I clicked my tongue to Thunder and gently pressed my knees into his flanks to encourage him to walk forwards. Once we started along the back path to the city, the countryside whirled by in a blur, and the wind soon dried my tears.

Epilogue

Twenty-first-century cars honked loudly as I dashed across the street. It felt odd to be wearing jeans and a hooded grey sweatshirt. I thought longingly of the corsets and billowing skirts I'd been wearing just a few days ago.

'Hey, lady – are you gonna move, or do you have a death wish?' a cab driver yelled through his window. Startled, I realized I'd paused in the middle of an intersection, crossing against the light. I shook myself out of it and ran the rest of the way across the street.

I was now only a couple of blocks from my destination – I could see it, just ahead. The serenity of the place I was headed for was like an island in a sea of concrete. It helped me ground myself and find some inner strength to go on to whatever might lie ahead. I knew I was an immortal. I'd finally made some peace with what I'd become. I didn't have the choice to turn back. I could only move forwards with my new existence. I wandered through the gates into the well-kept grounds and made my way to a site which had become very familiar to me over the last few days. I was surrounded by headstones in a tranquil cemetery. Ironically, the greenery reminded me of life and vibrancy when set against the concrete clatter of the nearby city streets. Here I stood among the dead, surrounded by life. It was quite the conundrum, but it brought me peace. I walked over to a familiar gravestone and knelt down in front of it, tracing the engraved words with my finger, as I'd done many times recently.

These were letters I knew all too well, even with my eyes closed. As my fingers traced them, I could almost feel him there with me. *Henley A. Beauford.* I traced them three times, as had become my ritual. I wished for them not to be real when I opened my eyes, but they were still there staring back at me like some cruel joke. I read the words beneath his name: *Innovative Businessman & Loving Husband.* I brought my fingers to my lips, placed a kiss upon my fingertips, and then transferred it to his name. 'I shall never forget you, dear Henley.'

Nothing seemed real. I waited to feel his familiar hand on my shoulder. He would turn me towards him and look at me. *Really* look at me. I'd gaze into his bright eyes and they'd tell me that my leaving had been nothing but a dream. He'd be here to stay for good and his lips would come crashing down on mine.

I sighed as I turned to the tombstone beside his. *Eliza P. Beauford, Loving Wife & Daughter.* For the first time, I really registered the dates of her death. She'd only survived a few years after she and Henley had married. Still, I was glad those two wonderful people had made even a brief life together, and hoped they'd found some happiness with each other. Briefly, I wondered whatever had become of Christine, but then laughed to myself as I realized it really didn't matter, and I certainly couldn't care less. The important thing was that Eliza and Henley had turned to one another, and I still loved them both dearly.

'You know, it's pointless to relive old memories. You'll soon forget them, anyway. Trust me, I know what I'm talking about.'

I hadn't heard Miss Hatfield walk up behind me, but this wasn't unusual. Sometimes I wondered if she was more than an immortal – whether she could just appear wherever and whenever she wanted. It didn't surprise me any more when she showed up out of nowhere. I moved over to sit for a while on the bench that faced the two gravestones.

'Yes, I suppose you're right. You usually are,' I admitted to her. The noonday sun gleaming behind her made her look like a silhouette against the sky.

'That's right. You're learning,' she responded. 'Well, do come along when you're ready. We must be off soon. Not everything has ended with the return of that painting. We have things to do, you know.' With that, she turned and walked away. I was a bit surprised she didn't just de-materialize, since I was ninety-nine per cent sure she could if she wanted to.

'I'll be along shortly,' I called after her. I stood and walked over to stand in front of the headstones to look upon them one last time. 'Goodbye, Henley.' I paused, but I knew what I had to say. 'I love you. I hope you're happy, wherever you are.' Then I turned to Eliza's. 'And the same to you, Eliza, my friend. I'd never encountered spirit and courage such as yours before. I'm glad you and Henley had a few years together, at least.'

As I turned to follow Miss Hatfield, a piece of paper, charred around the edges, fluttered to the ground. It appeared to have fallen out of the sky, but I knew it must have slipped out of my pocket. I bent down to pick it up and examined it with curiosity.

I remembered that when I'd exchanged my long gown for this sweatshirt, I'd taken this paper from the pocket of my dress and transferred it to my sweatshirt pocket, in a desperate attempt to somehow keep a part of Henley with me. I suddenly realized this was the paper I'd caught in the fire, and I didn't even know what it was.

For the first time, I really looked at it, turning it over to see if I could make some sense of what I'd recovered from the past. It looked older than ever before. I knew it was now about a hundred years old, even if it had taken a short cut. I turned it again, stroking it softly with a trembling hand. The paper was folded over and felt as though it contained something.

I was startled to find written on the outside of the folded paper, in very clear cursive handwriting: *To my darling Charles. With all the love in the world, Ruth.* The note to Mr Beauford from Henley's mother! As I unfolded the paper, I saw that enclosed was a photograph.

'Are you coming or not? We can't afford to be seen out in public so often. You never can tell who's watching.' Miss Hatfield was nearly at the cemetery gate, preparing to lead us to who knew where. She was still her impatient self.

'Just a minute,' I called out, hastily trying to stuff the photograph back into the folds of paper. But as I looked closely at the photograph, I gasped in shock.

The photograph was clearly Miss Hatfield. She was Ruth. It suddenly became obvious why she couldn't retrieve the painting herself, and had me remain, despite her misgivings, until I finished the job. She'd also possibly hoped for a connection with those she loved, if only through me.

I carefully slid the photo back into the folded paper, just as I'd found it. I saw flashes of my Henley's smiling eyes, heard the clear ring of his laughter when he was genuinely amused, felt his breath upon my face from our one passionate encounter. My cheeks flushed, and I did what I always did these days to centre myself back in the present and try to leave the past behind – I turned the ring with the blue stone around on my finger, quickly, three full revolutions.

I began walking, and hurried my pace to catch up with Miss Hatfield. She spoke to me without looking my way.

'Forget about it all,' she said. 'You didn't even belong there. You're an immortal – you don't belong anywhere.'

I stayed silent, but I could only think of Henley.

'Innovative Businessman' it said on his gravestone. A hint of a smile curved my lips when I remembered how he'd dreaded taking over the family business. Had I touched his life and changed the direction it was heading in? Had Henley kept a memory of me throughout his life, however small a thought it might have been?

I closed my eyes and couldn't help but laugh, because I knew that I'd changed him and played a bigger role in his life than I'd imagined. I laughed because I knew in that moment, somewhere in time, there was that boy I knew – the one with the clear blue eyes that crinkled when he laughed – and he'd kept a memory of a girl he'd once known. Someone who teased him back and looked forward to the verbal jousts they used to have. That boy kept a few words imprinted in the back of his mind, so when he walked in the park, he could remember her. And suddenly she walked alongside him.

'Henley?' I whispered.

I couldn't see him, but I felt him nearby, as if, in a different time, he was standing next to me, holding my hand.

'I love you.'

The wind carried my voice away, but I was certain he heard me. The trees around me bowed their heads in reverence for the words I uttered.

'I love you, too.'

Acknowledgements

I would like to thank my agent, Margaret Hanbury, and my editor, Marcus Gipps, for their enthusiasm and belief in the story I wanted to tell. Both took a risk on a teenage girl who barely gets her English essays in on time, and for that, I'm thankful.

A huge thank you to Henry de Rougemont, Gareth Howard, and Hayley Radford for all their support and encouragement. Thank you to Lisa Rogers, Charlie Panayiotou, Rabab Adams, Jennifer McMenemy, Sophie Calder, and the entire team at Gollancz for making this book a reality.

To Laura Ackermann and Anna Kreynes, a special thank you. There are days when I talk to you more than I talk to my own parents. Thank you for not getting sick of me yet.

Rhean, thank you for all your guidance, reading, and re-reading over the last few years. I think you've read this book more times than I have.

For putting up with me when I complain about my imaginary friends, thanks to Maya, Aelya, Fernanda, Corinne, Katie, and Michael. Thank you for not letting my imaginary friends be my only friends.

To my parents, I don't know what to say. There will never be enough words to thank you for all the times you've stood by me, counseled me, and consoled me. Thank you for all your love and patience.